FRAYED ENDS

SALLY J. LING

Flamingo Press

To contact the author, you may email her at:
info@sallyjling.com

Frayed Ends is a work of fiction. Names, characters, locations, and incidents are either the product of the author's imagination or are used fictitiously.

Cover designed by Andy Massari.

ISBN: 978-1-7371329-0-5

ACKNOWLEDGEMENTS

My sincere thanks to editor Kara Leigh Miller, Kimberly Pavlik, consultant, and the select individuals who assisted in the editing process by reading *Frayed Ends*.

TABLE OF CONTENTS

FRAYED ENDS

Chapter 1

Wednesday, 5:00 p.m.
Washington, D.C.

"Please, can you go faster?" I sat in the back seat of the Uber car, fidgeting, anxious to get to my apartment. I needed to shower and change and be at the White House Correspondents Association Dinner by 6:30 p.m. By the looks of the Washington, D.C. traffic, though, that would be impossible.

"I'm sorry, ma'am, but I have to go the speed limit. I can't afford to get another ticket. They'll suspend me." The female driver's dark eyes pleaded in the rearview mirror for my understanding.

Staying at the TV studio in D.C., where I was a news producer, put me way behind schedule; yet, I wouldn't have had it any other way. An intern from New York University needed some encouragement after she fumbled a critical interview with a Congresswoman. Everyone makes mistakes, and I tried to lift her spirits since she had lots of potential, yet time ticked away. If I didn't make it home by 5:30 p.m., I'd miss FaceTime with my parents that we had arranged by text earlier in the day.

While my parents and I exchanged frequent text messages, we hadn't spoken in weeks. Tonight would be our first phone conversation or face-to-face in a while. I was anxious to see them, even though I had to squeeze them into the day's packed schedule.

Out of breath from running up two flights of stairs instead of waiting for the perpetually delinquent elevator that operated on its own schedule, I opened the door to my compact apartment at 5:29 p.m. One minute to reach my parents, five minutes for the conversation, thirty-five minutes to shower and change, twenty minutes to get to the media banquet. If my parents didn't pick up on time, it would completely throw off my schedule, and I'd be late. I couldn't be late; I was one of the speakers. Admittedly a small part, but still, it was an honor to say even a few words at this illustrious event where I would stand in front of hundreds of my peers.

Taking a deep breath, I tapped my mother's contact name then the FaceTime icon.

Pick up, Mom.

I kicked off my shoes and started to undress. No answer. I tried again. Still no answer.

"Ugh! Why doesn't she answer her phone?" My words of frustration echoed off buttery yellow bedroom walls. I would have tried my Dad, but he never turned his cell phone on when out with Mom—technically challenged is what he called it.

I tried Mom a third time.

Tossing my phone onto my trapunto quilted coverlet, I decided to go ahead and shower and change, then try Mom one last time. If she didn't answer, I'd have to go.

Pulling my go-to scooped-neck little black dress from the closet, I hurriedly slipped it on. What used to fit comfortably on my size eight frame now snuggly hugged my curves.

When did this happen?

No worry. My shawl would cover whatever needed concealing.

Mascara and eye shadow added to my hazel eyes, blush to my cheeks, diamond studs to my ears, and my long brown hair pulled back to one side and fastened by an inlaid mother of pearl comb made me appear far more sophisticated than my usual in-the-studio casual jeans and ponytail. With three-inch black heels added to my five-foot-five-inch frame, I was almost ready to go. Just one last accessory.

I placed the front of my name tag—black with "Randi Brooks" engraved in gold—off my right shoulder and secured the magnetic back with a click. Picking up the phone, I tried my mother again. My pump tapped the floor as the phone rang. I scrunched my face in despair when the call went to voice mail. This wasn't like either of my parents. They never missed my FaceTime calls. Had they gotten busy and forgotten? Grabbing my shawl and handbag, I rushed out the door and into the waiting Uber.

While riding to the banquet, I remembered something. My parents installed security cameras inside and outside the house about three years ago, and I could access them on my phone. I had accessed them only once before when first installed, but now I wanted to know if my parents were home and simply forgot our phone date or there was another reason they hadn't picked up. I located the security app and pressed it. After putting in my password, a slew of small icons appeared indicating the cameras in each designated spot.

First, I tried the front porch cam that looked out onto the circular brick driveway. No cars there. Next, I tried cams in the other rooms. No one there either. Then I tried the cam in the garage. Mom's Buick was there, but Dad's space was empty. They must have gone out. Still, that wouldn't account for Mom not answering my call.

"We're here, ma'am," said the driver as he pulled up to the curb behind a line of other vehicles in front of the Washington Hilton. The hotel had been the site of the annual dinner for decades, even after President Reagan's attempted assassination by John Hinckley Jr., which occurred just outside the landmark in 1981.

"Thank you," I said. I slipped ten dollars into the front seat as an extra tip for getting me to the event on time, gathered my things, and bolted from the car.

Thankfully, I wouldn't be late.

Though the evening was full of excitement, not hearing from my parents lingered uncomfortably on my mind. I finally received a text just as the keynote speaker took the podium.

SORRY WE MISSED OUR FACETIME APPOINTMENT. LOTS GOING ON. WE'LL TELL YOU ALL ABOUT IT TOMORROW. LOVE YOU. MOM

Chapter 2

Friday, 4:00 p.m.
Boca Raton, Florida

I flopped face up onto my childhood bed and stared at the ceiling fan. The white blades rotated above me like the circling thoughts in my head. So much had happened in the last twenty-four hours. While I was glad to be home and alone, at least for the moment, I knew the tragedy I faced would probably take months, even years, to comprehend and deal with thoroughly.

Just twenty-four hours ago, Aunt Adele had phoned. I could barely understand her as she sobbed uncontrollably. "*Randi, I'm so sorry to tell you this, but your parents' car ran off the road into a canal last night. They didn't make it out. No one even found the car until this morning. You need to come home.*"

Home. Boca Raton, Florida. I hadn't been back in years. My job on Capitol Hill kept me so busy, so occupied I rarely took time off, even at Thanksgiving or Christmas. With breaking news occurring on a minute-by-minute basis between the current administration and Congress, both correspondents and producers were on call 24/7, a hectic schedule I both loved and hated. The excitement of working in Washington, D.C., with all its twists and turns and being among the first to get the lowdown on the political scene was intoxicating. But it was toxic as well. The demands and stresses of the job took their toll.

Relationships? I currently had none except for co-workers and contemporaries in the same line of work. Health? It took a hit, too—migraines and acid reflux. I took medication to make it through each day but hated working so hard, though I couldn't blame anyone but myself. My parents always told me, "Diligence pays off." It did. I rose quickly through the ranks at the station from college intern to post-graduate production staff, assistant producer, and producer. Now, at age thirty-three, I was five years into my producer position. I loved my profession but knew I wouldn't be able to take the pace forever. Maybe this diversion was just what I needed to break the unhealthy cycle.

What was I saying? That my parents' deaths were simply a welcomed distraction from my demanding and frantic life?

I turned over onto my coverlet and let the tears roll down my cheeks for the first time since hearing the devastating news. Robust sobs followed.

~

"Hey, Randi, how are you feeling?" A familiar voice poked through my sound sleep while a hand drew soothing circles on my back. Mom used to do that to put me to sleep as a child.

"Rachel?" As I turned over, the face of Rachel Cohen, my best friend from high school, came into view. I sat up quickly and threw my arms around her neck. We hugged as tears and sobs shook us both.

"I can't tell you how sorry I am. I talked to your parents just three days ago." Rachel grabbed a tissue from the side table and dabbed the tears from her perfectly blushed cheeks.

"It's certainly something you don't think about. You expect your parents to be there forever, even when you live far away. I mean, you understand that someday they will die, but not until they are old. Not when they're fifty-seven." Tears ran down my cheeks in rivulets.

"Have you eaten anything since you got home? Your Aunt Adele has food downstairs."

Aunt Adele had picked me up from the airport and driven me home. We tried to make small talk in the car, but we both knew my parents' deaths were the silent elephant in the room. We agreed to talk later after I rested. While I had gone directly upstairs to my bedroom to drop off my bags, I must have inadvertently fallen asleep when I fell onto the bed.

"How long have I been sleeping?"

"About three hours. Adele didn't want to wake you, given the circumstances, but I just had to see you even if I woke you."

"I'm glad you did," I said, smiling through the tears. Even though we'd only seen each other a half dozen times since my move to Washington, we used FaceTime every week to maintain our best friend status. I joined her in gushing over Todd when they first started dating and stood by her side at their wedding. During her pregnancies, I empathized with her and rejoiced at the births of her two children. I even listened to her busy philanthropic endeavors at the Boca Raton Historical Society while she learned of my "exciting" life—work, work, and more work.

"I'll head downstairs," said Rachel. "Come down when you're ready, and we'll grab something to eat." She hugged me, then pushed a loose strand of hair away from my eyes and smiled before leaving.

I looked about the room. It hadn't changed much since my high school days—same bed, same furnishings. Even my bulletin board had the same photos and mementos pinned to it as when I left. The carpet and blinds were the only things different, but I guess there was no need to make any additional changes to my room when there was another guest bedroom upstairs. Any company my parents had could comfortably bunk there or in the guest house.

After washing my face and pulling on a pair of jeans and a white tunic top, I descended the stairs. Adele and her husband Ron, and Rachel and her husband Todd were seated around the kitchen island. Food platers covered the black granite countertop.

"There she is," said Ron. He rose from a barstool and gave me a warm hug. "I'm so sorry, Randi." He kissed me on the cheek. The lingering scent of alcohol wafted in the air.

I nodded, trying to hold back tears.

"We're all here for you, Randi. Whatever you need," said Todd, who also hugged me. Time had indeed been kind to him. He'd grown into his chiseled face, complete with dimples, just the right kind of look for a successful financial planner. He matched Rachel in the good looks department.

"Hungry?" Adele asked. "There's plenty of food. Everyone has been so kind." She opened the refrigerator door, where various platters took up shelf space.

"I guess I am. I haven't eaten since this morning." I grabbed a couple of egg salad sandwiches, vegetables with dip, and a mug of coffee then went into the sunroom. Adele and Rachel followed, leaving the men in the kitchen.

"How did it happen? The accident, I mean?" I sat on the Rattan couch with its colorful cushions featuring orchid prints, my mind still foggy from sleep.

Adele and Rachel gave each other a "do you want to tell her?" look.

"The police are still investigating," Adele finally said, "but they think someone deliberately ran your parents off the road."

Egg salad caught in my throat. The lump went down when I took a sip of coffee.

"Deliberately ran them off the road? Who would do that? And why?" I looked expectantly at both women for the answer.

"They don't know," Adele said. "The police pulled the car from the water only yesterday morning. And, of course, there are the autopsies."

I sat back hard, almost knocking the wind from me as the realization set in that someone may have murdered my parents.

Just then, the doorbell rang. Adele rose to answer it. Rachel moved next to me on the couch and put her arm around me. In high school, she was the sister I'd always wanted. Mother had a miscarriage after me and then wasn't able to have more children. Rachel was the next best thing.

"I realize it's a lot to take in all at once, but know that Todd and I will be here for you every step of the way." Rachel squeezed my shoulders.

Adele returned to the sunroom, followed by a man.

"Randi, this is Detective Morgan. He's investigating your parents' case." She stepped aside to reveal a tall man dressed in street clothes.

I shot out of my seat and gulped air.

"Seth Morgan?" I gawked at the man then looked at Rachel. Her mouth was agape, and she appeared just as surprised as I was to see the boy everyone in high school called "Moron Morgan." He was the classic nerd—bright, awkward, socially inept.

"It's good to see you, Randi, though I wish it were under better circumstances. I'm so sorry about your parents." Seth cradled a notebook computer under his arm.

"Uh, we'll be in the kitchen if you need us," Rachel said as she guided Adele out of the room.

I was still blinking back faded high school memories when the realization hit me—skinny Moron Morgan had filled out into an attractive man—sandy hair, blue eyes, strong chin and nose.

"Can we sit down?" Seth asked. "I need to ask you some questions."

I dropped back down onto the couch. Seth sat in a matching armchair across from me.

"So, you became a cop?" I asked, not knowing what else to say.

"Joined the Palm Beach County Sheriff's Office right out of college. As you'll recall, I always loved solving mysteries."

We gazed at each other in silence as though remembering our high school days, he in one world, I in another.

"I've already spoken with your aunt, but I need to ask you some basic background questions."

Seth set up his notebook computer on the coffee table and turned it on. A sparkle caught my eye—a gold wedding band—something I hadn't expected.

"Of course. What do you want to know?" I pulled my hair back from the sides of my face and tucked it behind my ears.

"I understand that your parents own A Stitch in Time, a fabric store as well as the adjacent upholstery shop on NW 20th Street."

"That's right. My grandparents started it back in the 1960s when they moved to Boca. When they died, my parents inherited the business."

Seth typed into his notebook computer as we spoke.

"I understand your mother managed the day-to-day operations while your father managed the financial side of things. Is that correct?"

I let out a sigh and sat forward. "Seth, you've lived here long enough to know all that."

"I have to stick to protocol, Randi. Please, answer the questions."

I sat back. "Yes, Mom managed the store, but when she decided to expand several years ago to include quilting fabrics, she asked her sister, Adele Walters, to come down from Minneapolis and help out. My aunt manages the quilting fabric side of the business."

"Have there been any problems between your mother and your aunt?"

I stiffened. It seemed an odd question, given that my mother and aunt were very close. But then, how would Seth know that?

"Not that I know of. Oh, they squabble at times, just sister things. Nothing serious. They'd do anything for each other."

"Any problems with employees or any financial difficulties that you know of?"

"None that my parents shared with me. The business has always been profitable, and despite what people may think, my parents lived a very frugal lifestyle."

"What about any personal issues?"

I faded into the back of the chair. "Honestly, I have no idea. I haven't been back to Boca in five years, and although we talk fairly regularly and my parents visited me in D.C., I don't know much about their business or personal lives."

Had I just voiced the sobering truth—that my life had become so consuming I hadn't taken an interest in theirs?

"Do you know anyone who would want to harm your parents?"

My eyes widened, and I sat forward. "You think the accident was deliberate."

"There are skid marks on the pavement and grooves in the grass before their car hit the water. The rear of their car was crumpled, and there were tire marks from a second vehicle. It looks like someone rammed them then pushed their car into the canal."

Just thinking about my poor parents drowning in the canal brought tears spilling down my face. I brushed them away.

"Where did it happen?" I asked.

"Boca Rio Road, unincorporated Palm Beach County, not within the Boca Raton City limits. That's how the Sheriff's Office became involved." Seth cleared his throat. "Your parents may have been unconscious or at least stunned from the collision when they hit the water. If so, they may not have been able to get out of the car."

"Both my parents knew how to swim. If they were able to get out, I'm sure they would have made it to safety. If I remember correctly, there are condos right across the street from the canal and the turnpike just on the other side. Didn't anyone hear or see anything?"

"The apartments are on the south end of the road at SW 18th Street. The accident happened north of there, across from the entrance to West Boca Golf Club and at the beginning of the commercial section. Although we're canvassing the area to see if anyone heard or noticed anything or if there are any security camera tapes, I doubt that we'll have any positive results. The stores are set back from the road with their cameras pointed at the parking lots. Plus, the incident happened when all the businesses were closed. As far as the turnpike is concerned, there aren't as many cars on the road after midnight, and foliage obscures the canal."

"It happened after midnight? I didn't even know my parents stayed up that late."

"I understand you received a text from your mom Wednesday night."

"Yes. Mom said she was sorry she and my dad missed our FaceTime and that she'd talk to me on Thursday. That usually meant after work, but Adele phoned that afternoon with the news." I thumbed through my texts and showed Seth the one from my mother.

"Do you know what she meant by 'a lot going on'? Was it business or personal?"

I shrugged. "I have no idea. I asked Aunt Adele, but she didn't know either."

"We'll know a lot more after we complete the full investigation and autopsy. I'll keep you informed through it all." Seth rose and handed me his card. "I'm sure I'll need to speak with you again, but in the meantime, feel free to call me any time, especially if you can think of anything that could help our investigation."

I walked Seth to the door then went to the kitchen.

"Ron and I are prepared to stay the night if you like. We've brought our things." Adele pointed to their bag in the corner.

"Thanks, but I think I need to be alone. It's been a long day, and I need to process what's happened." I wouldn't have minded Adele staying, but Ron? I didn't want to put up with him.

"Are you sure?" Adele asked.

I nodded.

"Okay, but we'll be back mid-morning tomorrow. We need to talk about funeral arrangements." A cascade of tears tumbled down Adele's cheeks. She withdrew a tissue and wiped her red eyes. "I just can't believe my sister is dead."

I went to Adele and wrapped my arms around her. "I can't believe it either," I whispered.

Ron picked up their bag, put his arm about his wife's shoulders, and led her to the door.

"We're going, too. I hope you can get a good night's sleep." Rachel gave me a parting hug and kiss. "We'll drop by tomorrow afternoon to see how you are."

I followed them to the door and smiled as they left. When I turned around, I panned the home of my youth with its high ceilings, terra cotta tile floors, archways, and stucco walls. What was once a home filled with the warmth of love and glowing memories had now become a silent stranger.

I strolled through the house—the dining room, living room, den, sunroom—and onto the lighted patio. Even though I'd grown up there with plenty of love and laughter, it now seemed way too large, way too silent, and way too empty without my parents. I once asked them why they hadn't downsized after I left. Their answer: "We're waiting for grandchildren to fill it up." The realization that they would never experience that brought a stabbing pain to my heart.

"Yoo-hoo! Tootsie!"

I turned toward the high-pitched voice. My surprise turned to delight when I saw Leslie Davidson, who had called me that nickname ever since I was a child, limp across the patio with her cane. Our next-door neighbor, whom I figured to be close to eighty by now, Leslie was a pixie of a woman with long grey hair pulled back from her face and pinned against the back of her head with a hair clip. Severe arthritis in her hips crippled her, thus the cane.

When I was young, I spent time after school with Leslie until my parents got home from work. I also visited her on weekends. She was a descendant of one of the original Boca Raton pioneers who came to the obscure town in the early 1900s. I used to sit for hours listening to fascinating stories about Boca's early beginnings—pirates, rum runners, German spies, and secret military bases. To get to her house, I'd walk down the street and press the buzzer on her front gate. Many times she didn't hear it. Dad finally installed a secret gate between the houses behind the hedge in the back to access each other more quickly, especially in case of emergency.

"I'm devastated about what happened to your parents. We've been neighbors for decades, but your mother and I were more than that. We were family. I considered her like a younger sister, and we shared many intimate hours discussing our personal lives. Both your parents were so good to me. Ever since I lost Henry to a heart attack ten years ago, they've looked out after me. I'll miss them terribly." Leslie's voice broke and moisture formed in her eyes.

I wanted to give her a comforting hug, but tucked under her arm was a calico cat.

"What's with the cat?" I asked.

"What do you mean? He's your parents' cat. Now he belongs to you." Leslie extended the cat toward me, feet dangling. "I was feeding him until you came home."

"But I don't know anything about cats." Accepting the feline, I held him at arm's length and eyed him skeptically.

"Well, my dear, this isn't just any cat. Bigfoot is a very special cat. Ninety-nine percent of calicos are female, but your cat is male. That makes him part of the elite one percent. Besides, he came all the way from Key West. Look at his feet. Count his toes."

I cradled the calico in my arms while counting the toes on his white socks—six toes on one front paw, seven on the other.

"Why he's de…de…"

"Deformed?" Leslie let out a hearty laugh. "Silly girl, he's a polydactyl cat. That means he has more than the normal number of toes. It's unusual, yes, but he's not deformed. Some people call them Hemmingway cats because the great writer Earnest Hemmingway loved them and had them all over his Key West estate. The fact is they're still there. Bigfoot is a descendant of one of his cats. Your parents traveled down there and paid a bundle for him. They're very desirable cats."

I viewed Bigfoot with renewed respect—a male polydactyl calico. His green eyes returned a regal stare.

"So, how do I take care of him?"

"The litter box is in the utility room. The litter is in the cabinet, along with the scoop. His food is in the kitchen pantry. He eats in the morning and again at night, half a scoop of kibbles at each feeding. And don't forget to change his water daily. That's about all you need to know, at least about the cat," Leslie said.

"What does that mean? Is there something else I should know?"

"You'll find out in due time, dear." Leslie turned to go. "Let me know about the funeral. Toodle-oo," she called over her shoulder with a wave of her hand.

I watched as she shuffled across the pool deck and slipped back into the lush tropical foliage.

Bigfoot jumped from my arms and pranced toward the house. He entered through the kitty door I hadn't noticed before that led to the utility room. Regardless of his noble heritage, what was I supposed to do with a cat?

~

I awoke the following morning to a damp paw being dragged across my cheek. When I opened my eyes, Bigfoot was sitting on the bed, eyeballing me. As I sat upright, he jumped down and loped out the door. I scrambled after him in my bare feet, praying a toilet hadn't overflowed or a hose from the washing machine split. Downstairs in the kitchen, a puddle covered the tile floor where he had overturned his water bowl. Next to it, his food bowl was bare, the aluminum shining as though a cat's tongue had polished it. Bigfoot sat next to it, his tail swishing back and forth and his head swiveling between the empty bowl and me.

What time is it anyway?

The clock on the microwave glowed 9:30 a.m. Thankfully, I'd slept peacefully through the night, but clearly, it was way past Bigfoot's feeding time. I opened the kibble bag, placed a half scoop in his bowl, then sopped up the puddle and refreshed his water bowl. I hadn't had to be responsible for anyone or anything but myself for the last thirteen years. Taking care of a cat was going to be a challenge.

I climbed the stairs to shower and change so I could meet Adele and Ron. As I did, the urge to visit my parents' room overwhelmed me. I hadn't put so much as a big toe in it since coming home.

As I stepped into their bedroom, the fragrance of my mother's after-shower powder still lingered in the air. I closed my eyes and filled my lungs with the sweet aroma. In front of the full-length mirror, I envisioned my father fumbling with his tie as he seemed to do on numerous occasions and my mother rushing to his rescue. The blue and white Double Wedding Ring quilt that served as a bedspread still covered my parents' bed. Grandma Brooks had made it as their wedding gift. It was now well-worn, a bit faded, and torn in spots, but mother never considered replacing it. In the walk-in closet, my hands rippled across my parents' clothes. I remembered hiding behind them as a youngster during games of hide-and-seek with my father.

The strong memories caught me off guard. I slumped to the floor and wept.

Chapter 3

The celebration of my parents' lives took place four days later at Boca Raton Church, where I attended until I left for college. Though I hadn't stepped into a church since, except for home visits and would describe my faith life as woefully lacking, Pastor Drake comforted me with his kind words at both the funeral service and gravesite, where my grandparents had purchased several family plots. Friends, business associates, and neighbors jammed the church beautified by myriad condolence bouquets. My colleagues at the TV station sent two large sprays of flowers; each adorned a casket. I don't think I'd seen as many flowers in one place before. But then, I hadn't been to that many funerals either. The after-funeral reception took place at Boca Grande. With all her connections and a penchant for organizing events, Rachel, with Todd's help, took care of everything—planning, setup, catering, parking, cleanup. All Adele, Ron, and I had to do was show up.

Many of my high school friends attended, even some from out of town, which made the funeral reception feel more like a class reunion. And while a tragic event brought us together after fifteen years, connecting again with my former classmates proved wonderful. Customers and employees of A Stitch in Time and, of course, my parents' personal friends and neighbors attended as well. The celebration was crowded and loud, reminding me of the parties my parents used to throw around the pool. It was just what they would have wanted.

While making my way across the patio, a robust male voice behind me rose above the din of conversation.

"Excuse me. You must be Randi."

I turned to find an impeccably dressed man and woman. Their clothes alone, not to mention their shoes and her accessories, must have cost well into the thousands.

"I'm Leo Barlos, and this is my wife, Judith. Our sincere condolences on the loss of your parents."

Barlos. The name struck a chord somewhere in the recesses of my mind, but I couldn't quite put my finger on it.

"Thank you. It's nice of you to honor my parents by coming."

"I've known your parents for a long time, even before they purchased the property on 20th Street. We own the property next to A Stitch in Time…on both sides. If we can do anything for you, please don't hesitate to ask." Leo, a burly man with a round face, ruddy cheeks, and thinning hair, handed me his card.

"Thank you. You're very kind," I said.

As Judith moved into the crowd, Leo hesitated a moment.

"I'm truly sorry about your parents, especially your mother. She was an exceptional lady. You look just like her and are just as lovely." His voice choked with sincerity as he drew his chubby, manicured fingers down my cheek.

I jerked back as a shiver ran through me. Leo turned as though he hadn't noticed my reaction and blended into the guests.

What is that all about?

While looking at his card—Barlos Commercial Property Development & Management, Leo Barlos, President—a voice so soft it almost got lost in the clamor, called me.

"Miss Randi, you got a minute?"

I looked up to find Archie Withers, head of our upholstery shop, his wife Karen, and son Randall walking toward me. He had worked in the shop for thirty-five years and was our number one upholsterer. Archie's father worked for my grandparents when they first opened the fabric and upholstery store on Federal Highway in a pink shopping center known as Palm Plaza. Archie learned the upholstery trade from his father. When he passed away, Archie took over as head of the shop. He was a whiz when it came to taking an outdated piece of furniture and dressing it like new. None of the salespersons in the upholstery shop made a move without asking Archie first.

"We're so sorry about your parents," Archie said. "They were good people." He wiped his red eyes with a folded handkerchief.

I gave him, Karen, and Randall a warm hug. "I want you to know that my mother and father loved your family and always considered you part of ours."

"Your grandfather gave us our first big opportunity in Boca Raton when black folks had a difficult time finding jobs. We'd have nothing without your family."

"We'd have nothing without yours," I returned.

"Well, Miss Randi, when you come to the upholstery shop, please stop and see me. I need to talk to you."

"Of course, Archie, I hope to be there next week."

Archie bid me goodbye and exited through the crowded patio with his family. As my gaze panned the backyard with all its guests, they suddenly stopped when Seth Morgan came into view. He was speaking with Adele and Ron. I hadn't seen him since our first meeting. Nor had I seen him at the church or cemetery. I walked over.

"Hello, Seth. Thank you for coming. Looking for the killer amongst the guests, I assume?"

Seth grinned, crinkling his eyes. "Why would you assume that?"

"From what I understand, the killer will return to the scene of the crime or attend family gatherings. Perhaps you're trying to find him or her among the crowd?" I swept the air with my hand.

He laughed lightly. "You've seen too many detective shows."

"Perhaps."

Seth's gaze probed the crowd like a laser. "Excuse me, Randi, but I must speak with Pastor Drake." He moved to the other side of the patio, where the Pastor was talking with some guests.

After two hours, most of the people had left, including Seth, leaving only Rachel, Todd, a few folks, and the cleanup crew milling about the patio.

"Well, Tootsie, you should be proud that your parents had so many friends." Leslie sat next to me in a chaise lounge and popped a grape into her mouth.

"Between the service, burial, and this, I'll bet I've shaken over five-hundred hands," I returned in a low voice.

"Did you shake his hand?" Leslie flipped her head in the direction of a handsome, stubble-faced, well-tanned man dressed in a white shirt, camel blazer, blue slacks, deck shoes, and no socks. I could hear him conversing in Spanish with a couple on the other side of the pool.

"Can't say that I did. In fact, I don't remember ever seeing him before."

"He's hot, Tootsie. You should go over and introduce yourself."

I pulled back and looked incredulously at Leslie.

This is my parents' funeral reception. Why did she make such a suggestion?

Leslie turned, took my hands in hers, and looked me square in the face with her piercing grey eyes as though she'd read my thoughts.

"Look, I know you have a hectic life in Washington and don't have much time for men. I also know your parents have just passed away, and that's why you're here. But, after Henry died, a friend said something very profound to me, something I've never forgotten."

"What was that?"

"Life is for the living."

I blinked and swiveled back around only to find the man gone.

"I'm sure you'll see him again. See you, Tootsie." Leslie patted my hand before leaving.

Bigfoot padded out of the house and stopped in front of me. I hadn't seen him since the guests arrived. Too confusing, I suppose. He stared up at me.

Meow.

Oops! Did I forget to feed him again?

After satisfying Bigfoot's growling tummy and waiting for everyone to leave, including Rachel and Todd, I put on my bathing suit. I hadn't been in the pool since I got home with so many things to do—funeral arrangements, meeting with my parents' attorney and financial advisor, accessing their safety deposit box and bank accounts, registering my mother's car in my name, shopping for appropriate apparel for the funeral, and so much more. I was as busy here as I was on Capitol Hill, just a different busy. Now, in the quiet of the evening, taking a dip seemed like the perfect thing to do.

Can I still swim like I did when on the high school swim team?

Warmed by the Florida sun, the water enveloped me like a soothing hug. As I pushed off the end of the pool, I swam its length. Yep, swimming was like riding a bike. I did a flip turn and swam back. After a few laps, I turned over, closed my eyes, and floated, allowing the anxieties and concerns of the day to melt into the tepid liquid. I didn't know how long the euphoria of being weightless, motionless, and careless lasted, but when I opened my eyes, Bigfoot was sitting on the edge of the pool ogling me.

Meow.

"What? You've already eaten," I reminded him.

He pranced down the side of the pool and headed toward the guest house. As my gaze followed him, a yellow glow from the cottage peeked through the foliage. A guest from the reception must have left a light on. Then again, why would anyone have been out there? My parents always kept the guest house locked unless we had company staying there.

I climbed from the pool, toweled off, and wrapped the terry around me, knotting it in front. My feet left wet prints on the tile walkway as I strolled toward the cottage. When I got there, the front door was open. The living room light was on and Bigfoot already inside. As I stepped into the guest house, I froze. Several travel bags, shoes, piles of dirty laundry, and coiled ropes covered the floor.

"I'm sorry I didn't introduce myself at the reception. I just got back and was trying to be low-key."

I jumped at the voice behind me and wheeled around. The man in the camel blazer stood in the doorway. He held a thin ax with sharp teeth. I sucked air and stepped back. Keeping my gaze fixed on the blade, I almost tripped over the ropes.

"No, no," he said. Putting the ax on the coffee table, he held his hands up in a gesture of surrender. "That's for climbing mountains with ice."

I swallowed. "Just who are you? And what are you doing in my parents' guest house?"

"I'm Connor Romero, and this isn't what you think. I didn't break in. I live here."

I moved toward the coffee table and grabbed the ax. It bobbed up and down as I nervously held it in front of me.

"Live here? My parents didn't say anything about a man living in the guest house. You need to leave." I shook the ax at him and pointed to the door.

"Just wait a minute and listen." He combed his fingers through his thick, dark hair. "I realize this must come as a shock to you, but your parents leased me the guest house about four months ago. I can prove it if you let me get the agreement. It's right over there in the drawer." He pointed to the top drawer of the credenza and advanced toward it.

"You stay where you are. I'll get it." I moved toward the desk, keeping the ax in front of me, and my gaze fixed on him. I found the paper in the top drawer and quickly scanned it.

"See, your father leased me the cottage."

"Yeah, but it says here you don't have to pay rent."

"Ah, that's true. Your father said I could stay here as long as I needed in exchange for maintaining the landscaping and pool."

"Why would he do that?"

"Look, I'd feel far more comfortable talking to you if you'd put that thing down." He pointed to the ax.

I lowered it but didn't let it out of my hand.

"I'm an Army veteran originally from Las Cruces, New Mexico. I served three tours in Afghanistan as a CID Special Agent."

"What's that?"

"Agents are sworn federal officers responsible for investigating felonies. We conduct investigations to keep Army personnel and property safe. It was my job to know civil and military laws, conduct investigations, and sometimes get involved with hostage negotiations. Your father met me at the VA hospital in West Palm Beach. He did volunteer work there on weekends twice a month. I was getting discharged after several months of treatment for PTSD. The doctor said that a change in profession would be helpful since what I experienced was the worst in people. Your parents' gardener had just left without notice, so your father suggested this arrangement."

"Sounds like him, but how do I know you didn't write this and forge his signature?" I waggled the lease in front of me.

The man let out an exasperated sigh. "Look, if you don't believe me, call your Aunt Adele. Here, use my phone. I'll dial the number." He pulled the phone from his pants pocket, thumbed some icons, and offered it to me.

I put down the lease and grabbed the phone. Sure enough, Adele confirmed that Connor had leased the cottage. She apologized and begged me to forgive her for not telling me sooner, but with my parents' deaths and everything that had transpired in the last four days, it slipped her mind. Besides, Connor had been out of town. She hadn't remembered until she saw him at the reception. Even then, there were so many guests to attend to that she simply forgot to inform me.

I handed Connor back his phone.

"I believe you're Randi. I've heard a lot about you."

I reluctantly put down the ax. "Unfortunately, I can't say the same."

"Okay, but can we sit down now and talk? I believe you'll want to hear what I have to say."

"And why is that?"

"It's about your parents' unfortunate deaths."

"Just what do you know about it? You weren't even here." I eyed him suspiciously.

"How about we sit by the pool?"

Connor and I walked down the pathway, Bigfoot at our heels. We sat across from each other at one of the bistro tables. He leaned in.

"Someone killed your parents," he began.

Does he think I just fell off a turnip truck?

"That's old news," I said. "Even the police believe that."

"Yes, but they don't know why. I might."

Sure. And he might know where Jimmy Hoffa is buried, too.

"How would you know that?" I asked.

"I've lived here for the past four months, and I'm trained to be a good listener."

"So, the killer told you he was going to ram my parents' car and push them into the canal? Then you left to go mountain climbing and innocently forgot to tell the police?"

"Not exactly."

"Well, then, what exactly?" I gave him a hard stare, doubtful of everything he'd said thus far.

"Look, it all goes to motive. Understand the motive; you find the killer. Since I've been here, your father and I have talked a great deal. He's helped me make the transition from military to civilian life, and I've helped him, too, but in much smaller ways. I overheard your father arguing with someone a few days before the accident. I was cleaning the pool, and the patio door was open. The conversation was loud enough for me to hear their voices but not their exact words. All I can tell you is that it was a very heated exchange. The man your father was arguing with slammed the front door when he left and sped off."

I cocked my head to one side and narrowed my eyes. "Why didn't you tell the police?"

"At the time, there was no reason to. It was just an argument and none of my business. I didn't think much of it until today when I got back. I was pulling into Boca Grande when a cop who was directing traffic stopped me. I showed him my driver's license and told him I lived here, and then I asked him why all the cars. He told me what had happened to your parents, and this was their after-funeral reception. That's when I remembered the incident. I didn't even unpack the truck. I changed clothes as quickly as possible and joined the guests. I figured if I could hear the man's voice again, I might be able to identify him."

"And did you?"

"Yes."

I moved to the edge of my seat. "Well?"

Connor swallowed. "You're not going to like this. It belongs to Ron, Adele's husband."

I jumped up, hands on hips. "Are you saying Ron killed my parents?" As much as I didn't like him, I couldn't believe he'd do such a thing.

Connor jumped up as well. "Wait a minute! That's not what I'm saying at all! I'm saying he had an animated fight with your father just days before the accident. That's all. Don't you want to know why?"

"I need some time to process all this." I turned to go. Connor reached for me, his hand so hot it almost branded my arm.

"Look, Randi, I get that you're miffed about some stranger taking up residence on the property and implying your uncle could have something to do with your parents' accident. But can't we call a truce and work together on this? I could help you find out who had a motive to hurt your parents and why."

I pulled my arm away. "Good night."

Bigfoot followed me into the house. As I locked the doors, set the alarm, and got ready for bed, I realized I wasn't angry because my parents forgot to tell me about a stranger who was now living in the guest house or that he was insinuating my uncle may have a motive for killing my parents, though both bothered me. My racing heart and the lump in the pit of my stomach was because this man, this outsider, had spent more time and had more conversations with my father in the last four months than I'd had in thirteen years.

Oh, how I wished I could turn back time.

Chapter 4

The next morning while feeding Bigfoot, I got a call from my boss at the TV station.

"Hey, Steven. Nice to hear from you. Thanks again for the flowers. They were beautiful." I'd already sent my colleagues a Thank You e-card, but it never hurt to say it again.

"You're quite welcome, Randi. I just wanted to check in to see how you're doing and when you might be returning. Kevin's doing an adequate job filling in, but no one produces a news show like you do."

"I appreciate the compliment, and I'm doing okay, given the circumstances, but I don't know when I'll be back. I've got to get my parents' affairs in order, which means dealing with both the business and the house by meeting with their attorney and financial advisor. I had no idea how much there was to do." I paced around the island in the kitchen, hoping Steven would understand.

"It does sound as though you have your hands full. How about we give you a thirty-day leave of absence?"

I stopped pacing.

"That would be great, Steven. I've already used up some of my vacation time, so if I couple the rest of it with my comp time and leave of absence, another seven weeks should do it."

"You mean we have to put up with Kevin for almost another two months?"

I laughed. "He's not that bad."

"You're right, he's not that bad, but he doesn't hold a candle to my number one news producer."

"Flattery will get you everywhere," I said.

"So, it's agreed. You'll be back in seven weeks."

"Agreed." I didn't know if that would be enough time, but I didn't want to lose my job. I'd worked hard to get where I was.

~

At noon, I drove east in Mom's car to meet Rachel for lunch. How odd to be driving again. In Washington, I either used the Metro or a ridesharing service. My car, a Volkswagen Passat, typically sat parked in the garage adjacent to my apartment. Thankfully, the traffic in Boca was nothing compared to that in D.C., and the restaurant was only a mile away. Still, driving after such a long layoff was a bit nerve-wracking.

The Tin Muffin turned out to be a cute little café on Palmetto Park Road. Terrible parking, but great food. And if one enjoyed a little entertainment while using the restroom, this was the spot. Outlandish decorations of white and grey rabbits, multicolored eggs, green grasses, reed baskets, and yellow chicks still adorned the floor, walls, and table commemorating Easter more than a week ago.

"Are you sure two months will be enough time to take care of everything?" Rachel asked.

"I don't know, but I'll need to get back to D.C. by the agreed time."

"Do you love your job that much? Besides, now that you own the fabric and upholstery business, someone's got to run it. And you can't leave the house unattended."

"There certainly is a lot to think about." I took a bite of the chicken pecan quiche. Delicious!

As we ate, I told Rachel about meeting Connor, his overhearing a heated discussion, and that the voice he heard arguing with my father belonged to Ron.

"So, what do you think?" I asked.

"I think that you don't know anything about Connor. Maybe he's telling the truth, maybe not, but I think you should run a check on him, see what turns up. I doubt the internet would give you information about his time in the Army, but perhaps you can find helpful information in a local Las Cruces newspaper. I know you love your aunt and uncle, but there could be something to what Connor said. If there is, I'm sure you'd want to know."

We made plans to get back together in a day or two.

While Adele and employees at A Stitch in Time were holding the store together in my parents' absence, I needed to get up there and try to figure out what to do—keep it or sell. I grew up in the store and worked there until I went to college, so it wasn't as though I was utterly ignorant about the store's operation. The problem was the last time I worked there was the summer after I graduated from high school. I was sure things had changed significantly since then and figured on a steep learning curve; yet, I needed to absorb all I could to determine my next move.

I drove up to the store and, after parking, sat in the car, building up the courage to walk in. My parents had poured their lives into the business, and now they were gone. So many memories came to mind. I teared up just thinking about them but knew I had to be strong to figure out what to do with the business. I blew my nose, dabbed my eyes, and said a silent prayer.

I met with the staff, many of whom had worked at the store for over ten years. They all seemed willing to step up to help the business thrive now that my parents were gone, and I was so grateful for their support. Of course, Adele carried the most significant burden since she now took on the responsibility for both sides of the store, but I knew she couldn't do it for long. I needed to hire someone to help her; yet, I also needed to learn more about the store and its finances before deciding what kind of individual that needed to be. With my parents' deaths, the store lost its most valuable assets with intimate knowledge of both fabrics and finances.

After touring the store and spending several hours observing the operations, I reintroduced myself to the accounting staff, whom I had met at the funeral. Dad hired head bookkeeper Yvonne just before I left for college. This year she celebrated her fourteenth year with the company. She explained that Dad came by every Friday to sign checks for accounts payable and approve payroll, which a payroll company processed. That job now fell to me, then Adele in my absence.

Next, I went back to the upholstery shop that operated in a large, air-conditioned warehouse next to the store. A small reception area welcomed customers where staff provided estimates, generated upholstery paperwork, and customers paid invoices. I greeted the team then slipped through a door at the end of the counter that led to the shop's heart and soul.

I stopped mid-stride as I walked in. The shop was so spacious, clean, and orderly. Staff at stations located throughout the warehouse performed various services—fabric removal, design, layout and cutting, stitching, tacking, and more. Randall, who worked as assistant manager, had done a commendable job streamlining this aspect of the operation. Bolts of fabric ready for use protruded from bins along one wall. Next to a bay where deliveries came and went, furniture of all sizes and configurations sat on wheeled pallets forming a row. Numbers with paperwork attached to each piece indicated the next piece of furniture in line and the extent of its makeover. As usual, Archie hustled between stations, directing the upholstering in various stages. He waved a hand in recognition and immediately rushed over.

"Miss Randi, so good to see you." He enveloped me in a hug. "Come on back to the office. We can talk there."

A small enclosed room in the back of the warehouse served as his office. A bank of windows set high in the wall behind Archie's desk bathed the orderly room in natural light. We sat in two wingback chairs, turned to face each other in front of his desk.

"The shop is humming. It looks like you've got everything under control," I said.

"Yes, ma'am. All seems good." Archie's teeth gleamed behind his broad smile. "How are you doing?"

"The best I can," I said with a shrug. I'm sure he observed the tears in my eyes.

Archie took my hands in his calloused ones.

"Miss Randi, when my father died, I thought the world ended. He was such a pillar of strength in my life. We weren't just co-workers here in the shop; we were best friends. I miss him every day, especially when I open in the morning. It's so quiet, not a sound. But I can still see him and hear his voice. He'd clap his big hands together and say, 'Okay, Archie, let's get to work!'"

A tear ran down my cheek, recalling the two of them. When I took a break from the fabric store as a teen in the summer, I'd slip back into the upholstery shop and watch them. Seeing them laughing, pulling practical jokes on each other and the staff, and praising the Lord, all while getting their jobs done, taught me a lot about discipline, joy, and living in the moment.

"It's those sweet memories of my father that bless me every day. You'll find memories of your mother and father to bless you, too. Just know that Karen, Randall, and I are here for you and that we pray for you every night. We know what you're going through right now is a heavy burden, but God is merciful. He'll see you through." Archie patted my hand.

"Thanks, Archie. I wish I had your faith." I wiped the tear from my cheek. "So, what did you want to talk to me about?"

Archie fidgeted, and his gaze darted around nervously. "I sure do hate to mention this right now considering all that you're dealing with, but you need to know that something isn't right."

I sat back. "What do you mean?"

"Well," he said, scratching his head. "I don't deal with the invoicing, payments, and receipts of the shop. As you know, the front office takes care of all that. But what I know is how much furniture we take in and move out of the warehouse every thirty days. At the end of each month, your father always went over the shop's revenues with me. That's how we gauged how we were doing and whether we needed to add more staff, especially during the winter season when the snowbirds came down and our work multiplied. Your father also based bonuses on the revenues we produced. I never questioned those figures until recently. For the past few months, the revenues your father reported to me haven't added up to what I know we've produced back here. See, I keep a record. My father taught me to do it." Archie lifted a ledger book from the desk and placed it in my lap. He flipped it open.

"Look here," he continued. "This is a list of all the monthly revenues since the beginning of the year. The first column lists my figures. The second one shows revenues based on your father's report." He drew his finger down both columns. The columns listed the date, ticket number, type of service, and charges. "I didn't make up these figures, Miss Randi. These came right from the tickets before they went to the front office for payment."

I compared the two columns. They didn't match. Many tickets in Archie's column never showed up in the second column. If what I saw was accurate, thousands of dollars in revenues never made it into the monthly report. I was stunned to think someone would steal from the business.

"But how can this be? The process is computerized."

"I don't know, Miss Randi, computers and I don't get along. All I know is something isn't right. I was going to bring it up to your father this month, but the accident happened."

"Do you think my father knew about this?"

"Good heavens, no! He wouldn't have known anything about it unless I showed him my ledger. Up to this point, there was no need to do that as the figures pretty much matched every month."

I closed the book. "I'll have to do some investigating, and it may take me a while. In the meantime, keep this in a safe place." I handed Archie back the ledger. "Rest assured, we will get to the bottom of this."

"Yes, ma'am." Archie rose and walked me through the upholstery shop to the door. He hesitated upon opening it. "Just one more thing, Miss Randi, watch out for Leo Barlos."

"You know him?"

"No, ma'am, not personally, just by reputation. He's been here several times talking to your father."

"What did he want?"

Archie opened his mouth to answer, but Adele burst through the door before he could get one word out.

"There you are. I've been looking all over for you. Carla Simmons, one of Boca's premier interior decorators and a big customer of ours, is here. She wants to meet you." Adele grabbed my hand and pulled me toward the store.

I wanted to speak with Archie again, but by the time I finished talking with Carla, the upholstery shop had closed.

I fixed dinner when I got home, fed Bigfoot, and went out to the pool to take a swim and consider what Archie told me. My solitude didn't last long.

"Well, have you had enough time to process it all?"

Dressed in a pair of khaki shorts and a sweat-stained tee, Connor stared down at me from the coping around the pool. In his hand was a pair of branch pruners.

"You do have a habit of sneaking up on people."

"This isn't sneaking. It's coming right out in the open. Believe me, I know how to sneak up on people."

That's comforting.

"Well, I have had a chance to think about things, and I do want to find out what happened to my parents. If that includes people I love, I want to find out that, too." I figured if I played along with his suggestion that we work together, I'd be able to find out what he knew, and he might be able to shed light on some of the things I learned. In the meantime, I'd go online and do a little peeking into Connor's background.

"Good. Then let's put our heads together and see what we can come up with. I'll go take a shower and be back in a jiffy."

While Connor got ready, I exited the pool, dried off, and threw on a beach dress and sandals. By the time he returned, I was ready. His hair slicked back from his tanned face enhanced his dark smoky topaz eyes and gave him a sexy look.

Hmm. Not bad. Not bad at all.

"What if we talk over coffee and dessert?" asked Connor. "I discovered this little café on the beach that serves to die for peach cobbler a la mode."

I looked down at my tropical print beach outfit. "I'm not dressed to go out."

"You're perfect. It's Florida, and we're going to the beach."

We drove south along A1A to Deerfield Beach in his candy apple red Ram pickup and found a metered parking space. Located adjacent to the pier, the cozy café, more like a diner, had a commanding view of the ocean. We sat in a booth next to the windows and ordered cobbler and coffee. As we waited for the dessert to arrive, I gazed out into the twilight that was about to blink into night. A couple and their little girl wearing shorts and a tee left footprints in the sand, while other beachgoers clad in bathing suits took a final romp in the surf.

The scene took me back to my early childhood days when my parents used to take me to the Boca beach on Sunday afternoons. While Mom nibbled on a sandwich and read a paperback under her umbrella, Dad and I built sandcastles, embellishing them with liquid sand we let drip off our fingers into artful stalagmites. One night during turtle nesting season, the three of us combed the beach with Gumbo Limbo Nature Center guides and observed a female loggerhead laying her eggs in the deep hole she fashioned with her flippers. That same season we viewed with awe scores of hatchlings clawing their way to the sand's surface and racing toward the ocean. It was an extraordinary sight.

"I've had a chance to do some digging and know a bit more about the investigation," said Connor, shaking me from precious childhood memories. His mouth closed around a spoonful of peach cobbler topped with ice cream embedded with specks of vanilla bean. He closed his eyes and savored it. When he opened his eyes, he pointed to my dessert. "Your turn."

I took a generous portion. My smile and "Umm" said it all.

"You do know Detective Morgan is leading the investigation for the Sheriff's Office," I said.

"I do, but it won't hurt to have another pair of eyes on the case." Connor ate another heaping spoonful.

"And I'll have to tell him what you said about my dad and Ron arguing. I'm sure he'll want to speak to you."

"I understand." He washed down his cobbler with a sip of coffee.

I put down my spoon. "You don't have to do this, Connor. You're not a CID agent or in the Army anymore."

"I know, but I owe it to your father." His tone was one of conviction.

"How's that? Dad wasn't one of your comrades."

Connor caught my gaze.

"Your father helped me when I needed it the most. Now it's my turn to help him. In the Army, we have a creed that says in part: 'Never leave a fallen comrade.' That statement isn't just for pulling a soldier off the battlefield. It also means standing shoulder to shoulder in times of need. I'm just living up to that with your father."

"So, what have you found out?" I ate an ample portion of the sweet dessert.

"The vehicle used to ram your parents' car was a truck. They know that because of where the crumpled back end started in the Avalon, above the bumper. Only a truck, and a heavy one at that, going at a considerable rate of speed, could have caused that kind of damage. It would be as though they were standing still, and a car rammed them at forty-five miles per hour."

"You saw the car?" My spoon dangled in midair at the revelation.

"Even though I'm no longer a CID agent, I still have connections." He gave me a wink and a smile.

His cute overt gesture sent a trace of warmth through me. I cleared my throat.

"The police said that my parents could have been unconscious before their car hit the water. Wouldn't the airbags have inflated?"

"Not in a rear-end collision. Front airbags only deploy in a front end collision."

"So, how could they have been unconscious?"

"They must have hit the steering wheel or dashboard. Do you know if your parents consistently wore their seat belts?"

"As far as I know. At least Mom and Dad always wore them when I was in the car." I washed down a bite of the delicious cobbler with a sip of coffee.

"When I spoke to Adele at the reception, she said you tried to FaceTime your parents the night of the accident and didn't get an answer."

"Yes, that's right. I remember how frustrated I was that Mom hadn't picked up."

"Did that seem odd?"

"They'd never missed our FaceTime before."

"And did they call or text later that night?"

"I was relieved when Mom texted me and said she'd call me the next day. That's the last I heard from her."

"Anything else you can remember?"

I closed my eyes, thinking back over that night. Yes, there was something else, something I hadn't told anyone, not even Seth. But then, I hadn't recognized its importance until now.

After Mom didn't answer her phone, I accessed the Boca Grande cameras to see if I could locate my parents. Cameras had tapes, didn't they? Could the one in the office have caught the argument between my father and Ron? If so, it would corroborate Connor's allegation. My eyes shot open, and the blood drained from my face. Connor gazed at me with concern.

"Are you feeling okay? You look pale."

"I'm sorry, Connor, it's been a long day. I hope you don't mind, but I need to go home." I grabbed my purse and stood, leaving half that scrumptious cobbler still in my bowl.

Connor caught my hand. "Why the abrupt departure?"

"Please, Connor, just take me home." I shuffled from one foot to another while he paid the bill. I couldn't wait to get back to the house and see for myself whether the mystery man was Ron.

Thankfully, the restaurant wasn't far from the house, yet the drive home seemed like an eternity. I wanted to explain my actions to Connor, but the prospect that my aunt's husband might be involved in my parents' deaths sickened me. Swallowing in rapid succession seemed the only antidote to keeping bile from rising in my throat. It also made it impossible to speak. As Connor pulled into the driveway, I unbuckled the seat belt with trembling hands.

"I don't know what upset you, Randi, but I can see you're physically distraught. Please let me help." He reached for my hand.

I pulled away, opened the truck door, and rushed toward the house without so much as a thank you or goodnight.

My parents kept a file drawer in the office full of paperwork—installation and repair invoices, operation manuals, warranties, etc.—on all the house appliances. I fingered through the files until I found the one on the surveillance cameras. Aside from learning how to access the tapes, the instructions said the cameras kept tapes for two weeks before recycling and recording over the first day. Since the incident occurred just over a week ago, the system should have recorded it, and I'd be able to see what happened.

I brought down my laptop and logged onto the security company website. After providing my password, I typed in the date Connor said he overheard my father and Ron arguing. I tapped the icon for the garage and fast-forwarded the tape to the evening. Dad's Avalon was in its spot, but mother's Buick Regal was gone. She must have been out for the evening. Next, I viewed the office.

My father and Ron entered the room. Dad took a seat behind his desk. Ron sat on a chair in front of him. At first, everything seemed peaceful, like a normal conversation. Five minutes later, my father wrote a check and handed it to Ron. He looked at it, jumped up, and threw his hands in the air. Bending over the desk, he shook an angry finger in Dad's face before turning and stomping out of the room. From the other cams, I followed his exit through the house to the front door, where he took an angry parting glance in my dad's direction before getting into his car and speeding out of the driveway. Back in the office, Dad's shoulders slumped, and he put his head in his hands. Too bad the system didn't have audio, but at least there was definite proof what I'd just seen fitted Connor's account of the evening.

While at my father's desk, I decided to look at his checkbook to see how much he paid Ron. I found it in the top drawer and thumbed through the check stubs—$2,000! For what? The comment line was blank. Paper bank statements were my next stop. Since Dad was old school, he still kept paper copies filed chronologically by date in a file drawer. The past six months revealed random checks written to Ron, some in even more significant amounts. Oh, how I wished my father were still alive to unravel this.

I knew I couldn't ask Ron for an explanation. If he had something to do with my parents' deaths, I could be questioning the killer. I also couldn't ask Adele. She might not even know about the checks, but would she tell the truth or lie to cover for her husband if she did? To believe my aunt and uncle could be involved in something as nefarious as this crime seemed incredulous, primarily since it involved Adele's beloved sister. But other than my aunt and uncle, who might know about the payments? Only someone who was close friends with my parents and especially my mother. Someone she confided in. Leslie.

A dark moonless night hovered above me as I made my way, flashlight in hand with Bigfoot padding after me, through the secret gate and onto Leslie's property. She didn't answer on the first ring, but an outside light came on with the second one. She opened the door the length of the chain lock.

"Tootsie! What brings you here this late?"

I could barely see past her, but what the hallway light revealed dumbfounded me. The foyer was piled high with boxes. Only a narrow path in which to access the front door was clear.

"I need to ask you some questions about my parents. May I come in?"

"Of course," Leslie said.

When she slid the chain off the door and opened it, my mouth fell open. The foyer wasn't the only space that appeared filled with containers. As she led me through a narrow path back to the kitchen, boxes, bags, and plastic bins seemed squeezed into every hallway and room along the way. We sat in a small breakfast nook adjacent to the kitchen; it seemed the only place that wasn't jam-packed. As a child, I had spent plenty of time in Leslie's home, yet I didn't remember all the boxes.

"What do you need to know?" Leslie asked. She made no effort to explain the containers.

"Do you know of anything between my father and uncle that may have led to a misunderstanding?"

"You mean, like money?"

I jerked back in surprise. "I guess that's a good place to start." One thing about Leslie, she pulled no punches.

"Before I get to that, what do you know about why your aunt came to Boca Raton?" Leslie's long grey hair framed her face as it fell below her shoulders.

"Only that Mom asked her to come down when she expanded the store. She needed more help and believed it might be a good way to lure her sister to Boca so they could spend more time together."

"There's more to the story than that, Tootsie. Your uncle was suffering from depression. He'd lost several jobs in the past and even his current one. Your parents thought if Adele came down to help in the store, they could at least help support her financially and otherwise while trying to get Ron the medical and psychological assistance he needed."

"I had no idea and can't believe my parents kept this from me." The thought brought a twinge of pain to my heart.

Leslie looked at me with loving eyes and ran a wrinkled palm across my cheek. "They didn't want to worry you, nor did they want it out. Your parents were very dedicated to family and would do anything within their power to support your aunt and uncle."

"So, what happened?"

"Ron started gambling. It didn't matter what it was—horses, sports, or cards, though dogs were his favorite. He went to either the horse or dog tracks almost every day during the racing season while Adele was at work. He became addicted and accumulated considerable credit card debt. When Ron asked your father for a loan, your father agreed, but only if Ron sought help for his addiction. He never did. After a few months, your father cut him off."

"Did Mom or Aunt Adele know about the loans?"

"Your mother did, of course. She's the one who told me. She was so upset but couldn't bring herself to tell Adele. I don't know if Ron told Adele about them. What I do know is your mother didn't want her sister embarrassed because of Ron's debts."

"So, my parents enabled Ron to continue his bad habit by paying his debts?"

"You can look at it that way. Or, you can look at it from your mother's point of view; she was trying to protect her sister."

Admirable, but what about tough love? All they did is perpetuate an already bad situation.

"Do you know when my father stopped payments to Ron?"

"Just before the accident, I believe." Leslie stiffened as though a light bulb came on. "Do you think the payments had something to do with your parents' murders?"

"I don't know, but it is curious." I rose to go. Leslie put a hand on my arm.

"Just remember this, Tootsie, things aren't always as they seem."

As I walked back to the house, I tried to put things in perspective. None of this made sense. If Dad had already cut Ron off, what would have been the motive to kill him? Anger? Or something else? Then I recalled something that might have a bearing. In mother's revocable trust, she left Adele a handsome percentage of some stock she held. As the successor trustee of my mother's trust estate, I had to present my mother's death certificate to the broker before he could put in the "sell" order. I hadn't done that yet. Adele knew about the inheritance, but did Ron? Could that have been another motive? Things weren't looking good for Ron.

"Have a nice visit?"

Startled, I pointed the flashlight toward the pool. Connor stood there, arms crossed, feet apart, jaw tightly set.

"Can't a girl have a private walk?"

"Wait a minute, Randi," Connor said, striding toward me. "You were the one who rushed out of the restaurant earlier. Now you show up walking back from Leslie's place. What gives?"

"I wasn't trying to be rude, Connor, but I remembered something when we were at the café that I needed to check on. Once I did, I had to speak with Leslie."

“Anything I can help with?” asked Connor, his voice laced with concern.

“I’m not sure. Let me sleep on it, and we can talk in the morning. How about breakfast at about 8:30 a.m. on the patio to make up for tonight? I’m cooking.”

~

With pillows propped behind me and my computer perched on my lap, I sat in bed and accessed Ancestry.com to see what I could find out about Connor. I followed his lineage back several generations, but nothing stood out in his Las Cruces background. After high school, he attended New Mexico State University and joined the Army when he turned twenty-one. Since I would need Connor’s military service number, Social Security number, or other identifying information that I did not have, I couldn’t verify his military service. However, I accessed archival newspapers and found several articles on him, mostly about his mountain climbing. One item in a local community newspaper included a photo and story about his wedding, something he never mentioned. He didn’t wear a wedding ring, so what happened? Other than that, his past remained somewhat unknown. I didn’t intend for it to stay that way.

Chapter 5

While I set the patio table with juice, water, and coffee, Bigfoot chased brown Florida lizards around the patio. Connor showed up right on time wearing shorts, a Miami Dolphins tee, and flip-flops.

"Pool cleaning this morning," he said. His eyes sparkled in the morning sun.

"Please sit down. The food will be out in a minute."

In Washington, I hardly cooked. Well, hardly microwaved would be closer to the truth. With my crazy schedule, I mostly ate out or ordered in. To be back in the kitchen was nice, but I had to prepare something simple—bacon, eggs, fruit cup, toast—since my culinary skills took a nosedive as my career advanced. The enticing smell of sizzling bacon and eggs frying wafted through the kitchen.

"So, how do you like the landscaping and pool business?" I asked once the food was on the table.

"Well, it certainly is a change from investigating crime scenes, yet in some ways, it's quite similar."

"How so?" I buttered my toast and slathered it with orange marmalade.

"See the azaleas over there?" Connor flicked his head in the direction of some bushes.

I glanced at the greenery he had indicated. Which ones were the azaleas? Everything on that side of the pool looked the same to me.

"Some of their leaves have brown tips, and the foliage has become sparse. I need to know why, so I can counter what's happening. In a way, it's no different than a whodunit. Only this time, I'm investigating plants instead of people."

"And they can't talk."

"Exactly!" he said with enthusiasm. "It's not like I can walk up to the plants and say: 'Hey, little azalea, I know you're not feeling well. Is it your soil? The fertilizer? Too much water? Not enough? Too much sun? Too much shade?'"

I let out a hearty laugh at his rendition of a parent speaking to a baby, inflections included. He laughed, too. We wound up with tears streaming down our faces. Nothing like a good belly laugh to remind me of what Leslie had said: "Life is for the living."

"So, what's it like to be in the Army, to travel the world, see different cultures? Was it exciting?" I asked, wiping away the joyous tears.

He finished his breakfast and pushed his plate away. With elbows on the table, he intertwined his fingers.

"The only experience I've had is in Afghanistan, but each culture has its own history, mores, and expectations. As well, each culture nurtures its future by feeding its citizens the things that help it grow—jobs, economic stability, education, a place in the global community. This growth is exciting to see.

Unfortunately, these cultures also exhibit tensions that tear them apart—political unrest, religious differences, inflexible traditions, lack of economic support. Is it fascinating to explore a new culture? Absolutely. It's also heartbreaking to see how behind the times they can be."

"But you dealt mostly with crimes committed within the military community, right?"

"We responded to any issue a serviceman or woman was involved in, whether on the base or in the local community."

"I understand how dealing with that for so long could take its toll on an agent."

"It was tough, but if I hadn't gone through all that and been sent to the VA in Palm Beach where I met your father, I'd never have met you or had such a good breakfast." He gave me one of his cute winks and sly smiles.

"And you think flattering the cook will get you another meal?" I grinned and let out a chuckle.

He shrugged. "Maybe."

I cleared the table and returned to the patio.

"Last night, I asked if I could help you with anything. You needed to think about it. Have you come up with something?" Connor sat back and placed his elbows on the arms of the chair.

"Perhaps." I didn't want to go into Ron's indiscretions, but maybe he could help with something else. "What do you know about accounting theft?"

"Whoa," Connor said, his palms up in defense. "That's not my bailiwick." He rubbed his beard. "But I do have a friend who's a forensic accountant. If you can tell me what you think the issue might be, I'll relay the message and see what my friend has to say."

I did my best to explain the mysterious accounting discrepancy in the upholstery shop.

"Okay, I'd suggest first looking at the person who has access to the computers after hours. Then I'd consider any individuals who cash out the customers and close out each night."

"But that's the entire upholstery front office and maybe the bookkeeping department, too!"

"How many?"

"Six. Five full-time and one part-time."

"Sorry, but until someone can access your accounting program to see how this occurred, that's all you can do. In the meantime, I'll get in touch with my friend. By the way, I'll need your cell number to get back to you."

We exchanged phone numbers, and then Connor rose to go.

"This was enjoyable, Randi, and I wish I could linger, but it's time for me to get back to the pool and my plants."

"I enjoyed it, too," I said.

While putting the plates in the dishwasher, I looked out at the pool. Connor was bending over, checking the chemicals in the water. I smiled, watching him. To sit with a handsome accomplished man at a café on the beach last night and to have breakfast with him this morning was most enjoyable. As I performed a final wipe of the counter, the phone rang.

"Hey, Seth. It's good to hear from you. Tell me you have good news on my parents' case."

"It's probably not the good news you're hoping for, but I've been thinking about you and want to take you somewhere.

I believe this will help you through your time of grief. Can you meet me in front of the house in a half-hour?"

~

When Seth arrived, I hopped into his Sheriff-provided vehicle.

"Have you driven down Boca Rio Road since you've been home?" Seth headed south down SW 12 Avenue until we got to SW18th Street, then drove west.

Just him saying the name of the road and canal where my parents died brought a lump to my stomach and an ache to my heart. I'd filled my days with so much busyness trying to hold it together that I hadn't had much time to think about the fact that my parents weren't here anymore. Now the scene that took their lives was soon to be directly in front of me.

"No, and I'm not sure I want to." Tears rose in my eyes. "You're not taking me there, are you?"

"Loved ones of victims say it helps bring closure when they visit the site of the accident."

"Why do you call it an accident when you know it wasn't?" My tone sounded much harsher than I intended.

"I'm not trying to diminish what happened, Randi. It was just a figure of speech. I told you I'd keep you informed of our progress, and this is part of it. I wanted to explain just what happened, and no better way to do that than to show you where it happened."

We drove the rest of the way in silence. When he turned north onto Boca Rio Road, my whole body stiffened, and my heart began to race. After a half-mile, he pulled the car onto the shoulder of the road, crossed over the sidewalk, and stopped on the grass. Yellow crime scene tape at the canal fluttered in the breeze.

"If I'd known you were going to bring me here, I wouldn't have come." I felt my blood pressure rise; my breaths came in gulps. Clenched fists with white knuckles pressed against my thighs.

Seth reached across the seat and wrapped his hand around mine. Warmth permeated my trembling body as he gazed into my eyes with tenderness.

"You know I'd never do anything to hurt you, Randi. I brought you here because this is an opportunity for you to start healing. Are you ready?" asked Seth.

I drew a deep breath. "I guess."

We exited the car and walked along the rutted grass. Seth pointed at the tracks as he spoke.

"These indicate that your parents were heading north when they were struck hard from behind. The vehicle pushed their car off the road here and then continued pushing it until it went into the canal."

The tire marks went from the road to the grass to the canal, where the land dropped off several feet straight down into the water. Deep ruts marred the bank where the tow truck had pulled the car out. The sound of vehicles whizzing by on the Florida Turnpike across the canal became background noise as I stood there mesmerized by the sparkles of sunlight dancing on the canal's surface. The liquid seemed so peaceful, yet I knew my parents had lost their lives below its tranquil surface.

Standing on the bank, hypnotized by the water, something white caught my eye. I wasn't in the habit of picking up muddy pieces of crinkled paper, yet, something compelled me to do so, as though it had some connection to the case. Turning the object over, I brushed dried mud from its surface with my thumb. I let out a gasp as the image appeared. It was a photo Dad took of Mom and me in our bathing suits at the beach. They took me there for a picnic to celebrate my seventeenth birthday. It was my mother's favorite photo of the two of us, and she always carried it with her. It probably slipped out of her bag during the accident and fell out of the car when they pulled it to shore.

The picture took me back to another time, one filled with my parents' unconditional love and an unparalleled feeling of security. At that moment, I was in a dream or having an out-of-body experience, one where I was hovering above watching myself. The whole scene didn't seem real, and yet it did. My head swirled with memories and emotions.

"Randi, are you okay?"

I raised my eyes to meet Seth's. His furrowed brow and piercing eyes expressed deep concern as he wrapped his arms around me and held me up. He led me to the car and helped me inside.

"I'm sorry. I didn't realize how difficult this would be for you." Seth offered me a bottle of water and a tissue.

"Obviously, neither did I, but I am glad you brought me here." I took several sips of water and blotted the tears I didn't realize had run down my cheeks. I tucked the photo carefully into my purse.

"There's more I need to tell you. Would you like to have coffee somewhere?" Seth asked.

I looked at him and smiled. "That would be nice."

We headed back toward the house and stopped at Duffy's, a local restaurant and sports bar. Being 11:15 a.m., they were open, but the lunch crowd hadn't yet arrived. Except for the background music, the place was quiet. We sat across from each other in a booth by a window and ordered.

"The vehicle that hit your parents' car and pushed them off the road was a Ram pickup truck. We know that by the red paint left on your father's Avalon."

"Have you found the truck?" I was still a bit dazed but tried to shake it off.

"No, we're checking repair shops in the tri-county area, but so far, we haven't come up with anything concrete from Miami-Dade, Broward, or Palm Beach Counties. That's where you come in."

"Me? What can I do?"

Seth shifted in his seat. "How well do you know Connor Romero?"

I almost choked on my coffee.

"How do you know him? And what does he have to do with this?"

"I know he stays in your guest house. I know he has a red Ram pickup truck. I know he took you out for dessert last night."

My jaw dropped. "Are you having Connor followed?"

"Just trying to find out if he's involved."

"Are you suggesting he had something to do with my parents' deaths? He wasn't even in town when they died. He didn't get back from mountain climbing until the day of the reception." My voice rose above the music in a sharp and pointed tone.

Seth jerked back and splayed his hands. "No reason to get defensive, Randi. Just doing my job."

Annoyed, heat rose up my neck and settled onto my cheeks. "For your information, Connor has some info that could prove very important to the case." As soon as I blurted that out, I wished I could take it back.

"What's that?" Seth reached into his breast pocket and pulled out a small notebook and pen. When he flipped it open, a fleshy white band had replaced his gold wedding ring. I stared at his finger, then at him.

"We're separated. It's been coming for some time," Seth said, not looking up from his notebook. "Now, what does Connor know?"

I'd already let the cat out of the bag, and Connor knew I'd have to tell eventually. I told Seth about Connor overhearing Ron's argument with my father, what Leslie said to me about his gambling, and what I'd found out about the money Dad was paying him.

"So you see, if it hadn't been for Connor, we wouldn't have known any of this."

"Thanks for the information. I'll need to see the tape, stubs, and bank statements so I can verify what you've told me, but that doesn't clear Connor. I need you to let me know if you see or hear anything suspicious."

I sat back in disgust, my arms crossed over my chest. "You mean spy on him?"

Who am I? Mata Hari?

"I wouldn't quite put it that way. I'm just asking you to keep your eyes and ears open."

"Thanks for the coffee." I got up to leave. Seth put a hand on mine, stopping me.

"Look, Randi, we don't know who killed your parents or why. Now that you're their heir, you could be in danger, too, since we haven't uncovered a motive. I'm just trying to keep you safe." Seth's eyes locked onto mine.

"I'll keep that in mind. Now, could you please take me home?"

As if I didn't have enough to worry about, now I had to wonder about Connor's possible involvement in my parents' murders. I didn't know who to trust, and trusting a man was an issue I already had a difficult time with.

~

I spent the rest of the afternoon at the store with Adele. Everything seemed to be chugging along nicely. We agreed to promote one of the sales staff to manager of the quilting fabric side and move Adele over to the upholstery fabric side. We'd hire another sales associate for the quilting fabric side. That way, both areas could operate more efficiently, and it would take a significant burden off Adele. I wanted to stop in and see Archie, but once again, by the time I finished my business in the store, the shop had closed. I made a notation on my phone calendar to see him tomorrow.

Just as I opened the front door, I received a text from Connor: MY TURN. DINNER AT 7:00 P.M. MY PLACE. HAVE NEWS.

That gave me just enough time to feed Bigfoot, shower, and change before going to the guest house.

As I let the warm shower rain over me, I couldn't believe my life could ever get busier than Washington, but Boca Raton proved me wrong. Several days had passed since the conversation with my boss, Steven, and I had just over six weeks left to pull everything together before I had to get back to my job. It would be a challenge; there was still so much to do.

Wearing tropical print harem pants, a sleeveless fitted turquoise tee, and lace-up sandals, I made my way toward the guest house. Bigfoot trotted after me, disappearing into the bushes when I stopped to pluck a red hibiscus bloom and tuck it behind my ear.

"Right on time. I love a punctual lady." Connor planted a warm, soft kiss on my cheek as he greeted me at the door.

I'd like that a little more centered, please.

The open-concept guest house had two bedrooms that shared a bathroom to the left of the open area. Furnished very tastefully in wicker furniture, Connor had placed several knick-knacks and photos around to make the place his own. A beautiful table setting—white tablecloth, midnight blue placemats, gold chargers with white dinner plates, and crystal wine glasses—adorned the dinette table in the small dining area.

"Wow! It looks like you're expecting someone special."

"Just my landlord," said Connor nonchalantly with a wink. "Please have a seat on the couch and enjoy some appetizers and wine while I finish dinner." He gestured to a partially filled wine glass and a small plate of appetizers on the coffee table. He looked comfortably domestic with a dish towel tucked into the waist of his khaki pants.

The small crab cakes with lemon sauce melted in my mouth, and I could have made a whole meal of the savory starter. I wanted to know more about Connor's background and family, the part I couldn't find out online. Now seemed an appropriate time.

"You never told me about your childhood, though when we first met, you said you were from Las Cruces."

"Yes, Las Cruces, New Mexico. Oldest child. Two sisters. Camille and Cathy."

Hmm. Connor, Camille, and Cathy. His parents must have a penchant for "Cs."

"Quite a different climate than Florida. It's mostly desert, isn't it?"

"Desert and mountains, but it's stunning in its own way. Think sunrises and sunsets against a backdrop of mountains that change colors from yellows to pinks to reds and purples. It's a sight to see."

"Sounds lovely. Is this a photo of it?" I picked up a framed picture from the coffee table. A young man and blonde woman were standing in the desert, red mountains, more like tabletops, rising behind them. An abundance of small red and yellow flowers bloomed at their feet.

"Yes, just after the rain. That's when the desert flowers bloom."

I recognized Connor but not the woman. "Is this one of your sisters?"

Connor hesitated. "No, she was my wife."

I placed the photo back down. "You said 'was.' Did something happen to her?"

"I think dinner is ready," Connor said, bringing it to the table. He offered a prayer in Spanish before we began our meal of lobster, new potatoes, asparagus, salad, and crusty French bread. I let him talk about growing up in Las Cruces while I stuffed myself. He never did mention his wife again—a conversation for another time, I guessed.

"How come you joined the Army?" I asked.

"My great grandparents originally came from Mexico as rancheros, people who worked on ranches and tended cattle.

When they became US citizens, they were so proud to be part of this country that they challenged all the boys in the family to serve in the military. It was their way of giving back and thanking the country for the freedom they experienced. My great grandfather became a foreman of a ranch and eventually owned a small ranch. My grandfather inherited it, and then my father. While I could have stayed on the ranch and helped my father, I wanted to honor my great-grandfather's wishes. Once I joined the Army and got into crime scene investigating, I became hooked. I kept on re-enlisting but eventually burned out. That's how I came to the Palm Beach VA."

"Why didn't you go back to New Mexico? Don't they have a VA there?"

"Yes, but I wanted to go somewhere I didn't have a history, so I could concentrate on getting better. I know having family around is helpful, but I didn't want to get distracted by too much family."

Does he include his former wife in that "too much family"?

Connor cleared the dishes and served dessert—key lime pie.

"Did your accounting friend get back to you?" I sliced a wedge of the pie. The creamy yellow filling was sweet and tangy, and the graham cracker crust firm—a perfect ending to an excellent meal.

"So this is how something like this works," said Connor. "The work order is generated by the computer, indicating the deposit and essentials—fabric, padding, embellishments, and so forth. The system updates the work order as the piece of furniture goes through each station during the reupholstering process. Final payment is received on the completed work either by cash or credit card, and the account is balanced. With me so far?"

I nodded. It wasn't rocket science.

"Everything shows up like it's copacetic. The customer has his merchandise and a receipt from the upholstery shop, the transaction is closed, and as far as the customer and shop staff are concerned, all is well. When the system posts transactions at the end of the day, some are wiped out, and these revenues are transferred into an alternative bank account. It's very clever and typically undetectable. You're fortunate Archie kept a paper trail of each transaction; otherwise, you would have never known."

"So, how can we catch this devious person or persons?" I placed my elbows on the table and leaned in.

"That's a bit more difficult. A programmer has altered the accounting software to remove certain transactions on the upholstery shop side and transfer the revenues into the alternative account. Of course, the process is password protected. And typically, a sophisticated process like this involves more than one person and includes someone on the inside with a password."

I pulled back in surprise. "You mean someone on my staff is the thief? Most of the employees have been with the shop for years. It's difficult for me to believe any of them would steal from the company."

"Yet someone did. While this person may not have manipulated the software, they arranged access to it. You'll need to hire someone like my friend who can go in and follow the transactions. The good news is my friend has vacation time coming and would be glad to travel here, for a fee, of course, and take a look at your system. The second bedroom in the guest house would provide adequate accommodations." Connor gave me a broad grin.

"That sounds great. Please ask your friend what his fee would be, and we can go from there. I need to get this corrected as soon as possible. Right now, the perpetrators don't know we're on to them, but as soon as they find out, the whole process will stop, and we'll never catch them."

"If the fee is acceptable, my friend can be here in two days. Is that fast enough?"

"Sounds great."

To trust someone so quickly was out of character for me, but I needed to get some answers. My father trusted Connor, and so far, I hadn't seen anything to challenge that trust. Besides, I'd already been in Boca for nine days. Time was flying by, and there was still so much to do.

While Connor cleaned the table and stacked dishes in the dishwasher, I looked at his photos more carefully. One had him in climbing gear standing in front of a snow-covered peak. I chuckled to myself as I recognized the ice ax he held in one hand. Another had him dangling from ropes while scaling the face of a barren mountain that I assumed was in New Mexico.

While viewing his photos, I happened to look down at some folded papers on the credenza. Something startling caught my eye. The top form was a repair bill for Connor's pickup truck's front end—grille and headlights—dated the day after my parents' deaths

Didn't Seth say the truck that rammed my father's car was a red pickup? And didn't Connor tell me he didn't get back until the day of the reception? It didn't add up. If someone repaired the truck the day after my parents' murders, that meant Connor was in town when the incident occurred.

A numbing cold crept through me. Was this what Seth meant when he asked me to keep my eyes and ears open?

With trembling hands, I lifted my cell phone from my pocket. One quick photo was all I needed, yet my hands shook so much I could barely hold the phone. I looked back at Connor. He was still busy at the sink with the dishes. I tapped the photo button.

Darn! Blurred! I needed another shot. I poised the camera.

"Hey, you interested in a walk around the neighborhood?"

I jumped at Connor's voice, fumbled the phone, and dropped it. Quickly picking it up, I stuffed it back into my pocket. I hadn't gotten a second shot, but I knew what I saw. I wheeled around.

"Gee, that would be nice, but wouldn't you know it? Just when I'm having fun, I've developed a headache. I need to go." I slipped hastily around the furniture and headed out the door.

"Wait a minute, Randi," said Connor, chasing after me.

"Sorry, Connor. Everything was lovely. Maybe we can do it again sometime." I hurriedly ran down the path toward the house amid a whirl of confusion. I let Connor's subsequent phone calls and text messages go unanswered well into the night.

Chapter 6

In the morning, I opened the front door only to find my car hemmed in by an assortment of garden equipment—several ladders in front, a wheelbarrow, and two garbage cans behind. Connor stood by the driver's door, hands on his hips, blocking any hope of my getting into the car. Dark circles under his eyes indicated a severe lack of sleep.

"I need to get to the store," I said, stepping off the stoop. "Please remove that stuff from the driveway." I flicked one hand toward the ladders while reaching into my purse with the other for my phone.

"Not until I get an explanation," Connor countered. "Why did you leave last night so brusquely? And why didn't you answer my calls or texts? Friends don't treat each other that way."

I stopped abruptly; his words stung. "Look, Connor, there's no reason to play dumb with me. I saw the invoice for the repairs on your truck."

"So now you're going through my personal belongings? Landlords may have some privileges, but that's not one of them." His eyes flashed with anger.

"Seth said a red pickup pushed my parents' car into the canal. Your truck is red and repaired the day *after* the incident. I have proof." I held up my phone. "If you don't get those things out of my way, I'll call the police."

"So, you believe some hotshot detective who thinks I may be the one who pushed your parents into the canal? Unbelievable!" Connor lowered his head, shaking it.

"What am I supposed to think?"

"Did you bother to notice the location of the repair shop? Obviously not, Miss Detective, because if you had, you'd have seen the repairs were made in Maine. Maine! That's a long way from Florida, sweetie. That's where I went climbing with one of the premier climbers in the US, Freddie Williamson. You can call him if you like. Here, let me text you his phone number." Connor yanked out his phone and tapped several buttons. "Someone backed into me in a parking lot up there, damaging the grille and smashing the truck's headlights. I couldn't drive back to Florida at night without lights, could I? Besides, the truck that rammed your parents' car wasn't red. It was grey. Don't believe me? Check the report."

I stood there, dumbfounded.

Grey? Why had Seth told me it was red?

"Look here, I'm going to follow through on my commitment to bring in the forensic accountant, and I'm going to help you find your parents' killer. It won't be because of you, though. It'll be because of your father and how kind he was to me. I owe it to him. After that, I'm out of here." Connor moved the ladders from in front of the car and stomped toward the backyard, pushing the wheelbarrow.

"Lover's spat?"

I turned to find Leslie staring at me. Bigfoot sat next to her, swishing his tail and looking as perplexed as I felt.

"How long have you been there?"

"Long enough to get the gist of that conversation," she said, walking toward me.

"I think I made a terrible mistake." A ribbon of heat crept up the back of my neck.

"Isn't your first. Won't be your last. Come on, Tootsie, let's go inside. I think you need time to calm down before you go to the store."

The coffee was still hot, so I poured both of us a mug. We sat at the kitchen island.

"To ease your mind, why don't you call this Williamson fellow in Maine? Then you'll know for sure whether Connor's telling you the truth," Leslie suggested.

I put in the call. Sure enough, Connor had been climbing with his friend in Maine, and his truck was damaged in the parking lot.

"What do I do now?" I asked.

"Depends upon how much you value your relationship with Connor."

"I enjoy his company, and he's been very helpful."

"Then, the next step is yours. Gotta run, Tootsie." Leslie patted my hand and left.

I phoned Connor, but all I got was his voice mail. I left an apology and also sent him one by text. When I returned this evening, I'd tell him in person—nothing like eating crow, and a big plate of it at that.

While walking to the fabric store from the parking lot, I received a text from Connor informing me of the fee for the forensic accountant. I agreed to the estimate, and his buddy would arrive tomorrow afternoon. He said nothing more.

My first stop was the upholstery shop and Archie. Several days had passed since I'd seen him, and I wanted to catch him up on what was going on. Plus, we never finished our conversation about Leo Barlos. I found him at the bay, arranging new furniture that had just arrived for reupholstering.

"How are you doing, Miss Randi? We've been praying for you." Archie gestured toward his office. We continued our conversation as we moved in its direction.

"Thanks, Archie. Right now, I can use all the prayers I can get. How are things here?"

"Very busy, as you can see, but I really won't know how well we've done until the monthly report comes out. Then we can compare what it says to what we've done."

We sat down next to each other in the chairs in front of Archie's desk.

"We're going to have some help soon since what we're experiencing is over both our heads. I've hired a forensic accountant to look into the matter. He should be here tomorrow."

"Good timing," said Archie. "It's the end of the month, and he may be able to catch the culprit in action."

"Most of his work will be off-site at a computer, but he may need to come in to speak with you. If the staff asks who he is, you can tell them he's a special customer."

"Will you need my ledger?"

"Please make a copy of it. I'll pick it up tomorrow morning and have it ready when the accountant arrives."

Archie nodded his head. "Sure thing, Miss Randi."

"Now, about Leo Barlos. You were about to tell me something about him when I was here last."

Archie hung his head and was silent for a moment, then he looked directly at me and spoke in a soft voice. "The Bible warns us about wolves in sheep's clothing, people who profess to be one thing but are something else. That's what Leo Barlos is. He's very charming on the outside but ruthless on the inside. He's been after your father to sell this property for as long as I can remember. He wants to tear down the buildings and put up a block-long strip mall. He can't do that without this property since we're right in the middle of the land he already owns and wants to develop. Don't be surprised if he approaches you one day about it."

"Thanks for letting me know." I moved to get up, but Archie placed a hand on my arm, stopping me.

"Miss Randi, I didn't mean Mr. Barlos is ruthless in a business sort of way, though he's that, too. I mean, he's very heavy-handed and will stop at nothing to possess this property." The seriousness of his statement showed in his penetrating brown eyes.

"I'll be ready for him, Archie."

"I hope so, ma'am."

I spent the afternoon in the fabric store and checked my phone several times for messages. Other than the forensic accountant's notice, I didn't get any calls or texts from Connor. I couldn't blame him, of course. I had done a terrible thing insinuating his involvement in my parent's deaths. I tried to put it out of my mind, but better said than done. For a person used to being in control, I seemed to be anything but.

Rachel invited me to dinner, so I went right there from the store. After eating and while Todd got the children ready for bed, Rachel and I sat on the patio, glass of wine in hand, and talked. I told her everything that had happened.

"Why would Seth lie?" she asked. "Do you think he's still carrying a torch for you and is trying to put a wedge between you and Connor?"

"Thing is, there's nowhere to put the wedge. Connor and I were friends; now I don't know what we are. Maybe simply landlord and tenant." I took a sip of wine.

"Well, I think you need to confront Seth and find out why he told you the car was red when it was grey."

"I intend to. In the meantime, what can you tell me about Leo Barlos?"

Rachel sat forward. Cupping her wine glass in both hands, she swiveled it.

"Good old Leo. We call him Baron Barlos," she said. "His parents came here in the early 50s and started with several pieces of property they bought from the closed Boca Raton Army Air Field. They were forward thinkers and saw the potential in Boca, buying up former base buildings and acreage right and left. They converted some of the buildings into apartments and rented them out to newcomers to the area. Other buildings became storefronts, which they leased to retailers."

"I remember Leslie showing me aerial photos of the community before and after the war. What a difference a few years made. In the late 1940s, there were only around 700 residents in Boca. By 1960, there were houses everywhere." In my mind, I could still see the images.

"Leo inherited the company from his parents and methodically expanded the portfolio. He now owns about seventy percent of the commercial property in the city and makes no bones about the fact that he wants to own it all. With his power, financial status, and influence, he's highly sought after for charitable boards and serves on several. He's well connected politically and wields a lot of power and not just in Boca. He's made considerable contributions to political campaigns in state and national elections. People either love him or hate him." Rachel pressed the wine glass to her lips and took a swallow.

"How about you? Do you love him or hate him?"

"I hate his holier-than-thou attitude and bullying techniques," she said without hesitation. "He's no different than a thug, in my opinion. On the other hand, he has made a big difference in the community by giving away millions of dollars to local charities. But then, even the murderous Al Capone proved to have a philanthropic streak when he opened the first soup kitchen in Chicago during the Depression. Of course, Capone was concerned about the common man since he was the son of a barber. Barlos comes from money and gives it away only to impress people and wield power."

"How far do you think he'd go to get his hands on a piece of property he wants?"

"Pretty far, I think." Rachel cocked her head to one side. "What are you thinking? That Leo's involved with your parents' deaths because he wants your property?"

"There's nothing to indicate his involvement, but hearing what you and Archie have said today doesn't ease my mind." I poured more wine into my glass.

"Well, be careful. I've heard horror stories about people who didn't sell out to the Baron. Oh, I almost forgot, you did get the invitation to join Todd and me at the Historical Society gala on Saturday, didn't you?"

"I know you mean well, but I don't know if I'm up to it, Rachel." With everything that was going on, attending a nonprofit money raiser was the last thing on my mind.

"Look, Randi, you can't become a hermit and go just between the store and house. Getting out and meeting new people will be good for you. There are so many who want to meet you. We'll pick you up around seven."

I sighed. "Maybe."

When I got home, I fed Bigfoot. I could tell he wasn't happy about eating so late, but taking care of a cat just wasn't part of my routine yet. The fact that neglecting him wasn't doing him any favors either and my feeling guilty made me ponder whether he would be better off in an alternative home.

I summoned the courage to talk with Connor and went to the guest house. His truck wasn't in the driveway. I was relieved in one way, but not in another. I still needed face-to-face time, and the sooner, the better. A note on his door let him know I had stopped by.

Snuggling in bed with my laptop, I typed in the name Leo Barlos. Lots of sites popped up, mainly relating to the company advertising the availability of office, warehouse, or storefront space. I found more salacious stories in the newspaper archives, where a slew of articles from local newspapers addressed property disputes. The reports suggested that intimidation, threats, property damage, and even personal injury were tactics Barlos used to squeeze property owners into selling over previous decades. None of the property owners pressed charges against him, though. In the end, they all sold, mainly because selling was easier than spending copious amounts of time and money fighting him in court. I had no reason to suspect Leo Barlos in my parents' deaths, yet Archie's and Rachel's warnings seemed sincere.

~

I made a quick stop at the fabric store and upholstery shop in the morning, where I picked up a copy of Archie's ledger. Next, I went shopping at a local organic market. I'd fix a nice but simple meal for Connor, the forensic accountant, and myself so we could talk about how the process would unfold. I sent a text to Connor, inviting him and his buddy for dinner at 7 p.m. That would give them enough time to get home from the airport and relax a bit before coming to the house. He sent me a text: WE'LL BE THERE.

Marcia, my parents' housekeeper, came at one o'clock. Since the funeral reception, she hadn't been at the house but started back on her regular schedule of once a week. I knew the house wouldn't get that dirty in a week with me being the only person living in it, yet for some reason, I wanted to keep the same routine as my parents. Besides, with my busy schedule, I couldn't clean the house with the attention to detail Marcia did.

I preset the table in the dining room, selected several flowers from the garden, and placed them in a vase. The table looked most presentable for a first impression. A knock on the back door alerted me that Connor and his accountant buddy had arrived.

When I opened the door, my eyes nearly popped from my head. Before me stood the petite and attractive blonde-haired woman in Connor's photo of the desert—his former wife!

"Hi, Randi. This is Sarah Samuels, the forensic accountant," Connor said without a hitch.

My mind sputtered for a few moments before I came to my senses. "Please come in." I sent Connor a stern look as he crossed the threshold.

He gave me his cute little wink and grin as he passed me. "I never said my friend was a man. That was your assumption," he whispered.

Ugh! Such cockiness!

Over cheese and crackers, the two talked and giggled like long-lost friends. While we talked about the upcoming assignment over dinner, the meal proved to be more of renewing the old acquaintance between them than a business meeting that included me. By the time they were ready to leave, I was thoroughly peeved.

"It was a lovely dinner, Randi. I'll see you in the morning." Sarah gave me an air kiss as she left.

"Thanks for making Sarah feel at home," said Connor. He stuck out his hand. I kept mine by my side. He shrugged. "Suit yourself."

I watched the two of them walk away, arm in arm, toward the guest house. Had I been a kettle, I would have spouted steam.

I spent the rest of the night trying to calm down and think rationally about the evening. In reality, Sarah was charming. Did I care if the forensic accountant was a man or a woman? If the person was qualified and could do the job, wasn't that all that counted? Yes, except for two things. First, Connor didn't tell me his "friend" was his good-looking ex-wife. And second, she was staying in the guest house with him!

~

Sarah came to the house the next morning. I gave her a history of the business, a list of who works where and has access to the computer system, and explained that my father analyzed the reports at the end of each month. I also explained how Archie found the discrepancies by keeping records of his own and gave her copies of the ledger.

"I don't know if Connor told you, but along with being a forensic accountant, I'm also a programmer. I used to develop and customize accounting software. Now I work for the government to fight white-collar crime and put bad guys away. Both of my skill sets will help us discover how the transactions became deleted, the money transferred to a different account, and who is doing it." Sarah continued to flip through Archie's ledger.

Beauty and brains. A dangerous combination.

"So glad Connor knew just the right person to call," I said behind a smug smile.

"I'll set up at the dining room table in the guest house for the duration of my stay. If I need to speak with Archie, I'll let you know."

"Sure. I'll be glad to take you to the shop."

Yeah, and while you're there, maybe Archie can reupholster you in ugly fabric.

I wanted to know about her and Connor's relationship and what happened to their marriage, but I couldn't bring myself to pry. I had already done that with disastrous results. I walked her to the door.

"Thank you for coming. I can't tell you how overwhelmed I've been since..." My sentence trailed off into nothing, and my lips began to quiver. I hadn't thought about my parents' deaths in days, but somehow at this moment, the overwhelming sense of loss hit me big time.

"Let's sit down," Sarah suggested. We sat on the couch next to each other. She took my hands. "Look, Randi, we never get over losing people we love, but we do learn to move on. Grief is like a Jack in the Box. We stuff it down and close the lid, but it pops up again at the most unexpected times. Sometimes it's a smell, or a phrase someone says, or a song. Other times it's completely unrelated."

I grabbed a tissue and blew into it.

"You know Connor and I were married, right?"

I nodded.

"After his second deployment to Afghanistan, I decided I could no longer live with his long absences. There was no doubt we loved each other, but it was as though my life had been put on hold. His commitment to the US Army and my marriage expectations didn't mesh. He loved what he was doing. How could I ask him to give it up? On the other hand, he knew what I needed didn't include an absentee husband. We agreed to go our separate ways."

Hmm. An amenable split. That doesn't happen often.

"It was like a death to me," said Sarah, bringing her hands to her heart. "I grieved for a long time. I was doing fine until seven months later. While driving a bit fast down the street, a cop pulled me over. He asked my name. Without hesitation, I said, 'Sarah Romero,' even though I had changed my last name back to Samuels several months earlier. It was then the grief of the divorce hit me like a blow to the stomach; I burst into uncontrollable tears."

"I'm sure that was quite a shock to the officer. What happened?" I asked, dabbing at my eyes.

"Fortunately, the cop understood, but the point is, it takes time to heal from losing someone we love through any personal trauma. What you're going through is doubly difficult since you lost both parents at the same time from the most painful of circumstances. Grieve whenever you need to, and be kind to yourself." Sarah hugged me before leaving.

In my eyes, she moved from merely being Connor's "friend" to a very compassionate and extraordinary human being.

For the next several days, Sarah worked diligently, following the transactions. She only came by when she had a question. I didn't see Connor except through a window when he worked in the garden around the house. The fabric store consumed my time, and I continued my familiarity with the material and operations. I even made numerous transactions at the register. In many ways, being back at the store reminded me of the summers I'd spent there.

I always enjoyed the upholstery side of the business, including the texture and design of the fabric. After Mom added quilting fabrics, a whole world of possibilities opened up that introduced new customers to the store. It now offered quilting classes from beginner to experienced and quilted clothes making. I was amazed at the ingenuity of the accomplished sewers who combined the upholstery and drapery fabrics with quilting fabrics to create some fabulous clothing and quilt designs. My goal was to have an annual display of these artful creations one day.

Chapter 7

Saturday was here before I could blink. In the morning, Rachel took me to several boutiques to find something appropriate for the historical society's gala theme, "Denim and Diamonds." After two hours, she finally settled on her rendition of what I should wear—an off-the-shoulder washed denim top that buttoned down the front paired with deep cuff white stretch jeans and white lace-up heels.

"You look stunning," said Rachel as I pivoted in front of the tri-panel mirror.

"I don't know, Rachel. Don't you think it's a little over the top for me?"

"You've been keeping yourself locked up in a news production studio too long. It's time you started to live."

That night, my mother's rhinestone necklace plus her diamond earrings, bracelet, and ring added bling to my new outfit as I took a final look at myself in the mirror. I still had curves in all the right places, and with my hair clipped back on one side and appropriate makeup, I looked pretty attractive.

Like high school, though, I would never hold a candle to Rachel. She could wear a sack and look beautiful, even after birthing two children.

After feeding Bigfoot, I sat on a bench at the front of the house and waited for Rachel and Todd to pick me up. Except for the media banquet a few weeks ago in Washington and the funeral, I hadn't been this dressed up in years. I was more of a laid-back kind of girl, letting my professional abilities speak rather than any physical attributes I may have. To be truthful, I played them down from my makeup to my attire. I knew what went on behind closed doors at the television station.

A wolf whistle jolted me out of my musings.

"Quite the outfit," said Connor. He stood in his usual work attire and looked me up and down. Though I was sure he meant his whistle and gawking as flattering, I couldn't help but feel like I was being served up as hors d'oeuvres to executives at the station back in Washington.

Before I could respond, Todd screeched to a stop in the driveway.

"Get in!" Rachel shouted through her open window.

"What happened?"

"The upholstery shop is on fire," she yelled.

Panic rushed through me like an electric current. I jumped into the car, and Todd took off.

"How did you find out?" I asked, my voice trembling.

"When the police couldn't reach your parents, they called Adele. She couldn't get you, so she called me."

"Oh, my gosh! I turned off my phone when I was in the tub and forgot to turn it back on." I hurriedly pulled out my phone and turned it on. "It also never occurred to me to put my name on the property in case of an emergency. No wonder the police couldn't contact me."

When we got to the shop, we scrambled from the car. Two ladder trucks and medic units surrounded the building. Adele and Ron, along with Archie and his family, watched from a distance as the fire department sprayed the flames. Dark smoke billowed from the building, its acrid odor permeating the air. Ashes swirled around us. Fortunately, the fire had damaged only a small portion of the back of the warehouse. The rest of the shop seemed intact, though water and smoke damage were inevitable.

"Oh, Miss Randi, this is terrible," Archie said. His wife and son watched the destruction with tears running down their faces.

I gave each of them a hug. "We'll be okay, Archie. Your faith and determination will see us through."

"And God's help, Miss Randi."

"That, too," I said. "Do the firefighters know how it happened?"

"They're not sure, but they think an accelerant might have started it. Several firefighters said they smelled gasoline," Adele said.

"Arson? Why would someone want to burn the upholstery shop?" Rachel asked in disbelief.

Archie, Rachel, and I looked at each other. Though not spoken, I was sure the name Leo Barlos was on the tips of our tongues.

"Not the kind of outfits I'd wear to a fire," said a familiar voice behind us.

Rachel and I turned to see Seth walking toward us.

"We were going to a gala when we got word. How'd you find out about it?" I asked.

"Professional courtesy," he said. "The Boca police knew I was working on your parents' case. If this is connected, we need to know."

Rachel's brows shot up. "Is that what you think? That the two events are linked?"

"Too early to tell," said Seth. "Excuse me." He walked toward one of the firefighters.

We remained transfixed until the fire was mostly out, though the fire crew still attended some smoldering areas. Archie and I moved closer to the building, walking through wet sand and mud mixed with soot. I saw several broken windows and a damaged side door firefighters entered to put out the fire from inside the warehouse. I gasped when I realized the significance of the fire. The portion of the structure that burned was Archie's office.

"The ledger!" Archie and I exclaimed in unison.

He ran toward the office, but a firefighter stopped him. "Sir, you can't go in there. This is a crime scene until it's cleared." He pointed to a technician who was making plaster casts of footprints outside the window.

"But I have to check on something important," Archie said. He tried going around the first responder but was blocked.

"It won't be until Monday at the earliest," said the firefighter. He escorted Archie back to where I was standing and then helped cordon off the area with yellow crime tape.

Archie looked dejected. "At least we have copies."

"That's something to be thankful for," I said.

Seth walked over to us. "You'll need to take care of that door and window to secure the building. After firefighters clear it, you'll be able to go inside. They'll keep me informed of what they've found, and I'll keep you in the loop. You might as well go on to your gala."

I looked down at myself. Soot smudged my white pants, and mud ruined my heels, not to mention my hair and clothes smelled like smoke.

Adele and Ron went home. Randall stayed at the warehouse while Archie took off to get some plywood to board up the building. He said they'd stay there all night if necessary. Rachel and Todd drove me home and helped me put together a list of priorities to tackle. Contacting my insurance company topped the list, followed by the security company. Thankfully, the fabric store remained unscathed due to the nighttime sea breeze that blew the smoke and fire westward, away from the store. Tomorrow, I'd assess the damage to see whether we needed to relocate the upholstery shop or we could stay in the building during repairs.

After everyone left the house, I hoped Connor would come by or at least call to see how things were.

He didn't.

~

Mid-morning on Sunday, Archie and I met at the warehouse. He'd been there all night, securing the building then sleeping in his truck to make sure no one broke in. We walked the exterior of the structure to evaluate what damage we could see from the outside. Two firefighters, who had been there since dawn, finished gathering evidence and performed their final inspection. Upon departing, they allowed us to enter the shop a day earlier than we expected.

I gasped and brought my hand to my face as the odor of waterlogged burnt wood assaulted me. I wish I'd brought a mask. Fortunately, I had on a tunic tee and lifted the hem to cover my mouth and nose.

Archie stood next to me as we inspected the interior of the shop. Water covered the floor in the back where the office, mostly gutted and charred, used to be. Archie's desk was still standing but burned to a crisp, as were the other office furnishings. The fire's intense heat had practically vaporized the ledger, leaving only blackened pieces of soggy paper that liquefied in our fingers.

Outside the office by the bay, furniture waiting to be upholstered was intact. Unfortunately, smoke, the smell of which still hung heavy in the air, had permeated the fabric on the shelves and furniture pieces in various stages of the upholstery process. We would need to discard all this fabric and start over, an expensive proposition. Yet, our insurance would cover the damage. On the positive side, fixtures and equipment at the stations were salvageable, though all would need cleaning and some touch-up.

"We'll have to move out for a while, Miss Randi, until the building can be repaired and cleaned."

"I agree, Archie. We also don't want your staff to work in such smelly surroundings."

"Tomorrow, I'll look for a temporary place and start making arrangements to move the equipment. Hopefully, we can find something close by," said Archie.

"A crying shame," said a deep booming voice. Leo Barlos, dressed in his Sunday best—another hand-tailored suit of luxurious material—walked through the shop toward us. I was surprised he'd do so, considering smoke vapors might adhere to his expensive suit. But then, no problem. He could readily afford another one. He stopped, clasped his hands behind his back, and scanned the interior.

"I was at church when a friend texted me the news. Thought I'd stop by to see how I could help. Looks like you might need another place to operate while the building is repaired. Good thing you happen to know someone in the commercial property business." His rosy cheeks vibrated as he let out a muted laugh.

"We're not sure what we'll need as we just touched base with the insurance company. The appraiser will be here this afternoon."

"Well, I'm sorry this happened, especially so close to you losing your parents. If you need warehouse space, don't hesitate to call me. I'm sure we'll be able to find something for you." His smile seemed sincere, but his reputation convinced me there was an ulterior motive behind the grin.

"Thank you, Mr. Barlos, that's very kind. Archie and I will be sure to give you a call if we need you."

Leo looked me square in the eye. "Oh, you'll need me, Miss Brooks. You'll need me." He turned and left without further conversation.

Archie and I walked outside; I removed the makeshift mask from my face.

"I'll make sure we find someplace Leo Barlos doesn't own," he said, looking at me with a stern expression.

"Good idea," I said, though I knew our selection close to the store would be limited.

"Miss Randi, the firefighters were talking before they left. They said someone broke the window of the office then threw a Molotov cocktail inside. They found broken glass from the window and the broken bottle. From the smell, they said it had gasoline in it. That's how the fire started."

"So, it was deliberate?"

"Seems so, Miss Randi. They hope to find fingerprints on the broken pieces of glass but said it depends if the culprit was an amateur or professional. The professionals wear gloves so there won't be any prints."

"Archie, did you tell anyone about the ledger?"

"Goodness no, Miss Randi. Not a soul."

"Seems funny someone would burn the only section of the warehouse that held evidence against the accounting thief."

"Yes, ma'am. Sure does."

A man wearing a mask walked up and introduced himself as the insurance company's appraiser, hampering further discussion. Archie and I stayed to answer questions and show him around until he left an hour later. By that time, the emotional stress had zapped every ounce of strength from me.

When I got home, I tried to relax by taking a swim, but there were too many matters swirling in my head—my parents' deaths, Seth, Ron, Connor, Sarah, Leo Barlos, the accounting theft, the fire. How was I going to sort it all out? As the Capitol Hill news producer, I was used to juggling locations, prioritizing reporters, and editing scores of video within a tight timeframe. Still, the last two weeks had taxed every ounce of my mental and emotional being. If I was going to finish my business here and get back to my job in D.C. within the allotted time, which at this point seemed like an absurd notion, I needed some answers and fast. The first answer I needed was why Seth lied to me about the color of the truck. I climbed from the pool, wrapped a towel around me, and phoned him.

"How's the building?" Seth asked.

"Well, we'll have to find another place to work while they clean up and repair the warehouse, but we should be back there in about a month. It could have been worse."

"If I can help in any way, please let me know."

"Any news on locating the truck?" I asked.

"Not yet, but we're still looking. Sometimes these things take months."

"I've meant to ask you about something you said earlier. When we went to Boca Rio Road, you told me that the vehicle that pushed my parents' car into the canal was a pickup truck and that it was red."

"Red? You must have misheard, Randi. I'm sure I said it was grey."

"And I'm just as sure you said it was red." My tone was one of conviction.

"Well, no harm done. The color is grey. It's in the report."

No harm done! Maybe not to him, but I had seriously bruised a relationship I was beginning to enjoy. Had Seth set me up because of jealousy? We hung up on a sour note.

"Tootsie, I hope I'm not disturbing you." Leslie shuffled over to a patio chair and sat down. I sat in one across from her.

"You know you're always welcome," I said.

"The TV news reported the fire. I am so sorry."

"Fortunately, it only damaged a small portion of the building. We'll need to relocate the upholstery shop for a while, but it could have been a lot worse."

"Here, I brought you something. It took me a while to find it, but I know you'd like to see this." Leslie handed me a newspaper clipping with a photograph from the *Boca Raton*

News, a community newspaper that started back in 1955. It went out of business in the early 2000s only to rise like a phoenix online years later. There wasn't a date on the clipping.

"Is this one of your ancient relics?" I asked.

"Just one out of thousands," said Leslie with a laugh. "Do you recognize either of the boys?"

"That's my father," I said, pointing to the younger version of him on the left. He was wearing a high school basketball uniform and had his arm draped over another young man's shoulders, also in uniform.

"Do you recognize the other boy?" Leslie asked.

The handsome face had a hint of familiarity, but I couldn't quite place it. "Can't say that I do."

"It's Leo Barlos."

"What?" I looked closer at the photo. Sure enough, the face was a lot thinner, but the eyes were the same as were the ruddy cheeks.

"He and your father were best friends in high school. They had a falling out in their twenties and remained at odds."

"Why didn't you tell me this before?" I couldn't believe my father would ever have been best friends with such a devious individual.

"Didn't think it was important until now. With the fire and Barlos' reputation, I just remembered it," said Leslie

"Where did you get the photo?"

"From my boxes. You see, I've kept everything about the history of the city in those boxes. Why I have things you'll never find anywhere else. I don't even know why I kept this clipping, but I could say that about most of the papers and photos I have in the house. I keep thinking someday they'll be significant to someone."

"Why didn't you give all of it to the historical society?"

"Can't tell you how many times I've needed to find something. If they were in a building where I couldn't access them, I wouldn't be able to get my hands on things when I need them."

It made sense, but at what cost? A house so stuffed you could hardly walk through it? Not to mention how long it must have been since the place had a good cleaning. I looked back at the photo. The boys looked tired, yet they beamed as though they had just won an important game.

"Do you know what came between them?"

"I believe it was your mother."

I pulled back in dismay.

"My mother? Why?" Neither of my parents ever said anything about this.

"Your father never spoke about it, but your mother hinted at something long ago. Your father and Leo were both in love with her. She chose your father."

"My mother considered marrying Leo Barlos?" The revelation was as though I'd done a belly flop in the pool. It stung and pushed all the air from my lungs.

"He wasn't always the conniving character he is today. When Leo was younger, he was charming and most handsome. His character changed when your mother rejected him and married your father. It wasn't long before he turned into an angry and vengeful person. It's what drove him to become the powerful and wealthy man he is today. He wanted to prove to your mother that she married the wrong man."

I sat there, dumbfounded.

"Look, Tootsie, I don't know how this all fits into what's happened, but you needed to know. I don't think Leo had anything to do with your parents' deaths. While he may have wished your father ill and even had a part in the fire, he would never have hurt your mother. He always carried a torch for her. Unrequited love, I believe."

Looking back at my parents' funeral reception, I remembered how Leo became all choked up when he spoke about my mother and how he tenderly caressed my cheek. I thought it creepy at the time, but in light of what Leslie just told me, it seemed to make sense.

I thanked her for showing me the article and bid her good night, unsure I would have one.

Chapter 8

By mid-morning the next day, the appraiser had given us the go-ahead to relocate and a monetary amount to work with. As long as we were frugal, the insurance money would allow us to do more than repair the shop. We could upgrade it, too.

While Archie researched locations, the sales and shop staff notified customers of the fire and the delay in delivering their furniture. Fortunately, we still retained undamaged fabric in the store that went on most of the furniture, but some would have to be acquired, further delaying orders. A handful of clients picked up their items and went elsewhere, while most longtime customers were understanding and opted to wait for the shop to relocate.

After lunch, Archie met me at the upholstery shop where staff not making phone calls to customers were organizing and preparing the equipment and furniture items for transport to another location, even though we didn't quite know yet where that would be. He spread a map before me on one of the work tables. The smell of smoke mixed with water, like that of a doused chimney fire, still infused the air. Though we had the air conditioner on and the doors open, hoping the smell would dissipate, this time, we all wore masks.

"Miss Randi, Randall and I have looked at possible buildings from Delray to Pompano Beach. Several warehouses are big enough to accommodate us for a month or so, but each needs electrical work to satisfy our needs. It would take another week to have that work completed, plus each one is more than five miles away. These red dots indicate the location of these warehouses." Archie pointed at the dots.

"Hmm. The buildings seem so far away," I said. "Transporting the furniture to and from would take hours out of our production time."

"I agree. Now, there are several warehouses close by that already meet our electrical needs, but they're all owned by Mr. Barlos."

"Those are the green dots?" I asked, pointing to them.

"Yes, ma'am. I hate to say it, Miss Randi, but the ones he owns are probably our best bet. We could be in them and set up within the week." Archie's dark eyes searched mine, looking for guidance.

I let out a long sigh. "You know I hate to do business with that man, but we do have to be practical. I suppose we could stand him for a couple of months. If you think it's the right move, then go ahead. Make the arrangements."

~

"So, you've come to sign the lease?" Leo sat behind his massive desk in his enormous office, displaying a giant

Cheshire cat grin. To him, the taste of victory was like eating milk chocolate—sweet.

"Well, of all the locations Archie looked at, this one makes the most sense. It's close by and seems to have everything we need." I hated to acquiesce to this man, but we had no choice. We needed to be up and running as quickly as possible.

"Didn't I tell you, you'd need me?"

I was sure he would have let his underlings take care of such mundane business transactions as a tenant signing a lease. Yet, I knew he wanted to take care of this in person so he could gloat over our unfortunate situation.

"You did, Mr. Barlos. Now, if I can sign the lease and get the keys, I'll let Archie know he can start loading up."

"Before you sign and go through all the expense of reconstruction at your warehouse, you'd be remiss if you didn't consider moving your operation to this warehouse. You'll already be there, and I'll even sweeten the pot by making you a great deal on ample storefront space to relocate your fabric store. It's just across the street from where you are. I'll pay for your moving expenses and throw in several months of free rent. And, I'll make you a most generous offer on your property. Now that's a deal you can hardly refuse." Barlos sat forward in his chair and continued to grin.

"We appreciate your offer, Mr. Barlos, but we like where we are."

"I'm only making that offer once, Randi. If you walk out the door and don't take it, you'll regret it." He pushed his proposal toward me.

"Thanks, but no thanks," I said, pushing it back. "Now, please, the lease we agreed on."

Leo placed the accepted lease in front of me. Even though we hoped we would be back in the old building within a month, we had no idea what issues the construction crew might run into while repairing the warehouse. Knowing these things usually took longer than expected, we opted for a sixty-day lease to give us a cushion of time in case we ran into unforeseen difficulties.

"If you find you'll need to stay longer, let me know. I'm sure we can extend the lease," said Leo.

"Hopefully, we won't have to do that. What you're charging is a pretty substantial price. If it weren't for the insurance money covering it, I'm sure we couldn't afford it," I said, placing my signature on the line.

Leo handed the signed document to his assistant, then let out a husky laugh. "Come now, dear, what I'm charging you is fair. It's the going market rate."

"With a hefty amount of our desperation thrown in," I said with a raised eyebrow. Leo's assistant handed me a copy of the signed lease and two sets of the warehouse keys. I could hardly leave the man's office fast enough.

As soon as I got in the car, I phoned Archie, who went to work making arrangements for the move. He hired a crew of helpers and several trucks. Between them and Randall's logistics training, I hoped everything would be up and running by the end of the week. In the meantime, the insurance company took care of getting someone to clean up the upholstery shop, and they contracted a construction company to start repairing the fire damage.

In the middle of all this, Seth called.

"Hey, did you get my text?"

"I'm sorry, Seth. I've been so preoccupied with the lease on the new warehouse, I haven't looked at my phone. What did you want?"

"To come by and take a look at the video from the day Ron and your father talked. And I'll probably need a copy of it, depending upon what I see."

"Of course. Thursday afternoon would be great. It's the earliest I'll be available since Archie's planned the move to the new warehouse for Wednesday."

"That's fine. See you then."

~

On Thursday afternoon, I brought my laptop down from my room and set it up on the desk in the den in anticipation of Seth's visit. I brought in two chairs and placed them side by side in front of the computer. I also copied the bank statements and check stubs and had them clipped together for him.

The chime of the doorbell told me Seth had arrived. Upon opening the door, I found him gripping a large bouquet—roses, mums, baby's breath, greenery.

"What's this?" I asked, staring at the lovely flowers.

"You've been going through so much lately I wanted to brighten your day." His smile was warm, his eyes soft, as he presented the flowers and entered the house.

"Is this part of your protocol?" I walked to the kitchen to put the flowers in a vase; Seth followed.

"Not exactly. I just thought you could use a bit of cheering up."

Was this his way of apologizing for misrepresenting the facts about the truck? "Well, it's very considerate. Thank you."

I hadn't had a man bring me flowers in years. There was just no time for romance with my hectic schedule. Plus, I had sworn off men three years ago, ever since my break up with Michael. We'd had what I considered an ideal relationship for an engaged couple, and as far as I could see, we were headed toward the altar. But then came the blow. A misunderstanding? Perhaps. But I didn't take too kindly to him telling me he had to break our dinner date because of work, only to accidentally run into him later that evening having dinner with another woman at Valrico's Bistro. He said it was business. Yeah, and I knew just what kind of business it was—monkey business. Their closeness, intertwined hands, whispers, and soft kisses spoke of much more. I can't say it was my finest hour as I made my way to their table, took off my engagement ring, and mashed it into Michael's coconut cream pie. Then I wiped my whipped cream fingers on his silk tie.

I selected a lovely clear-cut glass vase, filled it with water, and placed the flowers in it, spreading them out to their fullest.

"There," I said, turning the container around and scrutinizing my handiwork. "I've got us all set up in the office in the den. Why don't we go in there?"

Carrying the flowers, I led Seth to the office. When we got there, I placed the vase on the front of the credenza. Just as I set it down, a ray of sunlight broke through the clouds, shined through the window, and landed on the bouquet. The color of the flowers became intensified. I looked at Seth, awed by the timing, as though it was an omen.

"Uh, maybe we should look at the tapes," I said, sitting in front of the desk and clicking the keys on the computer. Seth sat, too.

We viewed the tapes from the day in question, including my father and Ron's silent but animated time together. I also handed Seth copies of the paperwork.

"Unfortunately, Randi, this doesn't prove anything, except that your father was giving your uncle money, and they had a disagreement. Sure, it could be a motive, and naturally, I'll ask Ron about it as part of the investigation. I'll try to keep from revealing where I got the initial lead, but he may eventually figure it out. After all, you now have access to your parents' security cameras and entire financial portfolio. If Ron does realize we have this information and where it came from, your relationship with him could change dramatically. Just be prepared for that."

"Even if you tell him that looking into my parents' finances is a routine part of the homicide investigation?"

"Sure, I can tell him that, and it would be true, but he'll know you provided the videotape and your father's bank statements."

"He couldn't blame me for that if you asked to see them. Besides, can't you look at Ron's bank account and see his deposits?"

"Not without due cause and a court order."

I stood, nervous that this whole thing could blow up in my face.

"Please, Seth, do what you can to keep me out of it. If Ron thinks I'm pointing the finger at him, it will affect my relationship with him. Adele may find out about the payments and be furious that my parents didn't tell her, not to mention the potential disruption of the operation of the fabric store as a result." Though I handled crises and made tough decisions every day in my job in Washington, things here seemed to be spiraling to the breaking point. Bile rose in my throat.

Seth stood and looked at me. His eyes spoke of the desire to wrap me in his arms, plant a kiss on my lips, and tell me everything would be alright. It was what I needed, but now was not the time. I stepped back, breaking the brief spell between us.

"Seth, I want to suggest something that could save you a lot of needless investigating time and me the possibility of an issue with Ron and Adele."

"What's that?"

"You haven't found the truck have you?"

"Not yet."

"Well, what if you don't question Ron until you find the vehicle and driver? That way, if you find there is no connection between my uncle and the truck or driver, you won't need to investigate the bank accounts at all. It will just have been an argument between my father and Ron about money."

"Police investigations don't work that way. If there is a potential motive for a crime, we need to follow the trail until we eliminate that person as a suspect." Seth let out a sigh.

"But I'm not suggesting you shouldn't investigate Ron. Just postpone questioning him until you locate the truck and driver and find out if he's involved."

"That could take weeks or even months!" said Seth. "I'll do what I can, Randi, but there are no promises. I have a legal and moral obligation to follow all leads once a crime has occurred."

I walked Seth to the door. "Anything you can do would be greatly appreciated."

"One more thing," he said. "If we find that the argument isn't associated with your parents' deaths but is connected to another crime, we'll have to turn it over to the Boca Raton Police since it occurred in their jurisdiction."

"I understand, but please don't tell them until you let me know."

"Agreed. Maybe after this is all over, we can see each other on a less professional basis." Seth looked at me with great expectation.

I laid a gentle hand on his arm. "Seth, you still have a lot to go through in your own life. Let's not get ahead of ourselves."

He smiled and kissed me on the cheek.

"You're right, of course. Good night."

After Seth left, I sat in the office and put together a budget for restoring the upholstery shop. The insurance coverage would offset the shop's loss, but no one could reimburse us for our time. That was lost forever.

Around 10:00 p.m., I got a text message from Sarah. She was finished with her investigation and wanted to meet tomorrow morning to give me the final results. I hoped her research would finally resolve one of the mysteries I faced.

~

"Well, I'm all packed and ready to go. As soon as we complete our meeting, Connor is taking me to the airport." Sarah settled into her seat at the breakfast table and placed her valise on the chair beside her. "Connor told me about the fire. Do they know how it happened or who did it?"

"They're still investigating, but it looks like it was deliberate."

"I'm so sorry to hear that, especially since it came on the heels of the accounting theft and what happened to your parents. Are the crimes related?"

"No one knows yet. It will take weeks to sort it all out. Please know how much I appreciate your taking your vacation time to come and help me. I know you probably spent most of it with your nose not far from your computer."

"We did get out a couple of nights for dinner. Boca Raton certainly is a lovely city." Sarah pulled out a stack of papers from her case and set them on the table.

I wanted to ask her where they had eaten, but did I really want to know where Connor took her and what kind of time they had?

"So, what did you find out? Who's doing this?"

"It's been an interesting journey, and it took me longer than I anticipated, but I believe I've identified the conniving thief, at least, the person who did the programming work. We still need to verify who he was working for, but I've got a lead on that as well. First things first, though." Sarah thumbed through the papers.

"Coffee while we work?" I asked. Sarah nodded. I went to the kitchen and returned with two mugs of coffee and the accouterments.

Sarah added milk and sugar to her coffee and took several sips.

"First, let me explain a couple of things about the process. There are several languages a programmer can use, depending upon the application. For instance, if you're developing a video game, you typically use C++, Python, Perl, or several others. If you're creating a database, you might use SQL. Identifying the kind of language a programmer uses gives me an idea of the person's skill level.

"Second, while most programmers don't leave a signature, some do. It's not a name like we'd think of, but more of a style. The closest I can come to as an explanation is handwriting. Some people write in large letters, some small. Some slant their letters to the left, some to the right. Well, in programming, although they aren't using cursive, they do leave telltale signs behind in how they construct their lines of programming. This is part of a programming signature. There's a whole lot more that goes into it, but that gives you a smidge of an idea."

"So, what did you learn about this programmer?" I was anxious to know everything about him.

"I'd say that he's quite sophisticated. To manipulate software such as an accounting program without detection, one would need a lot of knowledge and experience and the morals of a hyena. That said, I think we found the African plains carnivore."

"Really? Who?" I leaned forward to make sure I caught the name of the person.

"He calls himself Hermes. Hermes was a Greek god of lots of different things—roads, thieves, travelers, athletes, and more. He was the son of Zeus and Pleiad Maia. He's also known as the god of boundaries and the transgressor of boundaries."

"How apropos," I said, puckering my brow.

"The good news is that he's located right here in Boca Raton. His real name is Kenneth Donovan. He's a professor who teaches programming at Southeast Florida University."

"What? A professor would stoop so low as to risk his career and reputation to do something like this? Inconceivable."

"Motive is a powerful thing. Since the professor has no connection to your parents or their business, at least none that I've found, it's my contention his motive was simply the old-fashioned almighty dollar. But the question remains, whose dollar is it?" Sarah asked with raised eyebrows.

"So, you're saying someone with a connection to my parents hired Hermes to manipulate the program, erase the transactions, and transfer the funds to another account?"

"Exactly. Someone with a grudge. But, he or she would have needed inside help. Hermes could have figured out the password to the business system, but it would have taken too much time. He needed someone to help him, someone who already had a password and access to the system."

"Could you tell who?"

While each employee had access to the system, they could only access areas pertinent to their job. Only two staff members had administrative access—Yvonne, the bookkeeper, and Adele, the manager. Sarah flipped a couple of pages and pointed to a name.

I jerked back, my eyes wide in disbelief.

"No! Not Adele!" I said, trying to deny that my aunt would have any part of this.

"I'm so sorry, Randi. I know this isn't what you wanted to hear, but it is what it is. I'm not saying she knowingly let someone use her password to defraud the company. It could be the person who used it did so without her knowledge."

"And the person who may have done this?"

Sarah flipped another page and pointed to a second name. “This is who I suggest, given the circumstances.”

A long sigh escaped my lips as I stared at Ron’s name, though somehow it didn’t surprise me. He had motive and opportunity, as far as I could tell.

“There’s something else you need to know,” said Sarah. “I believe someone else is behind this, someone with big money. Hermes wouldn’t have risked everything without substantial compensation.”

“How much are we talking about?”

“Tens of thousands. Since the thief hasn’t yet transferred enough money from your account to make up for the cost of paying Hermes, though, over time, the loss would have been substantial, the banker behind this project was someone who could afford to lose that kind of money.”

“That narrows it down,” I said, believing Leo Barlos with his millions was somehow involved. I figured it was all part of his plan to get our property, though I didn’t know how he and Ron were connected. But the fact that Ron needed money to support his gambling addiction, Leo had plenty of it, and the password came from Adele made the dots appear much closer together.

“The papers I’m leaving with you document all my research. You’ll need them to go to the authorities.” Sarah handed me the papers.

I thumbed through them while she gathered her belongings.

“Just one more thing before I go,” she said. “Connor is committed to making sure whoever pushed your parents into the canal is caught. While I worked, he spent every waking hour trying to track that person down when not maintaining the property. I think he called every auto body shop in the area. Besides having developed a special relationship with your father, he's quite fond of you. Please don't do anything foolish, like taking this into your own hands. He's extremely knowledgeable about these things. Let him help you."

I paid Sarah the balance of what I owed her, and we said our goodbyes with a hug. Bigfoot jumped onto the windowsill next to the door. Together, we watched Sarah and Connor pull away from Boca Grande, heading for the airport. I was sad to see her go.

"Bigfoot, it's time to put the cuffs on these conniving thieves," I said. He arched his back as I stroked his silky fur from head to tail.

Meow.

I couldn't help but sense he agreed.

An hour later, I drove to the leased shop to see how Archie was doing with the setup. Despite the burdens he now shouldered, everything seemed to be progressing quite smoothly. The staff was scurrying around arranging workstations, tools, material, and furniture. The setup wasn't ideal, but they could manage for a month or so until we could get back into our shop. Archie gave me a tour of the temporary setup.

"Each station has electricity and is ready to go," he said. "The furniture readied for reupholstering is lined up by the bay door. What replacement fabric we have is stacked there on the makeshift shelves, and we've ordered the fabric we don't have. Miss Randi, we've got the weekend to fine-tune everything, but by Monday, we should be open for business."

"Quite an accomplishment in such a short time." I patted him on the back. "How's the cleanup and construction going at the old shop?"

"I've got Randall overseeing what's going on over there. That way, he can set up the shop to make it run more efficiently. He's also getting my office put together so I can work better there, too. I'm so proud of him. He's using all that college education to bring us into the twenty-first century. By the time he's through, we'll be more productive than we've ever been."

I could see by Archie's smile he was very proud of his son.

"I know this may sound strange, Miss Randi, but God always has a way of turning negatives into positives. In our case, the fire became a blessing. We're now able to start from scratch and design our stations to be far more efficient than before, and it's giving Randall a chance to apply his education in a practical setting. I believe he was becoming a bit bored, but now he has renewed enthusiasm and is coming into his own."

"I'm sure it's gratifying to see your son excel. Oh, and by the way, the forensic accountant finished the report. We now have proof to go after the persons responsible for the accounting theft."

"That's good news. Anything I can do to help?"

"You're kind to ask, but you've got your hands full here, Archie. Besides, this is something I need to take care of myself, and I intend to, starting Monday."

"I wish you God's speed, Miss Randi."

When I got home, I poured myself a glass of wine and took it out to the patio. Settling into a chaise lounge, I rested my head back and breathed in the night air infused by a hint of night-blooming jasmine. Closing my eyes, I envisioned myself back in D.C., running around the studio, making sure the night's production was on track. Then reality hit me.

Once everything settled down, how could I possibly oversee the fabric store and upholstery shop from Washington? I'd either need to fly down every month or hire a manager in my absence. Of course, Adele would be the most likely candidate, as she knew more about the business than I did. With everything going on right now with Ron, though, I didn't think that would be a wise decision. The other alternatives were selling the business or quitting my job and moving to Boca permanently. While I enjoyed being back in the fabric and upholstery business, did I want to do it full time? Once all the problems died down, would I be satisfied with the everyday routine? For the rest of my life? I was far more comfortable in a fast-paced environment. Besides, every time I watched the evening news, my heart ached to be back there. I missed being a part of the TV news business. After all, what was more vital to the American public than learning what was happening in the nation's capital? My job wasn't ideal, but it had more pluses than minuses.

I added two more phone calls to my Monday to-do list—my parents' business attorney and my new financial planner, none other than Rachel's husband, Todd. I was confident they would help me make the best decision possible for my economic well-being and the future of A Stitch in Time, as well as the people who worked there. In the meantime, I outlined my plans to confront the players in the financial scheme.

About 7:00 p.m. that evening, I decided to drop in on Connor. Since the fire, I hadn't seen him except when we had the brief encounter in the driveway, and I didn't want to leave the deep chasm between us. I enjoyed his company and our talks and hoped enough time had passed to talk civilly to each other once again. With a bit of trepidation, I knocked on the cottage door. He opened it dressed in casual, going-out clothes. I stiffened.

"Oh, I'm sorry. I see you've got plans. Perhaps another time would be better." I turned to go—disappointment mixed with a pinch of loneliness.

"Wait a minute, Randi." Connor caught my hand, his grip warm and strong. I turned to find his brow creased and his dark topaz eyes compassionate. "Don't go," he said. He gently pulled me into the cottage.

"But aren't you going out?" I blinked back mist in my eyes.

"I am. But I was going alone. Perhaps you'd like to join me."

My heart began to pound. "Are you saying you forgive me and that you're inviting me on a date?"

"Would that be overstepping the landlord/tenant relationship?"

"I suppose not," I said, keeping my smile in check. "Can you give me a few minutes to change clothes? By the way, where are we going?"

Connor winked. "It's a surprise. Just dress comparably to what I have on." He swept his hands down his clothes—blue pants, tropical print shirt. "I'll meet you at the truck."

I was back in fifteen minutes dressed in black pants, a short-sleeved black tee accented with rhinestones, and a colorful batik swing jacket.

"Perfect!" he said as I slid into the truck. "Now, for a great adventure. By the way, you do like seafood, don't you?"

"Love it," I said with a smile.

We drove south down Federal Highway through Deerfield Beach and into Lighthouse Point. We turned east and wound our way through a residential neighborhood until we arrived at a small parking lot on a canal that held about twenty vehicles. At the end of the lot was a dock with a sign: "Wait here for the launch to The Cap's Place. Tonight's skipper: Captain Madison."

After a few minutes, a small vessel with a canvas canopy skippered by the lone Captain came into view from the east and tied up at the dock. About six of us awaiting transportation to the restaurant took our seats along the sides of the boat as Captain Madison motored the vessel eastward. The balmy night held a gentle breeze while a full moon floated above us, creating a silvery path on which the boat seemed to glide.

As Captain Madison guided the launch toward Cap's Place, he told us Theodore "Cap" Knight originally owned the establishment that had been used as a speakeasy in the late 1920s during National Prohibition. The illegal liquor, transported by boat from the Bahamas, was brought up the Hillsboro Inlet, tied to buoys, and sunk in the water to escape detection by authorities. When Cap needed a bottle for his patrons or friends, he rowed out to the buoy and pulled up a bottle. The establishment became a gambling joint in the post-Prohibition era.

As a native Floridian, I knew Cap's Place was a South Florida landmark, though I'd only been there a couple of times while living in Boca Raton. Still, as we arrived at the restaurant's dock, the buildings looked as though they hadn't changed in all the years I'd been away or the nine decades before that. Built of planks of Dade County pine, wood no longer available, the structures had withstood Florida's gnawing insects, numerous hurricanes and tropical storms, and time to miraculously survive.

After disembarking, an elevated wooden walkway led us to a bar on the left brazenly built at the height of Prohibition. It consisted of one large room of pine-paneled walls with three large picture windows looking out onto the Intracoastal. Old photos of the establishment from its early days hung on the walls. On the counter behind the bar sat the rusted, original cash register.

"I found the restaurant online. I wanted something out of the ordinary with some history. Who knew it would be so interesting." Connor and I gazed at the portrait of Captain Knight that hung on a wall behind the bar.

"Well, you chose the right place to satisfy both those needs. Wait until you see the restaurant."

We strolled down another boardwalk, where we entered the second building that served as the restaurant. It was divided into several rooms with the same rustic look as the bar, except for the white tablecloths and more formal place settings. The ceiling still had exposed beams from which fans with light fixtures hung. The hostess seated us in an intimate room of about five tables.

"Oh, when you order, make sure you get the hearts of palm salad. It's historic as well," I said, perusing the menu.

"Does that mean I'll be eating trees that are almost a hundred years old?" Connor's face puckered as though he'd eaten something rotten.

I laughed and slapped his hand playfully. "No, silly. It's just that Captain Knight used to serve his guests hearts of palm salad because it was a specialty of the house. It's still a specialty, though I'm sure the chef uses fresh palms. The heart comes from young palmetto palms that are indigenous to South Florida. It has kind of a nutty flavor. Some Floridians call it swamp cabbage and make it into a stew using onions, celery, pork, stewed tomatoes, and seasonings."

"Sounds interesting. Hearts of palm salad it is."

We ordered drinks—wine for both of us.

"I appreciate your asking me to come with you tonight. I needed a distraction from the issues I've been dealing with."

"I'm sure you did. Sarah worked hard to find out who was involved with the theft at the upholstery shop. Was she able to pinpoint who it was?"

"She didn't tell you? I figured she'd confer with you during the process since you were the one who recommended her."

"She's a professional, and you're her customer. She doesn't involve others in the process unless she has permission. Now, if you want to tell me about it, that's your prerogative." Connor leaned forward and looked at me as though waiting for the inside scoop.

Thankfully, our drinks arrived to disrupt his line of thought.

"Why didn't you come by to see how things were after the fire?"

"I've kept abreast of the investigation in my own way. I didn't want you to think I was prying into your personal business."

Connor looked at me with a blank expression, but I knew what he was referring to—the truck repair bill. So far, tonight had been a lovely evening, and I wasn't going to ruin it by talking about that again.

"Sarah said you were hard at work, trying to find the truck and its driver. Any results?"

"I'm making headway."

"Really? Seth tells me he doesn't have any leads."

"Well, that's the police for you. Hard at work doing nothing except bringing flowers to the daughter of the victims."

I was speechless; prickles of heat rippled across my shoulders. "You were watching when Seth came to the house?"

"It wasn't like I was lying in wait for him. I was working in the front yard when he arrived. It didn't take much to put two and two together. So, are you two in a relationship now?"

I removed the napkin from my lap and placed it on the table. "Connor, with all due respect, whether we are or not, is none of your business." I was about to get up when he put a hand on mine and looked me straight in the eyes.

"You're right, Randi. It's not. I don't know why I even said that. I'm sorry." His eyes spoke of earnestness.

"Why is it when we get together, there's always something that turns a pleasant evening into one of regret?"

"Maybe it's because we like each other but are terrified to do anything about it because we've both got trust issues and are afraid to be honest in our feelings."

The truth took my breath away.

Our dinner arrived, and we ate our hearts of palm salads and broiled pompano with fruit salsa with little but polite conversation. The launch took us back to the parking lot, and we rode back to Boca Grande with few words between us. Honestly, I didn't have a clue what to say. I liked Connor a lot and would have enjoyed a closer relationship with him, but how do I do that with a man who always seems to push me right to the edge of my anger?

Once home, I got out of the truck and waited for Connor at the walkway.

"Before I leave, I want to thank you for dinner. I'm sorry it didn't turn out the way either of us would have liked." I didn't say it in an accusatory fashion, but one laced with sincerity and remorse.

"Maybe someday, we can quit putting up walls and be open with each other," Connor said. "Until then, I'll respect your privacy, and you can do the same with mine. In the meantime, if I'm successful in finding the truck and driver, I'll let you know. After that, as I mentioned before, I'll be moving on."

"I understand," was all I could muster as a response.

The short walk to the house became lonelier with each step until Bigfoot jumped out of the bushes. I picked him up and snuggled him against me.

Meow.

Chapter 9

On Sunday, I spent considerable time writing down the pros and cons of approaching each of our financial theft suspects to decide which one I would speak with first. Leo Barlos would either talk or buy his way out of any involvement in the theft, and I was sure he had covered his tracks well, so he was third on my list. As far as Ron was concerned, I needed to keep as far away from him as possible since Seth was already investigating him for ties to the accident. In the end, Kenneth Donovan, a.k.a. Hermes, had the most to lose if his involvement was made public. He became numero uno on my list.

I phoned Donovan's office on Monday morning. Under the guise of being a potential student who wanted to know more about SFU's Computer Science program before registering for classes, I tried to make an appointment for

Thursday afternoon. Donovan's assistant told me he wasn't on campus on Thursday afternoons, so she made me an appointment this afternoon. After we hung up, I phoned my legal and financial advisors and made appointments to see them as well. Both would come to the house that evening to sit down together to discuss my future and the business. The day was going to be busy.

At 3:00 p.m., I headed toward Southeast Florida University. The sprawling campus sat on the north side of Glades Road and covered two thousand acres that were once part of the Boca Raton Army Air Field, a top-secret military base during World War II. Most of the war-time buildings were gone, but runways in several sections of the campus still served as roads and parking lots.

I checked in with campus security, received a parking pass, and headed toward Donovan's office in the College of Engineering and Computer Science. This contemporary architectural structure sat on the east side of campus. Upon exiting the elevator on the fourth floor, the administrative assistant pointed me down a hallway to the third door on the right. It was open when I arrived, and Professor Donovan was hunched over his desk, staring at his laptop computer.

"Knock, knock," I said at the threshold. "I'm your 3:30 appointment." I presented a smile.

He jerked his head up. "Oh, come in. I'm just finishing up something. I'll be with you in a moment."

As I stepped into his cluttered office, he worked feverishly on his computer, his fingers flying across the keyboard as though he was playing Rachmaninoff Piano Concerto No. 3. His head of long dark hair dangled in his face and swayed to the movement of his hands as though he was the concert pianist. Lifting his right hand high above the keyboard, he depressed a key with such flair he looked as though he hit the final note of the concerto.

"Now," he said, looking up, "what can I do for you?" Though I figured him for the late 40s, he had an attractive boyish face with dark brown eyes. He pushed his chair back from the desk, stood, and stretched his arms over his head as if repositioning his spine and slim body from having sat for so long. He was well over six feet tall, and his casual attire appeared to be from an expensive line of men's clothing.

"May I sit down?" I asked, looking for a chair clear of papers.

"Of course. So sorry." He moved gracefully around the desk, swept up a load of papers in his arms, and plopped them onto his desk. "Please," he said, gesturing to the chair.

While I sat, he returned to his executive chair behind his desk, closed his laptop, and folded his hands on top of it.

"I know I said I wanted to speak with you about the Computer Science program, but that's not really why I came," I said.

"Then, why?" he asked, spreading his hands.

"I'm Randi Brooks. Does that name mean anything to you?"

He urged an unruly lock of bangs back to the side of his head, looked heavenward as though contemplating, and then at me. "Should it?"

"How about A Stitch in Time?"

Hesitation. "Nope. Don't know that one either."

Who is he kidding?

Though his words were glib, his narrowed eyes indicated clear recognition.

"You're sure?"

"Is there a point to all of this?" he asked, a distinct edge to his voice.

I pushed forward. "How about the name Hermes?"

"Ah, the Greek god," he said without hesitation.

"Yes, the Greek god of boundaries and transgressor of boundaries, like in computer programming transgression, especially accounting software." My stare was sure and calculated.

In one swift millisecond, the professor's brow furrowed, his eyes hardened into a piercing stare, and his lips stretched into a thin line. He rose and leaned over his desk to tower over me.

"This conversation is over. I'm going to have to ask you to leave, Ms. Brooks." Donovan extended his arm and long index finger toward the door.

"So quickly? Just when we were getting to know each other?" I withdrew some papers from my valise. "I think you'll want to sit down and listen to what I have to say, Hermes. Either that or I can leave and take these papers to the authorities. Your choice." I waggled the papers in front of me.

He sat.

"Now, what I have here, professor, is proof by a forensic accountant and programmer that you're Hermes, and you're the one who manipulated accounting software to steal thousands of dollars from my company, A Stitch in Time. I also know you had inside help, and I know who it is."

Donovan opened his mouth to speak. I waved him off.

"I know your inside help was Ron Walters. You do know him, don't you?"

Donovan hesitated; his eye twitched. "I may have met him once or twice."

"What about Leo Barlos? Know him?"

The professor's pupils widened at the mention of the real estate mogul's name.

"Know *of* him. Never met him."

Liar.

"Wasn't he the one who paid you?"

"Look, lady, you've got this all wrong." Donovan's gaze darted from my face to the papers, and his fingers fluttered nervously over the top of his computer.

"Really? We'll see about that." I got up and walked to the door. Just before leaving, I wheeled around. "Oh, and, Hermes, it would probably be in your best interest not to mention our little meeting. Good day."

As I walked to my car, I knew the conversation had stirred up a hornet's nest. I didn't know when the stings would reach me, but there was no question they would, as I was sure both Ron and Barlos would eventually hear about my visit. Beyond that, I didn't know how it would play out. To make sure I'd covered my bases, I planned to show the papers to my attorney and Todd when I met them later tonight and explain everything that had happened regarding the accident, financial theft, and fire.

The meeting wouldn't be just about Hermes. I wanted them to see the bigger picture in light of my parents' deaths, the incidents that followed, and my obligation to return to D.C. I was sure between the three of us, we would come up with adequate solutions to two of my concerns—how to best facilitate oversight of the fabric store and upholstery shop in my absence and my next move regarding the theft.

That night, during the two-hour meeting, I watched the money and legal man work together to help me resolve both issues. Regarding the business, I decided to retain full ownership in the fabric store but sell part interest in the upholstery shop. That would take a large chunk of the business burden off my shoulders. Though both men strongly advised me to take the evidence regarding the accounting theft to the police, I decided to wait until I gathered more proof. When the men left, I was perfectly at peace with my decisions.

At 2:00 a.m., the blare of the house alarm shattered my peaceful sleep. I jolted upright, my heart pounding. As I glanced around, the glare of the house lights blinded me. I held up my hand to shield my eyes.

What's going on? Is someone trying to break in?

Bigfoot scrambled off the bed and raced from the room. I jumped up, grabbed my phone and my father's old putter that I kept by my bed for protection. My heart raced as I searched the security app to see where the breach had occurred—the front living room picture window. Since we had hurricane impact windows, a burglar would have found it difficult to enter the house that way. Yet, an intruder may not have recognized the difference between those and conventional windows and tried to break it anyway, though I hadn't heard any shattering glass.

Standing at my bedroom threshold in my PJs—printed capris pants and short sleeve top—I peeked out the door and over the upstairs balcony. No one appeared to be in the house, but I did see someone's shadow move across the front window. Knowing the silent alarm would alert the police, who would be here soon, I unlocked the front gate from my phone to let them in. I shook as I waited at the top of the stairs.

Suddenly, multiple loud bangs came from the patio door. My body seemed glued to the floor in fright.

Is the intruder now at the back entrance?

"Randi? Randi? Are you all right?" I could barely hear Connor's voice above the alarm.

I descended the stairs as quickly as possible and opened the door to find Connor bare-footed and bare-chested, wearing only the bottom of his pajamas. He held a pistol.

Out of breath from fright and running down the stairs, I yelled to Connor over the blaring alarm. "Someone tried to get in. The police should be here soon." My fingers shook as I found the icon to turn off the house alarm on my phone. Now we could hear each other.

"Stay here. Let me check the house," Connor whispered.

He moved methodically through the downstairs, turning on lights and pointing his gun around corners as he went. Once he deemed the house secure, he opened the front door and moved outside into the yard. After a few minutes, he returned.

"And you were going to fend off the intruder with that?" He eyed the putter I held with skepticism.

I shrugged. "The best I could do under the circumstances."

"How about pepper spray or Taser?"

"Didn't enter my mind."

"Maybe it should have," he said.

Just then, lights from the police car flickered across the house as it pulled into the driveway. Any intruder was miles away by now, given the alarm, lights, and police presence. As we moved into the foyer, Connor pulled out a drawer in the hutch and placed his gun in it.

"I've got a concealed weapon permit, but why take the chance on questions?"

I propped the putter against the wall and opened the door for the officer. Connor and I stood on the threshold.

"Ms. Brooks?" The officer's name badge read Felix Lopez.

"I'm Randi Brooks, and this is Connor Romero," I said, suddenly realizing what Lopez must think, seeing both of us standing there barefooted and in our PJs. "No, no," I said hastily, "he lives in the guest house in the back. He came when the alarm went off."

"Yes, ma'am," said Lopez with a grin, shifting his gaze between Connor and me.

"Please come in." I stepped aside so Lopez could enter.

"Are you the Randi Books whose parents recently drowned in a Boca Rio canal? The case that Detective Morgan from PBSO is working on?"

"Yes," I said.

"And whose upholstery shop burned?"

"The same."

"Please let me say how sorry I am for the loss of your parents and the damage done to the shop," Lopez said. "Looks like you've had quite a time of it. Where did tonight's intrusion occur?"

"Well, no one got in, but my alarm company indicated the attempt happened in the living room." I led him to the picture window.

He looked around it using his flashlight. "Nothing inside. The glass wasn't compromised," Lopez said.

"I've got security cameras outside. We should be able to see the man and what direction he went after trying to break in." Still shaking, I brought down my laptop and accessed the front camera.

"There he is!" Connor pointed to a figure wearing a hoodie, who seemed panicked when the outside lights and alarm came on. The garment obscured the man's face, but there was no mistaking the figure carried a crowbar. He took off to the southwest side of the property.

"Let's see what we can find outside." Lopez led the way, followed by myself and Connor. He shined his flashlight around the window, pulled back bushes, and shined it along the ground. "I don't see anything here either."

"Well, he didn't have time to cover his tracks once the lights and alarm came on," Connor said. "There should be something here."

Just then, Bigfoot popped out of the bushes not far from us and sat in the driveway. He looked at us and swished his tail. As soon as he got our attention, he darted back into the bushes. A second later, he came back out and sat.

Meow!

He darted back into the bushes.

"Sounds ridiculous, but I think he's found something." Connor hurried toward the bushes. Officer Lopez and I followed.

Lopez pulled back the shrubberies and shined his flashlight next to the house. Sure enough, there was a footprint, along with several other impressions.

"Good job, Bigfoot," said Connor. "By the look of things, I'd say the shoes are a size twelve. See the horseshoe indention around the dimpled sole? That's the manufacturer's imprint. I believe you'll find it to be a Hampton Oxford, a moderately priced men's shoe sold by P.G. Bass Company. Not the kind of shoe a professional would wear if he were doing the job. The perp was an amateur."

Both Lopez and I looked at Connor in amazement.

"How'd you know that?" Lopez asked.

"Retired Army CID Special Agent," Connor said. "Shoes and their imprints were one of my specialties. Besides, I like shoes," he said with a wink.

I tried hard not to laugh since he typically wore flip flops.

"I'll get a forensic team over here to make a cast, dust for prints, and see if we can figure out where the perp got over the wall. The fire at the upholstery shop and this one may not be linked, but we don't want to take any chances." Lopez immediately called for Boca's Crime Scene Unit through his headphones. "Ms. Brooks, do you know anyone who would want to harm you?"

"Not really. As you know, my parents died in the canal, and we had a fire at the shop. Something is going on, but I don't think they're targeting me, per se. I just returned to Boca a few weeks ago. I haven't been back in thirteen years." I didn't tell him about my meeting today with Donovan, which would have opened another can of worms. Yet something came to me.

Is this the first sting from the hornet's nest I riled up in the professor's office?

"Why don't you take your cat inside? I'll wait for the forensics team," Lopez said.

I picked up Bigfoot and carried him inside, smothering him with verbal accolades; Connor followed us. Bigfoot jumped from my arms and ran upstairs. He must have figured his job was over.

"Why didn't you tell him about the theft at the shop? You can't dismiss that the accident, fire, theft, and this may be related," Connor said.

"I know, but I'm trying to handle the theft without police involvement. It's a sticky situation. Ron's involved and possibly Leo Barlos, who, by the way, is now my landlord. If he gets wind I'm onto him, he could change the locks on the doors of the warehouse anytime for whatever reason his conniving mind conjured up, and we'll be out of the upholstery business."

Connor combed his hand through his hair. "Randi, if Barlos is involved, this thing has already gotten way over your head. Don't go it alone. Let me help."

"Weren't you the one who said you were confining your investigation to the truck, then you were out of here?"

"You're the most exasperating woman I've ever met," said Connor. He retrieved his gun from the cabinet and stormed out the back door, leaving me in the foyer blinking.

I went upstairs and changed clothes in case Lopez wanted to ask me more questions once the others arrived. When I returned to the living room, I could see through the front window that Connor had changed clothes and was outside talking with Lopez. I joined them.

Crime scene techs made a cast of the footprint, dusted for fingerprints around the sill and on the window, took photos, and bagged whatever evidence they could find in the wee hours of the morning. In the kitchen, Lopez interviewed Connor and me separately, typing our statements into his notebook computer. He told us that tomorrow the police would canvas the neighborhood to see if anyone heard or noticed anything, and a detective would follow up with us.

In an hour, the commotion was all over. Lopez and the crime scene techs left, leaving Connor and me standing in the driveway. I closed the front gate with my phone.

"Would you like me to stay in the house tonight?" Connor asked.

I hesitated, not knowing how to answer. If I said yes, would he think that might be an invitation to do more than sleep? If I said no, would he think I was rejecting him?

"Your hesitation is the answer," he said. "I offered strictly for your protection, Randi. I had no ulterior motive." He walked down the driveway and around the house to the guest cottage.

I went back inside, turned off the outside lights, and reset the house alarm. What was holding me back from admitting that I cared for Connor? Why couldn't I give in to my feelings? The answer was Michael. He had done a number on me, and I feared being deeply hurt again. I didn't want to spend the rest of my life like this, afraid to let someone in, petrified to be vulnerable. I wanted to love someone and be loved in return. How was I going to break this unhealthy cycle?

Bigfoot snuggled against me as we bedded down for what was left of the night.

~

I shuffled between the fabric store, temporary warehouse, and upholstery shop during the next few days. Adele was doing a fine job managing the store, Archie was running full speed ahead in his temporary environment, and Randall was in his element directing the construction and refurbishing of the upholstery shop. Everything was running so well I questioned whether they needed me at all. That was a good thing since I knew I'd be returning to Washington in a few weeks. If I could only get these annoying crimes put to bed, I'd have peace of mind when I returned to my job.

So far, neither Seth nor Connor had any luck finding the truck or its owner, a crime that could take months, maybe years, to unravel. The fire remained unsolved, and while I assumed its connection to the accounting theft, I didn't know how. The Boca police hadn't gotten back to me regarding who tried to break into my house, but I knew Donovan was involved. I just had to prove it. I also needed to substantiate the connection between him, Ron, and Barlos. If I could, I'd be nearer to closing the case on the accounting theft.

While I could have purchased a new accounting program for the business and had the bookkeeping office switch over, I didn't plan to do that. I wanted those involved to think they were still getting away with something, and we weren't on to them. Of course, that would only work if Donovan kept his mouth shut. Once all the evidence was in place, I'd go to the police so they could arrest those involved in one fell swoop.

~

"Hi, Tootsie. Long-time, no see. Come in." Leslie, wearing a white terry cloth robe in the middle of the day, invited me into her foyer. We hugged each other.

"Are you ill?" I asked with concern.

"No, just didn't have the inclination to get dressed. Sometimes it's like that. I was going to have some herbal tea. Want some?"

"That would be nice," I said, following her to the kitchen and taking a seat at the dinette. Several amber pill bottles sat on the table.

"My meds," Leslie said. "They say older folks are living their golden years. To me, it's more like rusty years. After a certain age, everything in the body seems to oxidize. But you didn't come here to talk about my ailments. What's up?"

I told Leslie about the accounting theft, what Sarah turned up, my trip to see Donovan, and the attempted break-in. Leslie hadn't heard the house alarm or the commotion from the police. She slept through it all.

"I've got to find a way to connect Ron to Leo Barlos. I was hoping you could tell me something that might help."

Leslie poured me a cup of orange spice tea. I sprinkled it with sugar while she placed a plate of shortbread cookies on the table then sat.

"Perhaps." She hesitated a moment, appearing deep in thought, then took a sip of tea. "What do you know about dog racing?"

I brought my hands to my chest. "Me? Nothing, only that greyhounds are used."

"That's about all I know, too, except that owners euthanize as many as thirty-thousand dogs a year when deemed unfit to race or after they've been retired from racing. Eliminates mouths to feed. Thankfully, Florida residents voted to outlaw dog racing in the state next year for that reason alone, and there are Greyhound adoption programs throughout the country."

"I'm not following you. What does dog racing have to do with Ron and Leo Barlos?"

"That's where they met, at the track."

"How do you know that?"

"Your mother told me. It seems Ron goes to the track every Thursday for some special race called Run for the Money. It features dogs that are competing for money for the first time. He goes to check out the dogs for future races. Barlos is a greyhound breeder. He runs one of his dogs in every Thursday's race at the Palm Beach Kennel Club, the only dog track still open in South Florida."

"I had no idea Barlos bred greyhounds and was into dog racing."

"He needs something to do with all his money," Leslie said.

"Just one more reason for me to figure out how to put him out of business or in jail." I sat back in contemplation. "Tomorrow is Thursday. What do you say we take a little road trip to the Palm Beach Kennel Club tomorrow to check out Run for the Money? Maybe we can find Leo and Ron together. You up for it?"

Leslie's eyes brightened. A devious smile migrated across her lips, and she rubbed her hands together. "Can't wait!"

Chapter 10

Leslie and I headed north on I-95 toward West Palm Beach around 11:00 a.m. We decided to have lunch at the Track Restaurant at the Palm Beach Kennel Club and then watch the weekly Run for the Money. We hoped to catch both Barlow and Ron there, capture a snapshot of the two of them talking, and, perhaps, overhear a conversation.

We arrived at the track off Congress Avenue in about forty minutes and used the valet for parking the car. Since the club was a sprawling complex and we wanted to see it all—kennels, training area, clubhouse, card room—which required a lot of walking, the valet offered Leslie a complimentary wheelchair. That way, I could push her around without her getting tired or being in pain. She balked at the idea, but after seeing a map of the layout, she agreed. Surprisingly, the complex wasn't as congested as we imagined it might be, but we figured that was because of live streaming of the races and off-track betting.

After touring the kennels and learning about the dogs' training process, we entered the clubhouse. It was a long, three-story building that sat adjacent to the oval track. In the elevator on the way to the second floor, we stood next to a well-dressed elderly gentleman in an electric wheelchair. Leslie eyed it with jealousy.

"Vroom, vroom!" Leslie said. With spiked eyebrows and a devious grin of expectation, she looked at the man.

He turned to Leslie and nodded, indicating he was game. He moved the toggle switch on his electric chariot back and forth several times. The wheelchair jerked forward and back like a car at a drag race starting line. "Vroom, vroom!" he said.

Just then, the elevator door opened. The man eyed us one last time, then rammed the lever on his wheelchair forward. The contraption sprinted out of the elevator and down the hall, leaving us in an imaginary cloud of wheelchair drag racing dust and the sound of his hearty laughter ringing through the corridor.

Leslie and I looked at each other and broke into uproarious laughter.

"Well, this is a race track, isn't it?" she asked as I wheeled her down the hall.

The Track restaurant had a commanding view of the race track through its large glass windows. We were just in time to eat and watch the matinee races that began at 1:00 p.m. Run for the Money wouldn't start until 3:00 p.m., so we had a leisurely lunch. I had an Asian salad, Leslie French toast, though breakfast was long past.

As Carmen, our server, cleared our lunch dishes, Leslie winked at me and, without warning, turned to her.

"Dear, I'm looking for an old friend of mine. Leo Barlos. I understand he races his dogs here on Thursday afternoons. Where might I find him?" She gave our server a wide smile.

"Yes, ma'am, he's here every week. He dines in the owner's private dining room," Carmen said.

"And where is that?" Leslie looked around as if trying to spot it.

"It's down the hall. I can get the concierge to announce your visit if you like."

Leslie patted Carmen's hand. "That won't be necessary, dear. We'll go ahead and watch Run for the Money first. Then we'll have something to talk to him about."

"If you want to talk to Mr. Barlos after the race, you'll find him in the card room playing poker."

Leslie clapped her hands together. "Oh, what fun! And I'm sure his friend Ron would be playing with him. I've never been to a card room with real poker players. The card rooms I remember were for bridge, canasta, or gin rummy. But that was back in the day," she said with a laugh.

"I'm sure you had a lot of fun," said Carmen.

"We did, dear," Leslie said with all sincerity.

"We don't allow spectators in the poker room, but I know someone who might be able to get you into our special viewing room. It's got a two-way mirror, so you can see the players without them seeing you. It's for security purposes."

"Oh, could you?" Leslie asked, wide-eyed and grinning from ear to ear. "But, my caregiver and I wouldn't want to put anyone out or get anyone in trouble," she whispered to Carmen.

"Let me see what I can do," Carmen whispered back before she left.

"Your caregiver? Leslie, what are you doing?" I asked when Carmen was out of sight.

"Look, Tootsie, Carmen has a thing going with this fellow in the viewing room, so if anyone can get us in there, she can."

"How do you know that?"

"Didn't you see her blush when she mentioned her friend?"

I shrugged. "No."

"Well, that aside, don't you want to get close to Barlos without him seeing you and perhaps find Ron with him?"

"Of course."

"Well, then, just play along."

Leslie and I checked the day's racing form. Under the race heading, Run for the Money, we found Leo Barlos's name and that of his dog, Boca Bounty. The announcer introduced the race, and eight muzzled greyhounds in their racing bibs walked onto the track led by their handlers. Each dog was introduced, including the Kennel and owner, as they displayed their form in front of the spectators. Then they walked to the starting stalls. A booming voice announced, "Here comes 'Rusty!'" More like a stuffed dog bone, the fake bait circled the track until it passed the dogs. The starting bell sounded, and the dogs were off.

With raised arms and loud voices, spectators along the railing yelled encouragement to the dog of their choice as the canines sped around the oval track at breakneck speed, trying to catch "Rusty." When the dogs circled the track and passed the starting point, they headed down the home stretch toward the finish line. The 660-yard race lasted thirty-eight seconds. Boca Bounty came in second.

While the dogs that raced looked well cared for, the retired ones and the dogs unable to run were of concern. I knew Barlos was part of the accounting theft conspiracy, and I hoped there was some way to tie him to the fire. If he could be linked to even one of those criminal acts, I was hoping it would put an end to his contribution to this despicable sport.

As Leslie and I were ready to leave the Track Restaurant, Carmen approached us.

"I've got good news, ladies. Raymond has consented to allow you to watch the poker games from the security booth. You'll only be able to stay about ten minutes, but at least you can say you've watched the real poker players."

Leslie took Carmen's hands. "My dear, you've made me very happy."

"Please follow me," Carmen said.

I pushed Leslie out of the restaurant and down the hall. Carmen led us to a secure door that read, "Employees Only." She swiped a pass card and opened the door. Down another corridor, we came to a second secure door. Instead of swiping her card, Carmen knocked three times, hesitated, and then knocked twice. The door opened; a young man peeked out.

"Raymond, these are the women I told you about," said Carmen.

Raymond, a thirty-something serious-looking young man, stepped aside to let us in.

"Now, you two have a good time," Carmen said to Leslie and me.

"Thank you, dear." Leslie transferred a twenty-dollar bill to Carmen's hands as she left.

I wheeled Leslie into the room and pushed her toward the two-way mirror that took up considerable space. Raymond sat behind the mirror at an extended ledge and had a commanding view of the entire room below, which accommodated about twenty tables of five players each. At the time, about sixteen players sat at only four tables. A computer screen sat in front of Raymond, and we watched as he switched between close-ups of each table and the players. I assumed the other computer screens in the room dialed in on the other tables when they were filled and had a person like Raymond monitoring them.

"Isn't this exciting, Randi? Oh, and look! There's Leo." Leslie pointed at a table to our right.

Sure enough, Leo Barlos was looking at his cards and making a bet. And who was sitting next to him? None other than my Uncle Ron. Cautiously, I brought out my cell phone and showed it to Leslie. Knowing what I was about to do, she wheeled herself over to Raymond to distract him while I took photos.

"Raymond, dear, I'm a little confused. I understand Five Card Draw poker, but I see the placard on that table reads Three Card Poker. I didn't know there was such a game. Could you tell me how to play it?" Leslie looked at him with great expectation.

He took the bait. While he explained how to play Three Card poker, I casually took several photos of the table where Leo and Ron were sitting.

"Did you want me to let Mr. Barlos know you're here?" asked Raymond.

Leslie glared through the window at Leo. "Thank you, dear, but I don't want to disturb him while he's playing. I'll just give him a call later and let him know how wonderful Boca Bounty was. She came in second in Run for the Money, you know." Leslie's enthusiasm beamed.

I put my phone away and grabbed the handles on Leslie's wheelchair. "It's time to go, Mrs. Davidson. We've taken up enough of this nice gentleman's time. Besides, it's time for your nap." I just had to get in that little dig since I was now Leslie's caregiver.

"So soon?" Leslie said, eyeing me with faux disdain. "Well, thank you for your time, young man. You've been very kind." Leslie squeezed Raymond's hand and transferred a twenty into it.

"My pleasure," he responded as he pocketed the bill and walked us to the door.

I wheeled Leslie downstairs to the valet area, where we waited for the car.

"Did you get what you needed?" Leslie asked.

"I think so. At least we have proof that Ron and Leo know each other, but I still can't tie the two of them to the accounting theft. Donovan told me he'd met Ron but never mentioned they'd done business together. When I asked Donovan if he knew Leo Barlos, he acknowledged knowing *of* him since he lives in Boca but said they'd never met. Donovan was paid a large amount for the job, and Ron doesn't have that kind of money. That convinces me Leo is behind it, but I need proof. The only one that could provide that is Ron. How am I going to get him to admit Leo was the backer?"

"That's a tall order, Tootsie. Perhaps it will come to me while I'm napping," Leslie said with a laugh.

After dropping Leslie off at her house, I sent the photos on my phone to my cloud storage to access them at will. I had already started a folder on the accounting theft with the files Sarah sent me. I added the photos to it.

I opened one of the photos and enlarged it so I could see more detail. Leo and Ron, whom I could see quite clearly, sat side by side at the table looking at their cards. Stacked in front of them were several hundred dollars, maybe thousands, in $25, $50, and $100 chips. As I scanned the others at the table, the man to Leo's right looked familiar. His face, though, was turned to the man on his left, making his profile difficult for me to identify. I opened the second photo. It was still hard to make a clear identification. In the third photo, the man was looking straight on. I zoomed in and couldn't have been more shocked. The man was none other than Kenneth Donovan, the computer technology professor himself. Not only had he met Leo Barlos, but he also played poker with him!

The fact that they were in the card room on a Thursday triggered something in my mind. When I tried to make my appointment with Donovan for Thursday, the receptionist said he wasn't on campus on Thursday afternoons. That made sense. Ron, Leo, and Donovan probably met at the poker table every Thursday, like they did today. I had evidence of their connection with the photo, but it wasn't good enough to prove collusion. Maybe their meeting at the same poker table today was unplanned. Then again, maybe not. Either way, I needed more proof. And even though I now had ammunition to go back to the professor and pressure him for more information, first, I wanted to return to the Palm Beach Kennel Club to ask Carmen and Raymond a few more questions. Then I'd confront Donovan. I hoped he hadn't mentioned my visit to

Ron and Leo, but then, the professor's past deeds proved his trustworthiness left much to be desired.

I called the track to see when Carmen was working, explaining I enjoyed her service so much I wanted her to be my server again. As it turned out, she worked lunches throughout the week. I made plans to go back tomorrow with Leslie since she had developed a relationship with Carmen. After the trip, I hoped to have all the information I needed to catch the professor off guard and do a little arm twisting.

~

In the morning, I checked in by phone with Adele and Archie. All seemed well at the store, and things moved along nicely with the renovation at the shop. With peace of mind regarding that, Leslie and I headed back to the track. I played the caregiver's part once again as we sat at Carmen's table to stay in character.

"Back so soon?" she asked.

"Dear, you were so good to us yesterday, we just had to come back to see you." Leslie threw Carmen a big smile. "Besides, when you get to be my age, getting out and having a nice lunch is a luxury. But my caregiver here is the best. She takes good care of me." Leslie patted my hand. I rolled my eyes.

"Well, I'm glad to see you both. Want to try our special today? It is grilled salmon over a bed of linguini topped with a savory lemon sauce and served with grilled vegetables and a side salad." Carmen leaned in and whispered, "I'll even throw in dessert since you came all this way to see me."

Leslie clapped her hands. "You do know how to twist a woman's arm. We'll have two specials and iced tea."

"You love this, don't you?" I asked Leslie while Carmen put in our order.

"Not every day I get to be part of a big investigation. It makes me feel needed again."

"You're needed. It's like old times." I smiled at Leslie.

While relaxing after lunch, I withdrew a printout of Donovan's enlarged and cropped photo from my bag and slid it across to Leslie. Shortly after that, Carmen returned with our lunch bill.

"Carmen, dear, I wonder if you could help me? Do you recognize this man?" Leslie handed Carmen the printed photo of Donovan. She looked intently at it.

"I might have seen him but don't know his name or anything. Is he a friend of yours?"

"He is," said Leslie. "His name is Kenneth Donovan. He said we could find him here, but we haven't seen him. My caregiver tried to call him, but it went to voice mail. I know he plays poker. Perhaps he's in the card room?"

"If he's there, that's why his phone is off," Carmen said. "They don't allow cell phone use in the card room."

"Well, that's probably it. My friend got involved with a card game and forgot about us." Leslie furrowed her brow and pursed out her bottom lip in a big pout.

"Look, how about I ask Raymond if he's there?" Carmen offered.

"Oh, would you? That would be so kind of you, dear. We'll just wait here." Leslie looked at me and smiled.

In a few minutes, Carmen returned.

"Raymond says he's not in the card room today but was there yesterday. He played at the same table with your friend Mr. Barlos and plays with him every Thursday afternoon. Raymond was surprised you didn't recognize Mr. Donovan yesterday when you were here."

"We didn't have time to see everyone, dear. After all, we were only there for a short time. And me? I was having a wonderful conversation with Raymond about how to play Three Card Poker. Fascinating! Well, we must be getting home. My nap, you know. Carmen, dear, thank you for your help. Please give Raymond our regards."

We left a generous tip and made our exit.

I got what I came for, confirmation that Donovan and Barlos were more than casual acquaintances at a poker table. The time was ripe for a confrontation.

While driving home, I phoned Donovan's office to find out what time his classes were over on Friday. His assistant said his last class was at 3:00 p.m., and he usually left the office on Fridays by four o'clock. I had just enough time to drop Leslie off at home and hurry back to the university campus. I planned to catch the professor coming out of the building.

I skipped checking in with campus security and parked in a student lot. I figured campus police wouldn't be so vigilant on a Friday afternoon since most classes were over for the week and the parking lots significantly empty. I walked to a seating area not far from the Engineering and Computer Science building with the printed photo in my bag. A bench under a shady oak tree allowed me to view both the front and side entrances.

Feeling the need to blend in, I kept my eyes on my phone like most college students, only looking up intermittently to view students and faculty exiting the building. About a dozen or so came out before I noticed Donovan. He headed toward the faculty parking lot. Following him at a reasonable distance, I kept my head down, looking at my phone in case he turned around. I made my approach when he got to his car, knees knocking as I spoke.

"Hello, Hermes. Remember me?"

Donovan spun around. "What do you want?" His tone was rough, his eyes hard.

"Just a little of your time. You do have some of that, don't you? I mean, it's Friday. You've finished teaching for the week, so you're not in class, and yesterday you enjoyed playing poker in the card room at the Palm Beach Kennel Club." I smiled sweetly and let my words sink in.

"What do you know about that?" he said, softening his delivery.

"Quite a bit, surprisingly." I pulled out the photo of him at the poker table with Leo Barlos and Ron. "Looks like you lied to me, Hermes. You not only know Leo Barlos, but you also play poker with him every Thursday afternoon."

Donovan's gaze darted nervously from the photo to me. "So what? That doesn't prove anything."

"Really? How about conspiracy to commit grand theft? How about attempted burglary? How about accessory to arson?" I knew I was stretching things a bit with the accusations but figured I'd throw in the kitchen sink and see what happened.

"I didn't have anything to do with the fire. You can't pin that on me." Donovan sounded desperate.

"Maybe, maybe not. But once the university gets wind of what you've been up to, you can kiss your cushy professor job goodbye." As I looked at Donovan, I could almost see him weighing the options in his mind.

"Okay, okay," he said. He brought his hands to the side of his head and combed his fingers through his hair. "What do I need to do?"

"Tell the police how you met Leo and Ron and all you know about the accounting theft. Tell them how Leo backed the plan, and Ron played the go-between. If you're first to tell all you know, the D.A. may go easier on you." I didn't know if that was true, but I'd seen it on Law and Order SVU, so it must be true, right?

Donovan nodded. Droopy eyes and a downturned face revealed the defeat he felt.

"Someone will be in touch. I strongly suggest you don't tip your hand by saying anything to Leo or Ron. If you do, your advantage will disappear." I stuffed the photo back into my bag and left. Thankfully, my rubber legs got me back to the car.

I grinned to myself on the way home. I had just pulled off a brilliant coup and would let Donovan stew over the weekend. On Sunday, when I got back from my weekend in Key West with Rachel and Todd, I'd gather together all the evidence into one neat package to give it to the police on Monday. With the accounting theft solved, I'd be closer to heading back to Washington.

~

Leslie agreed to take care of Bigfoot while we were away, and on our early Saturday morning drive down to the Keys, I told Rachel and Todd everything. They were appalled I was so bold as to confront Donovan, but they also admired my courage. I didn't feel courageous at the time, just driven.

I hadn't been back to the Keys in twenty years, and many things had changed, including the islands becoming far more touristy, yet it was still the enjoyable, laid-back destination I remembered. We visited the Hemingway house and enjoyed talking to the docents and seeing Bigfoot's relatives. Other than that, we pretty much relaxed. Despite all the people, with the island's glorious turquoise waters, delicious food, and exciting shops, Key West was still fabulous.

Slathered in coconut-scented sunscreen, I sat in a lounge chair on Sunday morning soaking up the sun while Rachel and Todd guided jet skis over the tranquil ocean. I enjoyed having bronze skin up until the time I went to college. After that, my color faded into the typical northern pasty white. Even though I had occasionally relaxed by the pool since being home and developed a good base color, I hoped it would darken.

While drinking a tasty Bloody Mary, my phone rang.

"Hi, Tootsie. Enjoying your time?" Leslie's voice was perky.

"Good to get away," I said. "Gives you a different perspective on life. What's up? Is Bigfoot okay?"

"He's fine. The house is fine."

There was a long pause.

"Then what?"

"Debated whether I should call you since I knew you needed time away from all these issues but didn't want you to hear it on the news. Kenneth Donovan is dead."

My glass dropped onto the sand, tomato juice spilling out like pooling blood.

"What happened?"

"Pulled his car into the garage and left it running while his wife was away visiting her mother. They're calling it a suicide."

"Any note?"

"Not that they've said."

All of a sudden, tears poured down my cheeks, and I sobbed into the phone.

"What if I contributed to his death by confronting him on Friday? What if it pushed him over the edge? How could I live with myself?" I grabbed a tissue from my bag and wiped my eyes and nose.

"Listen, Tootsie, Donovan's death isn't your fault."

"Maybe he believed there was no way out." The tears continued to run down my cheeks.

"You can't control what other people think," Leslie said. "Besides, he's the one who got himself into this mess when he accepted the job. All you did was shine a light on the crime and make him take a good look at what he'd done."

"I didn't know Donovan and only spoke to him those two times, but he didn't seem like the kind who would take his own life." I dabbed at my tears.

"Maybe he didn't."

"What do you mean?" I said, dumbfounded by her statement.

"Maybe he had help."

"Like who?"

"Who had the most to lose if Donovan spoke to the police?"

"Leo," I said matter-of-factly.

"Well, maybe Donovan told Leo about your conversation on Friday."

"Why would he do that? He had nothing to gain."

"Not so, Tootsie. Perhaps he thought Leo could stop you from going to the police and exposing the scheme and all of them."

My mind raced. What Leslie said made sense on one level, and I didn't doubt for a moment that if Leo knew about my visits with Donovan and the nature of our conversations, he would take retaliatory measures. I was out of the area and temporarily out of his reach. Maybe his next best option was to get rid of the one person who could identify him as the backer and tie the whole thing together. Naturally, we had no evidence, no proof. Still, if there was even a remote possibility that Leo was involved with Donovan's death, investigating the crime had escalated to a point way over my head. I needed to go to the police, and I needed to talk with Archie. The upholstery shop could be in jeopardy, as well as Ron, Adele, and anyone else connected to the crime. My efforts to find who was responsible for the accounting theft had now officially become one gigantic disaster.

"Thanks, Leslie. We'll leave as soon as we can. I'll see you when I get home."

As soon as I hung up with Leslie, I called Archie and told him what happened and that we were on our way back. He said he'd have his son camp out at the old upholstery shop while he'd do the same at the leased warehouse. That way, if anyone tried anything, they'd be ready. I also called my attorney and updated him. He said he'd call his contacts at the Boca Raton Police Department and have someone meet us at the house upon our return. My last call was to Connor. He needed to know what happened in case he or the property was in danger. Repeated phone calls, though, went to his voice mail. My texts went unanswered as well.

While Todd drove as fast as he could, the four-hour ride home was excruciatingly long, and the sense of urgency pronounced.

Chapter 11

When we arrived at Boca Grande, a police cruiser was waiting for us. I opened the gate, and we all drove inside and parked in the driveway. After jumping out of the car, I rushed over to the police car only to discover Felix Lopez behind the wheel, the same officer who helped us during the attempted break-in.

"You're amassing quite a file, Ms. Brooks," he said as he exited his car.

"Not on purpose, I assure you. Please, I need to check on Connor. I think something's happened to him."

I ran inside and retrieved the key to the guest house. Then we all hurried down the path. When we arrived at the cottage, Lopez took the key from me and drew his weapon.

"Stay here," he commanded.

Todd, Rachel, and I huddled behind the shrubbery at the side of the guest house as Lopez knocked on the door.

"Boca Raton Police," he announced. "Open the door!" He waited for a response. When none came, he slipped the key into the lock.

Just then, the door opened. Leslie stood inside the cottage.

"Oh, my!" she exclaimed wide-eyed with mouth agape. Throwing her hands in the air, she dropped her cane and a bloodied compress. She stared at the gun.

Officer Lopez holstered his weapon and moved into the cottage. The rest of us followed. Connor lay on the couch; bloody cotton swabs sprinkled the coffee table. His face and lips were cut, red, and swollen; a bandage covered the side of his left eye. He looked dazed.

My heart ached to see him like this—so injured, so vulnerable.

"After Randi's phone call, I got to thinking I should check on Connor," Leslie said. "When I did, I found him on the floor. Someone did a number on him, but he wouldn't let me call the paramedics."

I handed Leslie her cane, wrapped my arms around her, and gave her a hug for thinking outside the box, then rushed over and knelt by Connor.

"What happened?" I scanned his face. By the looks of his red eye and lacerated lip, both of which were swelling, someone gave him several powerful blows. I hoped they hadn't loosened any teeth. Connor tried to move but grabbed his ribs and grunted in pain.

"I had just pulled into Boca Grande when a truck followed me in." The swelling of his lips and cheek left him with slurred speech. "A man got out. Just as I was about to ask who he was, he hit me and continued to rough me up. He said this was only a sample of what would happen if my girlfriend didn't back off. He meant you, Randi." Connor's piercing eyes spoke of the warning he'd given me days ago—"Don't go it alone."

"Go on," Lopez urged.

"I made it to the living room. Collapsed inside. Leslie found me. I think I have some broken ribs." Connor inhaled and winced in discomfort.

"Let me call the paramedics." Lopez reached for his mic.

"No!" Connor yelled, thrusting his hand out, palm forward.

"Connor, let them look you over," I pleaded.

"No medics," he reiterated with stern eyes.

"Okay, sir. Did you recognize your assailant? Can you describe him?" asked Lopez.

"About six feet. Dark hair. Dark skin. Khaki pants. Blue shirt."

"What about the vehicle?"

"Dark-colored truck." Connor licked his swollen lip. "He got in a couple of stomps to my ribs. Then I passed out."

"I'm calling a detective and the Crime Scene Unit. You may not want to go to the hospital, that's your choice, but this assault is now a police investigation." Lopez turned to me. "Do you think your security cameras might have caught the vehicle?" Lopez asked.

"There isn't a camera directed at the guest driveway, though the camera for the main driveway may have caught something. Can we take a look at it later? I want to stay with Connor right now," I said.

"We'll take care of Connor, Randi; you go with Officer Lopez." Rachel went to the freezer and brought back ice wrapped in a kitchen towel. She draped it gently across the left side of Connor's inflamed face.

Connor looked at me and gave a slight nod.

Lopez and I went to the house. I retrieved my laptop and, with shaking fingers, accessed the outside security camera from the front driveway. It showed Connor's truck entering the property, followed closely behind by a blue one, which left a couple of minutes later. Unfortunately, the video didn't show much detail, as foliage between the camera and vehicles obscured most of the view.

"The crime scene techs might be able to determine the make and model of the truck with close-ups through the gaps in the foliage, but they'll need access to the tape," said Lopez.

"Of course. By the way, there's much more involved here than meets the eye." I grimaced at Lopez, reluctant to reveal the whole story.

"Do you care to elaborate?"

"I believe Connor's assault and the death of Kenneth Donovan are tied together."

A surprised look came over Lopez's face. "You mean the Southeast Florida University professor who offed himself yesterday?"

"Yes, though it may not have been suicide. The warehouse fire, a theft at my business, and the attempted break-in here at the house might also be associated with it."

"You didn't mention your parents' deaths? Is it tied in as well?"

Lopez didn't say it sarcastically, so I took his question as well-intentioned.

"I don't think so, but the crimes I've cited could involve a high profile Boca Raton resident, someone whose influence reaches to the utmost levels of local government and possibly beyond."

Lopez's brows spiked above his eyes. "Like?"

I cleared my throat. "Leo Barlos."

I gave Lopez a brief overview of the crimes that had occurred and why I believed Barlos had involvement.

Lopez put his hands on his hips and let out a whistle. "Ms. Brooks, this is now way over my pay grade."

He accessed his mic and called for his Sergeant and CSU. We returned to the cottage, where I told everyone that I had informed Officer Lopez what I suspected. There was a collective sigh of relief that the events were now out in the open. Unfortunately, the star witness was dead, and there was only circumstantial evidence tying Leo Barlos to the crimes. Still, I wanted the police to have a complete picture of what evidence there was so they could conduct a thorough investigation. And, I didn't want any more of my friends to be in Barlos' crosshairs.

"Under the circumstances, I'm sure Mr. Romero can record his statement tomorrow when he's feeling better. The rest of you will have to come to police headquarters." Lopez looked from face to face. Everyone nodded in agreement.

"Did you call Ron and Adele?" Leslie asked.

"Oh my gosh! With everything going on, I didn't even think to call them, but if Leo is sending out warnings, they could be in jeopardy, too." My eyes pleaded for Lopez to do something.

"Give me their address. I'll have headquarters send a car over to check on them. In the meantime, see if you can get them on the phone," Lopez said.

I accessed my contacts and gave Lopez their address. While he called headquarters, I tried Adele. My calls went to voice mail.

"She's not answering," I said. "Rachel, please keep trying Adele's phone and send her a text. I need to check in with Archie and Randall and see if they're alright."

I was able to get Archie right away. He said everything was quiet where he was, and he'd just spoken to Randall, who indicated the afternoon was uneventful at the old warehouse. That was a relief. I hoped Adele and Ron were okay as well.

The CSU arrived along with Detective John Kester. While the investigators took photos of Connor's injuries, the parking lot, and blood spatter on the brick driveway with a shoe imprint, I gave the detective a brief account of everything that had happened. Afterward, everyone except for Rachel went down to police headquarters to answer questions and make statements. She stayed behind to take care of Connor.

I gave Kester the report from Sarah's investigation, photos, and copies of my investigation notes. A grueling three hours later, we left the police station. I dropped Leslie off at her home and returned to the guest house. Todd had just arrived and was getting ready to take Rachel home. She would go to headquarters tomorrow to make her statement. Before departing, we exchanged hugs. Connor was sleeping soundly on the couch, so I gathered a blanket and covered him. Exhausted from the day's events, I went into the second bedroom and dropped fully clothed onto the bed.

Morning came all too quickly. I slowly opened my eyes to discover I was in a strange room in a strange bed, and I'd never even crawled under the covers. I jerked upright, trying to orient myself. A couple of minutes later, my mind cleared. When it did, I remembered where I was—in the guest house with Connor on the couch. Bleary-eyed and on unsteady legs, I made my way into the living room. Connor had managed to push himself up to a sitting position but hadn't yet moved from the couch. I pushed the knick-knacks and the photo of Connor and his former wife to one side of the coffee table and sat.

By the looks of his face, he wasn't feeling too well. The reddened areas were now black and blue, and his eye and lip were extremely puffy. He tried to speak but found his lips pasted together with dried blood. I retrieved some cotton swabs from the bathroom, wetted them, and applied the water to his lips, gently wiping away the encrusted blood. All the while, his eyes searched my face.

"I need to go," Connor whispered once he got his swollen lips apart. He pointed toward the bathroom.

"I'll help you up."

He swiveled around and put his feet on the floor. With my help, he managed to stand. I could see by the grimace on his face he was in great pain. Holding his ribs, he hobbled to the bathroom with my help. When he was through, I helped him back to the couch

"Do you think you can eat?" I asked.

Connor shook his head and pointed to his swollen lips.

"Then let me get you a protein drink and a straw. I'll be right back."

Returning from the main house, I gave him the drink, which he eagerly consumed.

"I do think you need to have a doctor look at you, especially your ribs. There may be something else going on there. I'm taking you to the VA, and I won't take no for an answer." I gathered my things and headed for the door before he could object.

As we drove to West Palm Beach, Connor's injuries prevented him from saying much except when we hit a dip in the road. Then he let out a groan.

The doctors checked Connor and performed x-rays and blood tests. Other than the lacerations to his face, his battered torso, and two broken ribs, there were no internal injuries, and nothing unusual came up on the blood tests. Except for applying ice, taking pain relievers, and breathing deeply to avoid getting pneumonia, the doctor said there was nothing more he could do. Only time would heal his injuries.

We returned to the guest cottage.

"If you don't object, I'd like to stay to make some food and help in any way. You can decide when you're able to fend for yourself, or you want me to stay longer."

"I need a shower," Connor mumbled.

"And you need some help taking your clothes off?" I raised my eyebrows and gave him a sly grin.

Connor's eyes twinkled, and he tried to smile, but all he managed was a crooked grin on one side of his mouth.

Since I hadn't been in the room when the doctor examined him, as I removed his shirt, I was taken aback by the massive yellow and dark purple bruises covering almost the entire left side of Connor's torso. I was furious to think Leo Barlos had a hand in this and, no doubt, the other crimes. He had probably been getting away with things like this for decades, even profiting from it. It was time to stop him. I hoped the Boca police had enough ammunition to put him behind bars for a long time with my story and documents, yet I knew he was a slippery character.

I helped Connor to the bathroom and slid off his shoes and trousers. Although I'd seen him in Bermuda shorts without a T-shirt when he worked on the pool, I'd never seen him so exposed. I'm sure Connor appreciated the gleam of approval in my eyes, but he couldn't say much of anything. While Connor gestured to assure me he could take it from there, I went home to feed Bigfoot, get something to eat, and bring back another protein drink and some soup.

While walking back to the house, I looked at my phone. It was dead and needed recharging. Once inside, I plugged it in and listened to several voice mails from the police and Rachel. I returned each call and learned that Adele and Ron were safe, and Rachel had already been to headquarters to give her statement to the police. The last call was from Detective Kester, who wanted to know if Connor could come down and provide his information or wanted someone to come to the guest house.

Upon returning to the cottage, Connor had already showered and lay on his bed in a robe. He mumbled that he needed another day to recuperate before giving his statement, so I relayed his message. I brought him several ice packs, which I applied to his bruised side and face, and Tylenol for his pain. While he rested, I tidied up the cottage, threw his clothes in the laundry, heated some tomato bisque soup he could drink through a straw, and mused that Connor and I had just spent several hours together. So far, we hadn't fought or offended each other. Maybe there was hope for us yet.

Archie called and said everything was still okay at both upholstery shops. That was a relief. Barlos could have easily changed the locks on the new warehouse doors and stopped our business cold. Adele also called. She and Ron wanted to know why the police checked on them. I wanted to tell her the whole story, but that would have only exacerbated things. My explanation of Connor's assault and how the police reasoned it could somehow put them in harm's way had to suffice. As Adele was my aunt and only living relative, I wasn't ready for her to know of her husband's involvement in the accounting theft or that it possibly led to the professor's suicide, maybe murder, and Connor's assault. The truth would eventually all come out as the investigation progressed.

"Shoes!"

A loud murmur from the bedroom jolted me. I rushed into Connor's room and looked for his shoes. They were on the floor next to the bed.

"They're right here," I said, picking them up and showing him.

"No, no," Connor mumbled through his enlarged lips. "I recognized the shoes."

"Are you saying you know what kind of shoes the man who assaulted you was wearing?"

Connor nodded and spoke slowly out of the corner of his mouth. "Got a good look when he stomped on me. He's the same one who started the fire."

I looked at him in surprise. "How do you know that? You weren't there."

"Told you, have ways—plaster casts of footprints from the fire match. Call Kester. As long as he's here, I'll give him my statement."

In preparation for Kester's visit, I helped Connor move onto the couch in the living room. He sipped the tomato bisque soup through a straw while we waited. Kester came an hour later.

"Let's start with your statement," Kester said. He brought out a digital recorder and laid it on the coffee table. "Tell me what you remember from yesterday afternoon."

Connor repeated through swollen lips everything he could remember.

"So you weren't able to defend yourself, land a punch or kick?" Kester asked.

"No. The man's first two blows knocked me onto the driveway. After that came the boots—a Harrison 8 work boot manufactured by High Rise Boots that retails around $200," Connor said.

Kester let out a muted laugh. "Officer Lopez said you were a whiz at identifying shoe imprints. You didn't mention the man's boots when Lopez first spoke with you. How come you remember them now?"

"Not sure, except I know details come to victims in pieces and with time. After the thug knocked me to the driveway, I remember seeing the unique sole imprint as he lifted his leg. That's when I turned over, and he stomped me in the ribs. The pain was excruciating, and I passed out. It came to me while I was sleeping that the imprint from the fire and my assault were the same. The sole has a sort of arrowhead shape to it, with lines running through it. Here, let me draw it for you." Connor looked for a pen and piece of paper.

I grabbed each from the credenza and handed them to Connor, who proceeded to sketch the sole. When through, he passed the image to Kester.

Kester took a picture of it with his tablet, then tapped his device several times to bring up some images. He swiped through them, comparing Connor's sketch to those on his screen.

"These are photos taken of the footprint casts from the fire." Kester handed the tablet to Connor, who looked at the photos intently, enlarging each. "The next one is a photo of the bloody imprint we found on the driveway after your assault." Kester watched Connor's expression as he swiped to the next photo and enlarged that one as well.

"That's what I thought. The boot footprints from the fire match the bloody imprint from my assault and the ones I remember seeing." Connor handed the tablet back to Kester.

"Seems so. The problem is we don't know who was wearing the boots. With the internet, purchases are from hundreds of websites and stores, so it takes time to track down who bought the boots. The lab is still trying to identify the blue truck that followed you onto the property. If the lab techs can at least obtain some identifying mark—headlight, turn signal light, handle, etc.—they can narrow down the vehicle and go from there. Right now, all the evidence we have is circumstantial."

"Any news on who tried to break into my house?" I asked.

"I was getting to that. It seems the imprint of the shoes outside your window matches those worn by the deceased professor, Kenneth Donovan. Here's a photo of his shoes taken at the morgue." Kester handed me the tablet.

The photo showed Donovan's shoes had the characteristic indented horseshoe band around the dimpled sole like the one from the attempted break-in. I showed the image to Connor.

"Again, that's only circumstantial," Kester said. "If we can't put Donovan in the shoes at the scene, we can't prove a thing."

"I know he's the one who tried to break in. It makes sense after I confronted him about the accounting theft. I'm just sorry he's not around to tell you the whole story and identify the players. But then, he's not around precisely because of that," I said, returning the tablet to Kester.

"Rest assured, we're working hard on this case. Leo Barlos has slipped through our grasp too many times. Your case looks like the best opportunity we've had in years to slap the cuffs on this Teflon hoodlum." Kester gathered his equipment.

"If we can help in any way, let us know," I said.

"You've done your part," Kester said. "The best thing you can do right now is let the police handle the investigation and report anything new you might remember. By the way, any news from Detective Morgan on your parents' deaths?"

I shrugged. "He hasn't contacted me lately. I'm sure that means there's nothing new."

Kester rose and walked to the door. He turned just before leaving. "I'm very sorry about all your troubles, Ms. Brooks, but don't lose heart. These kinds of investigations take time, but the police eventually do get their man."

Connor spent the remainder of the day resting with ice packs on his face and torso. I went back to the house and fixed him something soft to eat—homemade mashed potatoes with sour cream. I also drove to the local McDonalds and brought him a vanilla milkshake. It would have to suffice until breakfast, when I would make something a bit more nourishing. As for my meal, I ate my Capitol Hill producer's special—a microwaved frozen dinner.

Chapter 12

The next morning, I fed Bigfoot, fixed some scrambled eggs for Connor, and brought them to the guest house. He was up, and color had returned to his formerly pallid face. Though his eye and lips were still swollen and discolored and his ribs bruised and aching, his countenance appeared brighter.

"Now that the police know everything and are handling the investigation, I feel more comfortable devoting my time to getting the upholstery shop up and running. Of course, my aunt dangles in the middle of Ron's indiscretions, and I wonder just how much she knows," I said.

"I'm sure the police will sort it all out once they gather enough evidence to arrest Barlos." Between bites of egg and sips of orange juice, Connor's words, delivered slowly, seemed pronounced with much more clarity.

"If Adele contributed to the crime by giving Ron her password, she'd be charged with a crime, too, and that will leave the shop without someone at the helm. Yet, I can't believe she'd willfully give him her password. Of course, I don't know her intimately, but I do know her well enough to say she'd never betray her sister."

"I believe that, too," Connor said. "I think somehow Ron got her password without her knowledge."

"But how do I know for sure?"

"You won't until the police confront Ron with the crime. As far as I can tell, they still have a ways to go before that."

"Do you think you can manage by yourself today? I need to get up to the shop and see how close we are to moving back in. I'll feel great relief once that happens, and we're out of Leo Barlos's clutches." I cleared the dishes and put them in the dishwasher.

"I'll be fine," said Connor. "You go ahead and do what you need to do."

I fixed some ice packs and handed them to Connor. "I'll check on you when I get back."

I went to the fabric store first to speak with Adele. Several customers were engaging the staff, and Adele was busy at the register, but we managed to find a few minutes between customers to talk.

"How's Connor?" she asked.

"Battered and bruised, but he'll be alright."

"Why in the world would someone want to hurt him?"

"The police tied his assault to a theft, and the people involved wanted him warned not to get involved." It wasn't a lie, just not the whole story.

"Then why were Ron and I involved? We don't know anything about a theft."

"Someone else doesn't agree. So how are things here? Any problems?" I asked, changing the subject.

"I know fires aren't good for any business, but it's been a blessing to ours. Our gross sales from existing customers have exploded this month, and many new customers have visited the store. Everyone has been so supportive. I guess having the fire sale didn't hurt either."

Both the upholstery and quilting side of the store offered fabrics for sale that needed moving. It proved to be a huge success.

"Well, you're the glue holding the store together. I can't tell you how appreciative I am for your loyalty." I hugged Adele.

"How's Archie doing? I've talked to him but haven't seen him in weeks. I guess he's busy getting the delayed upholstered furniture out and making sure the construction is on schedule at the old warehouse."

"As a matter of fact, I'm heading up to the temporary warehouse now to check on things. I'll be back later to help out in the store."

The drive to the temporary warehouse took me only a few minutes. As I entered the building, the sales staff was busy with customers, and as usual, Archie was scurrying around between stations. A long row of furniture waiting to be upholstered lined one wall. The shop was as busy as I'd ever seen.

"Miss Randi, so good to see you." Archie greeted me with a warm embrace.

"Wow, Archie! Things are certainly hopping here."

"Couldn't be better. I even hired two more workers to help us catch up with our orders. But the best news is that the construction at the old warehouse is almost complete. We should be able to move in this weekend."

"How wonderful! I'm heading over there now to see how Randall is doing."

"Just the two people I was looking for." Leo's booming voice was unmistakable as he waddled toward us. "I understand the work is almost complete on your old warehouse."

"Word travels fast," I said.

"To some, Boca may be considered a large city, but the business community is very close." Leo panned the warehouse and all the activity.

"We will be moving out sooner than expected," I said.

Leo leaned in. "I hope you don't expect to get a refund on your unused time." He spoke in a condescending tone.

I pulled back in disgust. Did he always have to act so pompous?

"Mr. Barlos, we're professionals and wouldn't even think about asking for a refund. We stand by our signed agreement," Archie countered, insulted by such a suggestion.

"Now, don't go getting all bent out of shape, Archie. It's nothing personal, just business." Leo gave him a wide grin.

"And I suppose the fire was just *business*, too?" Archie's eyes narrowed into a hard stare. I'd never seen Archie so combative.

Leo let out a loud laugh. "Are you trying to tie me to the fire? Good luck, my man. I was at church when I received word about it."

"Doesn't mean you weren't involved," Archie said. "You've been trying to get your hands on the Brooks' property for years."

"True, but I only use legal means to get what I want. I've never lowered myself to methods you're suggesting." Leo's tone was one of irritation.

"Harrumph!" said Archie, crossing his arms over his chest and turning his head away.

"I know you're a busy man and have other things to do. Thanks for dropping by. I'll see you out," I said before things could escalate. I walked Leo to the door.

"I'm sorry you didn't take my earlier offer. This warehouse is the perfect location for the shop, and the store would have been close by. Too bad," Leo said.

"Why have you been trying to get our property all these years? Surely there are other locations ripe for development?"

"Most of Boca is already developed, and while I own a lot of the commercial property, the purchase of the fabric store and upholstery warehouse has always eluded me. With your facility, I would be able to develop the entire block into a sizeable income-producing strip mall."

"Money. Is that all you think about?"

"Oh, I used to think about other things, but that was a long time ago."

"I know about your friendship with my father in high school. You used to be best friends. What happened?"

Leo hesitated and looked at me with eyes that indicated the past needed to be left there. "Betrayal," he spit in a harsh tone. His eyes turned cold.

"And my mother?"

Leo's countenance completely changed. It softened as though he drifted back to those days. "Now, there was a woman. She was beautiful, kind, and vibrant."

"But she chose my father over you."

Leo turned abruptly toward me. "Yes. I never forgave him. But it wasn't just that; there was much more to it."

"There always is when the heart's involved. The thing is, Mr. Barlos, my father and mother are dead. Don't you think it's time to let the anger go?" Tears welled in my eyes.

"Maybe someday you'll know the whole story." Leo blinked several times. Without another word, he turned and walked out the door.

Did I see a hint of a tear?

"What was that all about?" asked Archie.

"Old times, I think."

"I've called Randall. He's excited to show you the refurbished warehouse."

I gave Archie a parting hug. "I'm on my way."

When I got to the old warehouse, Randall met me outside at the door.

"Close your eyes, Miss Randi. I want this to be a surprise."

With eyes closed, Randall guided me inside to the sales reception area. I recognized the odor of new paint and freshly sawed wood from the refurbished counter.

"Okay. You can open your eyes now."

Soft blue-grey paint and contemporary photos of colorfully upholstered furniture hanging on the walls made the reception area warm, cheery, and inviting.

"Beautiful," I said, genuinely impressed by Randall's choices.

"Wait till you see the warehouse. Close your eyes."

Once again, Randall led me forward into the warehouse. The odor of soggy charcoal was gone, replaced by the smell of fresh paint. The sound of hammers and saws filled the air.

"Okay. Open your eyes."

As I turned a three-sixty, I hoped my wide grin expressed my astonishment and delight in the warehouse's transformation. The entire warehouse looked like a modern, efficient upholstery factory. Work stations, fabric bins, storage lockers, and the receiving area each had new furniture, accessories, and bright overhead lighting. Colored lines on the concrete floor indicated the direction the furniture would travel for the next stage of the upholstery process.

"Wait, that's not all. Come see Archie's office."

I followed Randall to the back of the warehouse. Archie's office was painted light celery green and furnished with a new desk, chairs, computer, storage cabinets, and shelving. Several pictures, similar to those in the reception area, hung on the walls.

"Has Archie seen this?" I asked.

"Not yet. I wanted it to be a surprise."

"Well, it certainly will be. You've done a marvelous job in pulling all this together. You can be very proud of what you've done, Randall."

"Finally, I got to use all of my talents and education. And it all came within budget from the insurance company."

"When will you schedule the move?"

"Over the weekend. We hope to be up and running by Monday. Ms. Rachel has planned an Open House to celebrate the occasion on Wednesday."

While I knew the staff would be moving back into the old warehouse at some point, the reality produced conflicting emotions I was unprepared for. On the one hand, I was glad to see the operations resume. On the other hand, my work here would come to an end, and I would return to D.C.

"Everything's wonderful, Randall. I'm sure you look forward to moving in and getting back to normal. Please let me know when you plan to show the warehouse to your father. I want to be here."

"Sure thing, Miss Randi. It will probably be Friday since we still have several small things to finish."

I gave Randall a congratulatory hug before I departed for home.

When I reached Boca Grande, I knew this might be one of the last times I'd drive onto the property, at least regularly. I sat in my mother's Buick in front of the house and looked out at the yard. Connor had done a beautiful job taking care of the property, and I had so enjoyed living back here. But being here every day would soon end.

The ring of my cell phone startled me and brought me out of my musings.

"Hey, I'm sorry I haven't been in touch as often as I'd like," said Seth. "Lots of cases to work, and quite honestly, there wasn't much I could offer on your parents' case."

I could hear tiredness mixed with regret in Seth's voice.

"That's okay. I've been busy, too."

"Yeah, the Boca police told me all about it, including the early morning pajama-clad duo."

"That's really none of your business." I figured the reference came from Officer Lopez when he investigated the attempted break-in.

"You're right. My bad. By the way, how is Connor? I heard someone assaulted him."

"He's quite sore but recovering."

"Good to hear," Seth said. "Now that you've turned the investigation over to the police, I guess you'll be returning to Washington."

"Soon. The warehouse is complete, and Archie is moving back in this weekend. The upholstery shop will be open for business on Monday. Rachel is putting together an Open House for the occasion."

"Please let me know when it is. I want to be there. And I'd like to see you before you go. Perhaps we could go to dinner."

"That would be nice."

Bigfoot must have heard me pull into the driveway. As I finished my phone call and got out of the car, he was sitting there, swishing his tail, staring at me. I picked him up, pulled him close, and planted a kiss on his nose. He lifted one paw and placed it gently on my cheek as though caressing it.

"I'll miss you, Bigfoot."

Meow.

He looked at me with his green eyes and purred softly.

"Let's go see how Connor is," I said, putting him down. He padded after me as I walked to the guest house.

When I opened the door, Connor was dressed and pacing the floor, a grimace on his lips, his arms wrapped around his ribs.

"I expected you'd be resting."

"Just got a call—a lead on the truck that pushed your parents into the canal. I need to meet the contact, but my ribs hurt too much to drive. Can you take me?"

Is this the break we'd hoped for? Will we finally discover the truck and driver that pushed my parents' car over the edge of the bank and into the canal?

"Of course I'll take you. Where do we need to go?"

"Lake Placid."

"New York!?"

Connor let out a laugh, then grimaced in pain. "And you claim to be a South Florida native. Lake Placid, Florida, just northwest of Lake Okeechobee." He tightly held his side.

"Oh, that Lake Placid," I said, relief washing over me. "Are you sure you're up to it? Your face is still quite swollen, and I'm sure it hurts, along with your ribs."

"We have to go, Randi. I owe it to your father to follow up on this lead."

"It takes two and a half hours to get there, and it's already three o'clock. With traffic, we won't make it there until after six. All the businesses will be closed."

"My contact said he'd wait."

"Well, in case it gets too late to drive back after the meeting, we might want to pack an overnight bag. I'll phone Leslie and ask her to take care of Bigfoot, and I'll let Adele know I may not be at the shop tomorrow. I'll meet you in front of the house in thirty minutes."

As I climbed the stairs to my bedroom, the idea that this trip might provide closure on my parents' deaths and justice to those responsible brought eager anticipation to my soul and tears of joy to my eyes.

In the middle of packing, I jerked up as a sudden realization overwhelmed me. If Connor and I could locate the truck and the driver, wouldn't that also mean his time at Boca Grande would come to an end? How would I reconcile the relief I'd experience at finding my parents' killer against the despair I'd feel of Connor's leaving when we were just getting to know each other? My parents were dead; he was alive. Leslie's words rang loudly in my ears: "Life is for the living!"

Chapter 13

I had been to Lake Placid only once before with my parents when I was in middle school. That trip was in the summer, the last weekend in July when the town held its annual Caladium Festival. My mother loved the leafy ornamentals in various sizes, designs, and mixed colors—white, green, pink, and red. In the 1950s, Lake Placid became home to dozens of caladium farms and soon held the honor of "Caladium Capital of the World." The plants were at their peak on the hottest and most humid weekend of the year. Thus hordes of plant lovers swarmed the vendors and took home thousands of plants. In the spring and summer, Boca Grande gave testimony to the fact my mother was one of them.

I hadn't driven out of Boca since I arrived and needed to reacclimate myself to the South Florida landscape. On the Google map, there was no direct route from Boca Raton to Lake Placid; the Everglades and Lake Okeechobee, Florida's largest lake, lay directly between the two cities. One either had to travel one hour south to take SR27 north through the Everglades and around the west side of the lake, or drive north on the Turnpike and take SR710 on the east side of the lake until it met SR70 in the city of Okeechobee on the north. We decided on that route.

Thankfully, we left early enough to miss most of the rush hour traffic through Palm Beach County and headed toward the lake on the four-lane divided highway. While Connor dozed most of the way, I enjoyed the pleasant drive through the sparsely populated countryside that the influx of northern transplants hadn't quite yet found. Just on the outskirts of Lake Placid, Connor woke up.

"He said he'd meet us at Ben's Barbeque on Main Street. Eats there all the time and says they have the best barbeque food around." Connor yawned and looked at his cell phone.

"Who? What's your contact's name?" I asked.

"Jimmy Jacobs, J.J. for short."

Connor proceeded to tap the address of the restaurant into my GPS. We followed the directions and pulled up to a rustic wooden building on Main Street. The sweet mouthwatering aroma of barbeque permeated the air as we stepped inside the busy establishment and waited at the hostess station.

"Just youse two?" The Raggedy Ann red-haired, middle-aged woman with Annie on her name badge grabbed a couple of menus and two bundles of napkin-wrapped silverware.

"We're here to meet Jimmy Jacobs," Connor said. "Could you direct us to his table?"

Annie looked at Connor with her green eyes and hesitated. “I would, honey, but I haven’t seen J.J. tonight.” She had a thick Florida drawl.

“I spoke to him a few hours ago. He said he’d meet us here. We drove up from Boca Raton to see him,” Connor said.

“Boca Raton, huh? Well, if J.J. said he’d meet you here, then he will. He’s always been a straight shooter. I’ve never known him to stand anyone up. Why don’t you and your lady here grab a table? I’m sure he’ll be along shortly.” Annie led us to a table in the corner and placed the menus and silverware at our seats.

Connor sat with his back to the wall, so he could see everyone who walked into the restaurant. I sat next to him.

“I’ll send J.J. over as soon as he arrives,” said Annie. “By the way, honey, you want some ice for that eye? It looks like quite a shiner.”

“Thanks. I’ll be okay,” Connor said.

“Suit yourself. Your server will be right with you.” Annie walked back to the hostess station.

“Why don’t you give J.J. a call and let him know we’re here?” I asked.

Connor pulled out his cell and tried J.J.’s number. The call went to voice mail. “Let’s give him some time,” Connor said.

I looked at my watch; 6:30 p.m. The server came by, and we both ordered sweet tea with lemon. While we waited for J.J., we scanned the menu. The barbeque dishes looked scrumptious.

Connor tried calling J.J. two more times, but by 7:00 p.m., he still hadn’t shown.

"How do you know this guy's legit? Just what exactly did he say to convince you he knew something?" I asked.

"I vetted him thoroughly through searches, references, and conversation. He appeared honest and to have important information."

"Well then, we'll have to take our chances he's on the up and up."

"He'd better be, or else," Connor said.

What does he mean by that? Did he bring his gun?

By 7:15 p.m., we were both restless.

"I think we need to go by his shop," Connor said. "Maybe I misunderstood him, and he's waiting for us there."

"Possible. But if J.J. is there, he'd still answer his phone, right?"

"One would think so."

We left a generous tip and paid for our tea. Connor put the auto body shop's address into the GPS before pulling out of the restaurant parking lot.

"Lake Placid Auto Body is just outside town. I've accessed Google Street View on my phone, and the business operates out of several white warehouse buildings with blue bay doors. Strange, though, the place looks too clean to be a busy auto repair shop, even though it's got great reviews. There's not a damaged vehicle or any cars in the parking lot. Every repair shop I've known has cars parked on the grounds behind chain link fencing and locked gates. Maybe Google took this photo before the place opened." Connor continued looking at his phone while I followed the voice on the GPS.

I drove back through town, took a couple of turns, and then headed south onto County Road. Lake Placid Auto Body sat about a mile and a half down and was easy to spot with its two white buildings and blue bay doors. I pulled up in front of the office.

"Doesn't look like anyone's here. There aren't any lights on in the office," Connor said, gazing out the windshield.

"Even if they were on, how could you see them? The window is tinted so dark. Probably because it faces the setting sun."

"Yeah, but let me take a peek through the window anyway." Connor got out and walked to the door. He cupped his hands around his eyes and peered through the glass, then walked around the building. A couple of minutes later, he got back in the car.

"Everything looks quiet. I don't understand this. J.J. seemed so honest and forthright." Connor drew his hands through his hair.

"Well, why don't we go back to the restaurant, have something to eat, and continue to try J.J.'s phone? If he doesn't answer, maybe Annie knows another way to contact him."

We drove back to the restaurant and entered for a second time.

"Back again?" Annie asked.

"Yeah, we may have mistaken our meeting place, so we went to the body shop. J.J. wasn't there, and the shop's closed," Connor said.

"Hmm. Sure ain't like J.J. not to take care of a customer, no matter what the time," Annie said. "Why, I remember once he got out of bed at midnight to help a young couple, just strangers passing through town, after they ran into a deer. Tore their car all to pieces. J.J. towed the car to the shop and worked on the car himself the very next day so the couple could continue their honeymoon. No, sir. Sure ain't like J.J. not to show."

"Well, we'll continue to try his cell, but we're also going to go ahead and have dinner. If you know of another way to reach him, we'd certainly appreciate that information. We don't want to drive back without seeing him. By the way, I'm Connor, and this is Randi," Connor said.

"Pleased to meet both of you. First time to Lake Placid?" Annie's gaze bounced between the two of us.

"His first time. He's from New Mexico. I'm a South Florida native," I said with a smile.

"A Florida Cracker. We've got lots of 'em 'round here, but there ain't too many in South Florida. Glad to meet you, honey. Let me show you to your table." Once again, Annie picked up menus and place settings and led us to a table. "You both want sweet tea with lemon, right?"

"Please," I said.

Connor tried J.J.'s cell. Again, it went to voice mail. Connor left him a message that we were at the restaurant. When he hung up, he ordered soft foods—sweet potato, baked beans, watermelon, and banana pudding. I selected baby back ribs with french fries, coleslaw, baked beans, and garlic bread. Each item was the best either of us had ever eaten at a southern barbeque restaurant. Maybe because we were both famished. Pleasantly full, we leaned back.

"How about some cherry cobbler a la mode?" our server asked as she cleared the table.

"Couldn't eat another bite," I said, patting my stomach.

As the server walked away to get our bill, Annie walked up.

"I tried a good friend of J.J.'s, but she wasn't able to reach him either. She's going to try his son. Youse going to stay overnight, maybe try the shop in the morning?" asked Annie.

"Probably, since we're pretty tired. Can you recommend someplace to stay? Maybe a B&B with a bit of character?" I asked.

"Oh, sure, honey. Red Rocker Inn is right on the lake and the cutest place you've ever seen. I'd call over there and see if Mabel has a room?"

"Better make it two," Connor said.

"Oh? Aren't you together?" Annie waggled her index finger between us. An uncomfortable silence followed. "Okay, then. I'll be right back."

Connor and I sat there tongue-tied until Annie returned.

"Mabel says she'd be happy to put youse up. I'll jot down directions while you settle your bill. In the morning, you might enjoy a walking tour of our murals. There are forty-seven of them on the buildings. Kind of a pictorial history of the town. We're famous for them." Annie handed us a brochure.

"Thanks for the suggestion. We enjoyed the couple we saw on our way in and will probably do just that," I said, looking at the brochure. Connor clutched his ribs. I knew today's activities were probably too much for him.

We found the Red Rocker Inn just as charming as Annie said. The outside lights invited us into a lovely old two-story wooden home where red rockers lined a wraparound porch. Connor and I couldn't get to our respective rooms fast enough and plop into bed.

~

We rose early and had breakfast at the Inn. Connor's bruises were less colorful this morning, and I could tell they were healing, though slowly. He phoned J.J. and then the body shop. Still no answer.

"I just don't understand this," he said, almost slamming his phone onto the table as if it was the phone's fault.

"I'm sorry to interrupt," said Mabel, "but there's someone here who needs to speak with you." She stepped back to reveal a slender, middle-aged man in street clothes. A sheriff's badge dangled from his belt.

"I'm Detective Clark. You two the ones lookin' for J.J.?" His gaze darted back and forth between Connor and me.

"We're the ones," said Connor, standing. "I'm Connor Romero, and this is Randi Brooks. We drove up from Boca Raton last night to meet him."

"I take it you didn't see him," said Clark, looking curiously at Connor's face.

"He said he'd meet us at Ben's Barbeque, but he never showed up. We tried his phone several times, but he didn't answer. Do you know where he is?" asked Connor.

"'Fraid so. Will you both come with me, please?" Detective Clark stepped aside and gestured for us to lead the way.

"Could you tell us what this is all about?" Connor asked politely.

"J.J.'s workers found him this morning in his office. Someone assaulted him last night and ransacked the place." Clark motioned toward Connor. "By the looks of your face, I'd say you've taken a few punches lately."

"It happened before we came. An unrelated situation," Connor said. "How's J.J.?"

"Sedated and in the hospital. His mechanics found him this morning when they came in for work. He was unconscious. The doctors will let us know when we can talk to him. It might be a while." Clark continued to stare at us as though we had something to do with it.

"I'm truly sorry to hear that, Detective. I hope he'll be alright. He was key to our being here," Connor said.

"Someone spotted the lady's car in front of J.J.'s shop last night. We need to ask you some questions." Clark stepped aside as though we were to go with him.

Is he suspecting us of having something to do with the assault?

"Officer, my car was there because we stopped to see if we'd gotten our meeting location confused. Connor looked around, but he didn't see J.J. You can ask Annie. We weren't gone very long. We came right back to the restaurant and had dinner when we didn't find him. Perhaps J.J.'s office has a security camera. Maybe you can check it."

"Well, ma'am, this isn't Boca Raton. Not every proprietor has surveillance equipment. Lake Placid is a rural community where everyone pretty much knows and trusts each other. We don't expect problems like this, except from an occasional outsider." Clark eyeballed me and gestured for us to head toward the door. A deputy stood there waiting for us.

Connor nodded at me, a signal to do as the detective asked. Lately, I'd been on the accusing end when dealing with the law, but now, it seemed, I was the accused. Having to walk through the Inn's breakfast guests with all their eyes on us like we were common criminals was unsettling.

Clark was silent as he drove us to the Lake Placid Substation on the north edge of town. Once there, he asked for our IDs and questioned me in a small compact interrogation room. Holding back tears, I relayed the whole story of my parents' untimely deaths in the canal, Connor's determination to find the killer, and Seth's part in all this. Clark said he'd have to call the Palm Beach County Sheriff's Office to corroborate my story. Hours seemed to tick by before he returned to the room, though the time was probably no more than thirty minutes. When he did, he brought Connor with him and gestured for him to sit in the chair next to me at the table.

"Well, I've spoken to Detective Morgan. He verifies your story, Ms. Brooks. I also spoke to Detective Kester of the Boca Raton Police Department. It seems you two have had a bit of trouble lately." Though Clark's steel gaze danced between Connor and me, his voice seemed to soften.

"That's an understatement," I said, "but with any luck, it's all coming to an end. We hoped this trip would bring some closure as well, at least to my parents' case."

Clark pulled out a chair and sat opposite Connor and me, the first time he'd sat down. He'd conducted his initial interrogation while standing, towering over me. I guess he'd learn that in the training academy as a way to intimidate those he questioned. He leaned in.

"Detective Morgan said he didn't know anything about this trip or your contact. He seemed a bit peeved."

I gulped. "That doesn't surprise me," I said. "Connor was investigating the death of my parents on his own. Did Detective Morgan tell you Connor was a retired Army CID Special Agent?"

Clark nodded. "What's the story with that, Mr. Romero? Why'd you get involved?"

"Randi's father was very good to me after my release from the Palm Beach VA for PTSD. He gave me a place to live and a job. When I became aware he and his wife had been pushed off the road and into a canal, I made a vow to try to find his killer. That's why we came here. For weeks, I've been calling every auto body shop in the tri-county area. When nothing turned up, I tried auto shops out of the area. It was random luck that I happened upon Lake Placid Auto Body. J.J. told me he had repaired a damaged grey Ram truck not long ago. When I told him why I was interested in talking to him further, he asked me to drive up. He was going to give me a copy of the repair paperwork. Maybe the person who assaulted J.J. took it. Maybe he was the driver, and maybe he wanted to cover his tracks. Is it possible for me to see the crime scene? I might be able to help."

"You can come along, but stay out of the way of my crime scene investigators. Ms. Brooks, I'll have someone drive you back to the Inn." Clark got up and started toward the door.

"Detective, Randi's my partner. She needs to come along." Connor grabbed my hand and squeezed it. "Besides, the reason we came to Lake Placid is because of the murder of her parents."

Clark turned when he got to the doorway. "Well, I did hear she was quite adept at gathering evidence in the other Boca Raton crimes. Sure, she can come. I'll call Mabel and let her know to keep your things as is in the Inn. I'll drop you there when we're through." He stood at the door, waiting for us.

Connor and I got up to go.

"Oh, by the way," Clark said as we moved past him through the door. "Detective Morgan will be joining us at the auto body shop within the hour."

An anxious lump formed in my throat.

Chapter 14

While Clark drove, all I could think of was how Seth would react upon seeing me. I was sure he would be furious on several levels—that I didn't tell him Connor was trying to find the truck on his own, that Connor had made contact with someone who might have done work on the vehicle, thereby proving Seth's investigative efforts inept, and that we'd taken this trip together to uncover a potential witness without informing him. Of course, the latter two issues only came up within the last twenty-four hours, and time was of the essence, so how could he expect me to inform him of those?

When we arrived at the body shop, two sheriff vehicles were already there, and the crime scene investigators were waiting outside with their bags. J.J.'s auto mechanics also huddled outside, expecting to get into the bays. I overheard Clark tell the mechanics they could work in the bays but could not access the office. They dispersed, talking among themselves. When Clark returned, he introduced Connor and me to his staff and explained our being there. He described

Connor's background with the Army, how he became involved with the case and then asked Connor to explain what they were looking for.

Connor cleared his throat. "J.J. said the man didn't want to go through his insurance company, so he left a hefty cash down payment and paid the balance in cash when he picked up the truck. We're looking for anything that will help us identify this man—fingerprints, scraps of paper with a phone number, notes, and especially the receipt. The man drove a grey Ram truck, model and year unknown, with front-end damage to the grille and headlights. J.J. said he completed the repair within the past thirty days. That's all we have to go on. J.J. was going to give me a description of the man and a copy of the receipt when we met. Perhaps when he's awake, he can tell us more."

The two CSI team members put on gloves and shoe covers at the office entrance, grabbed their bags, and led us inside. They also gave Connor and me shoe covers and him gloves so he could go into the room. He was to take a helpful role by looking for clues. Naturally, they had already done some minor investigation and dusting for fingerprints when they moved J.J. to the hospital but hadn't done an in-depth search. Clark pulled a chair from the waiting room and placed it in the threshold of the office for me to sit on. From there, I could see and hear what was going on.

The office was in disarray, with papers strewn over the entire room. Drawers were pulled from file cabinets and J.J.'s desk, chairs overturned, and a desk lamp smashed to the floor. The place looked as though a serious struggle had taken place. The CSIs were methodical about going through the papers and file cabinets where they gathered evidence into bags and boxes. In a desk drawer, they found a .38 registered to J.J. The assault must have happened so fast he didn't have an opportunity to pull it from his desk.

"Hey," said Connor. "I've found something on J.J.'s computer. It's on the shop's website."

All three officers went over to the desk and looked at the screen. I couldn't see a thing since the men blocked the display with their bodies.

"See," Connor said, pointing to an image on the screen. "I was toggling through his website looking at samples of his men's work when I ran into this—before and after photos of a grey Ram truck with grille and headlight damage that could be consistent with ramming a car. J.J. must take photos and post them to the website as a visual advertisement of his work. Of course, we don't know if it's the perp's truck, but it might be."

I sat up straight, ears perked. A spark of hope rose within me.

"We'll locate the webmaster and get copies of the photos. Men, see if you can find any paperwork that references a grey Ram truck. There could be more than one that J.J. worked on," said Clark.

Just then, the building's front door opened. Seth stopped cold when he saw me, his eyes pinched and full of fury. He took a deep breath and walked toward me.

I jumped up. "Can we talk?" I asked.

"Later," Seth said, a coldness in his voice I hadn't heard before.

"No, Seth," I said, moving between him and the office door. "Let's clear the air now."

Seth pointed to the front door. We walked out into the sunshine. The others were so involved with looking for evidence, they didn't even know Seth had arrived or that we left.

"Look, I know you're angry and feel betrayed, but it's not what you think. Connor only learned about this potential lead yesterday afternoon." I looked into Seth's icy blue eyes.

"And I guess neither of you has a phone?"

"Don't be patronizing, Seth. We both have phones, but Connor didn't know whether the information J.J. had was legit. He wanted to talk to him first."

"And you were all too willing to drive him up here."

"Look, it's my parents who were killed. Don't you think I would like to know who did it? Besides, Connor was assaulted, as you probably know, and has two broken ribs. He wasn't in any shape to drive, so I agreed to do it."

"And did you also agree to share a room with him?"

The hairs on the back of my neck stood up, and my face flushed with anger. It was downright annoying Seth would poke his nose into my business.

"So that's what this is all about? That I came up here with Connor, and we might have stayed overnight together?" I clenched my fists at my side.

"I told you from the beginning, I'm only trying to protect you."

"From what, Seth?" I said, hands on my hips. "I'm a big girl. I don't need your protection. Now, if you want in on what they find in there, you'd better check in with Detective Clark because this conversation is over." I turned on my heels, forcefully pulled open the door, and entered the building. Burning with resentment, I sat back down at the doorway.

A minute later, Seth came down the hall and stopped at the office door. Neither of us spoke. He poked his head into the office and introduced himself to Detective Clark and the CSIs. Then he introduced himself to Connor, sizing him up as he eyed his swollen and bruised face. I watched for several more hours while the CSIs combed through papers and drawers and packaged evidence they would take to the lab. They finally finished, taking their boxes and bags with them and leaving Detective Clark, Connor, and Seth in the room.

"Well, that's all we can do for now," said Clark, answering a call on his cell. While he spoke to the caller, a cold silence hung in the air between Connor and Seth.

"And if you don't find what you're looking for here, do you intend to continue your search?" Seth asked Connor.

"Not against the law, is it?" Connor replied.

"Not unless you get in my way. Then I'll arrest you for obstruction of justice," said Seth, a determined look on his face.

"You wouldn't have even gotten this far without my help. How about a 'thank you,' Detective?" Connor waited for an answer. None came.

"We're hoping J.J. can supply some vital information as soon as he's able," I interjected before the testosterone in the room got too thick.

Clark hung up his phone, a stern look on his face. "Sorry, but J.J. won't be able to help us. He's now in a coma. They don't know when or if he'll recover."

My hand flew to my mouth, trying to muffle a gasp. J.J. just became the first one to be classified as collateral damage. How many others would that term include before all this ended?

"So, we're right back where we started," said Seth.

"Let's wait and see if the crime scene boys turn up anything, then we'll know more. At least we may have photos of the truck," Clark said.

"Did J.J. have a wife? Kids?" asked Connor in a sympathetic tone.

"His wife died a year ago from cancer, and his son works with J.J. in the shop. I think he does the website," Clark said.

"If he put the photos up, maybe he met the guy who owns the truck and might be able to tell us something useful. And what about the men who worked on the truck? Have you questioned them?" asked Seth.

"Let me talk to them again," said Clark. He walked out the door and returned in about five minutes. "None of them saw the man. He dealt only with J.J. According to workers, the man brought the vehicle in before the shop opened, met with J.J., and picked up the vehicle after closing. Again, dealing only with J.J."

"That in and of itself would be red flags to me," Connor said.

"Well, it might be in the big city, but some people out here are very private and like to keep their business to themselves." Clark looked around at the office. It was still in disarray, minus the items the CSIs took.

"So, you think J.J. may have known this guy? That's why the arrangement didn't seem so unusual?" Connor asked.

"Can't say," said Clark with a shrug. He pushed some buttons on his phone and spoke to J.J.'s son, Rob. Clark expressed his condolences and let Rob know the men were through at the shop and that a deputy would stay there until someone came down to lock up, though staff wouldn't be able to use the office until CSIs cleared it. Clark also told him he'd like to speak with him tomorrow at 10:00 a.m. down at headquarters. With that arranged, Clark told Seth he'd meet him back at headquarters after he drove Connor and me to the Inn.

"I'll let you know if the CSIs find anything important. In the meantime, try to enjoy your time in Lake Placid. I'll see you in the morning," Clark said as he pulled up in front of the Inn.

"Everything resolved?" asked Mabel as we stopped at the front desk.

"Yes, ma'am. All's well," said Connor.

"Except for poor J.J," Mabel said. She looked at us and shook her head in remorse.

"Did you know him well?" I asked.

"We're all family here in Lake Placid, and most of us have had our cars at his shop at one time or another. He's the best auto mechanic around, and his crew is very skilled. Even the Formula One drivers and pit crew from Sebring bring their personal cars to him. J.J. has quite a reputation. By the way, your things are still in your rooms. Checkout was at 11:00 a.m., but considering the circumstances, you can gather your things and checkout now without paying for another night. I have your bill right here." Mabel pulled out the printed invoice.

"Thanks, but we'd like to stay another night if you have room." Connor smiled as best he could with his still swollen face.

"That would be fine, Mr. Romero. I'll adjust your bill for checkout tomorrow. I hope you won't let what happened to J.J. spoil your time in Lake Placid. It truly is a lovely town.

Have you seen the murals?" Mabel removed the invoice from the top of the desk.

"Not yet, but we're looking forward to seeing them," I said with enthusiasm.

Connor and I walked up the stairs to our respective rooms.

"How about we meet in the lobby in fifteen minutes? We can tour the murals and then go get a bite to eat."

"Sorry, Randi, but I'm bushed, and my side hurts. I think I'll put some ice for my ribs and lay down for a while."

"You do look a little ragged. Perhaps that would be best. Do you want me to bring you something back?"

"That would be great. Thanks." Connor kissed me on the cheek and slipped into his room.

After making phone calls to Adele and Leslie to let them know we wouldn't be back until tomorrow, I retrieved the mural brochure from my handbag. The leaflet suggested pulling into a small park in the center of town and walking the mapped route. The forty-seven murals covered buildings throughout the city and depicted Lake Placid's history as visualized by the different artists. I doubted I'd be able to see them all before my stomach howled for food, but I'd give the tour a half hour. After that, I'd head, once again, to Ben's Barbeque.

As I strolled down the streets, I was amazed at the artistry of the murals. They were life-sized, with some covering the entire side of two-story buildings. There were scenes of egrets and alligators from the everglades, a portrait of the town doctor when the community became established, men in boats catching bass in the lakes, workers gathering oranges during harvest season, and paintings depicting founding pioneers. The most impressive mural was one representing a cattle drive that took place back in the early 1900s. The mural stood thirty feet high and took up the entire side of what used to be a grocery store. The depiction came complete with an audio recording of mooing cows, pounding hooves, whoops from the cracker cowboys as they drove the stock, barking dogs, and cracking whips. The scene, along with the audio, made me feel as though I were right in the middle of the rushing livestock.

While I was mesmerized by the mural, my belly couldn't wait for me to see the rest of the murals. On the way back to the car to go to Ben's Barbeque for an early dinner, I stopped into the Florida Cracker, one of the cute little retail shops that lined Main Street. Being a Florida native, I knew the name referred to the proud heritage of Florida's early pioneers that migrated south from Georgia and to the Cracker Cowboys who cracked their whips during cattle drives.

A bell tinkled when I opened the door, and the shop smelled of orange blossoms. It reminded me of traveling across the state's center during spring when small white blooms cloaked the citrus trees, sending out the most intoxicating aroma. Farmers called it June bloom. I breathed it in as I browsed the shelves. I wasn't looking for anything in particular but hoped to find something as a memento of my time in Lake Placid. Several tourists browsed the store as well. As I looked through the shelves, a curved enamel candy dish depicting a white, red, and pink caladium leaf caught my eye. I turned it over to see the price. It was well within my budget.

"I'm sorry to disturb you, ma'am, but are you the lady who was looking for J.J. last night?"

I looked up to see a middle-aged woman with brunette hair cut in a bob standing next to me. Her hazel bloodshot eyes and streaked mascara spoke of recent tears.

"How would you know that?" I asked. Word traveled fast in this little town.

"Uh, we have a mutual friend."

I pulled back. "And that would be?"

"Annie." The woman looked around furtively. "Can I talk to you? In private?" She beckoned me behind a cloth partition that separated the store from a stock room while her co-worker took care of customers.

"I'm Mary Anne, a friend of J.J.'s." She spoke in a low voice as tears spilled down her cheeks.

Woman's intuition told me she was more than his friend.

"Are you his girlfriend?" I asked.

Mary Anne peeked out the curtain, then closed it. "Well, it isn't common knowledge, but, yes, we've been dating. We weren't ready to make it known to the community yet. He wanted to wait a few more months out of respect for his deceased wife. Annie is my best friend. She's the only one who knew we were serious." The soft-spoken woman dabbed at her eyes with a tissue.

I put my hand on her arm. "I'm so sorry about what happened to J.J. Have you seen him? How is he?"

"He's still in a coma."

"I'm sure he'll pull through. From what Annie told us, he's a strong man."

"Yes, he is. But are you saying you didn't meet him?"

"I just came into town yesterday. My friend and I were supposed to meet him last night at the restaurant, but he never showed. We didn't know something had happened to him until this morning."

"So, he was never able to give you a copy of the receipt?"

I pulled back in utter surprise. "What do you know about the receipt?"

"He told me about it. Said the man whose truck he repaired wanted everything very hush-hush but that someone had called about the repair and was coming up to look at the receipt. He didn't tell me who it was. I guess it was you."

My heart raced with anticipation.

"Did J.J. tell you anything about the man? What he looked like? Where he was from? What kind of truck he drove?"

"No, but he seemed nervous about this man. He'd never dealt with anyone quite like him."

"Did you tell this to the detective?"

"I haven't spoken to the detective. Besides, there's nothing to tell. I don't know anything, except…"

Mary Anne's coworker poked her head behind the curtain. "Mary Anne, there are customers who need your help. I can't do it all by myself, darlin'." She held open the curtain while we walked out.

"I'll have to speak with you later," said Mary Anne. "I know where you're staying." She dabbed her eyes as she walked out.

I paid for my souvenir and left.

As I entered the barbeque restaurant, Annie greeted me like a long, lost friend. "Good to see you, Randi." She looked around, arched her red brows skyward, and leaned in. "My boss told me J.J. was assaulted and is in a coma."

"Unfortunately, yes," I said. "It looks like someone wanted him silenced."

"What a tragedy. I just hope whoever did this doesn't find anyone else to..." Her sentence trailed off into nothingness as customers lined up behind me. She looked at me and straightened.

"What?" I asked.

"I'm sorry. I talk too much. You came here to eat." Annie led me to a two-top against the back wall. "Sweet tea with lemon, right?"

"Yes," I said, lifting the oversized menu and perusing the many choices.

"This seat taken?" The familiar voice of Seth Morgan rose above background conversation from the other customers.

"How'd you find me?" I asked in a not too friendly tone.

"It was dumb luck. I just happened to see you walk in." Seth pulled out the empty chair and sat.

"I don't remember saying the seat was available." My eyes challenged him.

"True, but I don't see Connor, and I think you may want to hear what I have to say." Seth looked at the menu he brought to the table with him.

"Yeah? And why is that? So far, everything you've said has ticked me off." I raised my menu high enough between us to block my view of Seth. I hoped he'd get the message.

He didn't. He put his hand on the menu and pushed it down. "Really, Randi, isn't that a bit childish?"

I placed the menu on the table and leaned in. "What's childish, Seth, is you jumping to conclusions about a relationship that doesn't exist." My eyes narrowed as I glared into his.

The female server with Mia on her name badge brought my tea.

"What'll you have to drink, sir?" She pulled a ticket from the pocket of her apron.

"I'll have the same," Seth said. "By the way, what do you recommend?"

"Can't go wrong with the fried catfish or baby back ribs. Best you'll ever eat." Mia, a fortyish heavy-set woman, poised her pen over the ticket.

"I'll have the catfish," I said. It came with hush puppies, coleslaw, and french fries.

"For you, sir?" asked Mia.

"Full rack of baby back ribs with all the trimmings." Seth handed the menus back to Mia. She left to put in our orders.

"By the way, did it register to you what Annie said?" asked Seth, leaning in.

I stiffened. "Were you eavesdropping on our conversation?"

"I have excellent hearing. Besides, I've been trained to be a good listener."

What is it about these investigators? Do they all have extrasensory hearing?

I crossed my arms over my chest. "Yes, I heard it."

"To refresh your memory, the hostess said that she hoped whoever did this to J.J. didn't find anyone else to hurt. I wonder who else J.J. told about the man with the grey Ram truck?"

I shrugged. "I have no idea."

"And why would the guy come back now and assault J.J.? If the man wanted to keep J.J. quiet, he could have done that when he picked up the truck."

I had pondered that question myself. What happened between the time the man picked up his vehicle from the repair shop and now that would make him feel threatened or give him a sense of urgency to make sure J.J. didn't talk to anyone? Naturally, he had to know the police were looking for him. Did he know Connor and I were looking for him, too? Or that Mary Anne knew about the receipt?

"It's probably just coincidence," I said flippantly, though I was sure it wasn't.

"Who knew you were coming here?" Seth looked at me expectantly.

"Only Adele and Leslie, and they'd have no reason to tell anyone."

"But what if one of them did, accidentally, of course?"

"I just got off the phone with both of them. Neither said anything about someone asking for me." I was sure he was overly cautious, maybe even a bit paranoid.

"You may want to check with them again." Seth sat back. His glare indicated I should follow his directive.

Reluctantly, I withdrew my phone and excused myself from the table. Walking outside, I phoned Leslie. She hadn't talked to anyone who asked about me. My next call went to Adele.

"Now that you mention it, there was someone who called for you at the store yesterday," Adele said. "He wanted to speak specifically to you about a big upholstery job for his motel. I don't remember his name. When I told him you were in Lake Placid, he said he'd call back."

I was surprised she would give out that information, but I knew it was an innocent oversight and didn't want to alarm her.

"Can you pull his number off caller ID? I think I'll return his call," I said, though I had no intention of doing so. I nervously awaited the number and typed it into the notes screen on my phone.

"Well?" said Seth when I returned to the table.

"Someone did ask for me." I held up my phone so that Seth could see the number.

He withdrew his cell and called Clark, explaining what had occurred, and asked him to check the cell number. He stayed on the line while Clark's staff did the research.

"It's a burner," Seth said, hanging up. "That means the man knew you were here."

Adrenaline surged within me.

"But how would he know about me?"

"Aren't you the daughter of his victims? Wouldn't you want to know who killed them? I'm sure he could put two and two together."

"But, I'm not the one who's been asking questions."

A cold chill ran through me. Connor! He's at the Red Rocker Inn alone. If this guy knows where I am, he'll certainly know where he is. I pulled out my phone and punched in his number—voice mail. I grabbed my bag and threaded my way through the restaurant, leaving Seth at the table just as Mia was bringing our meals.

"I'll be back," I called to Annie as I rushed out the door.

Chapter 15

When I arrived at the Inn, I bounded up the stairs. Connor wasn't in his room. I retreated to the front desk.

"Have you seen Connor?" I asked Mabel, out of breath.

She looked at me with concern. "Anything wrong?"

"I need to find him quick."

"I think he's down by the lake. Go that way. Out the back door and through the garden." Mabel pointed to a long hallway.

I dashed down the hall, out the door, and into a beautifully landscaped garden with strategically placed benches along mulched walkways. Beyond the garden lay a wide stretch of grass that bordered the lake. At the end of a broad dock that berthed several small boats, someone sat in a blue Adirondack chair. I bolted down the marina, my feet stomping on the wooden planks. At the noise, the person stood and turned around. Connor!

A tsunami of relief washed over me.

"You certainly know how to interrupt an enjoyable and serene moment," he said.

"I couldn't get you on your cell." My lungs heaved.

"Sorry, I turned it off, so I could sit here and enjoy the view and do some thinking."

"Well, please don't do that again."

"Enjoy the view or do some thinking?" he asked with an enigmatic smile.

"Turn your cell phone off," I said, annoyed he would even think about turning it off at such a crucial time.

"Excuse me?" Connor's stare and facial expression told me he didn't appreciate my motherly directive.

"Sorry. I was concerned when you didn't answer your phone because we believe the man who roughed up J.J. knows you and I are here in Lake Placid."

"Randi, what are you talking about?"

"Look, a man called the fabric store yesterday, and Adele told him I was here. His phone number goes to a burner. If he knew I was here, he'd know you were here, too. The man came back to silence J.J. Perhaps he wants to silence us, as well."

"How do you know the same man who called for you is the one who assaulted J.J.?"

"Doesn't it make sense? He had his car repaired in Lake Placid by J.J. He'd know from the obituary I was the daughter of the couple he killed. He found out from Adele I was in Lake Placid. Maybe he figured I'd found out something and would try to connect it to J.J. And now J.J. is in a coma. Doesn't it make sense to you?"

"On one level, yes. But I'm the one who made the calls, not you."

"Exactly. We figured if the man knew I was here, he'd know you were here, too."

"Who's this 'we' you keep referring to? And how'd you know the man's number goes to a burner?"

Oops. I hadn't wanted to go there, but I had already stepped in it. I took a deep breath.

"The 'we' is Seth and me. We were at Ben's Barbeque talking when it dawned on us the man might know you and I are here."

"So, you and Seth were at the restaurant together?" Connor raised an eyebrow and looked at me skeptically.

"Seems like you'd be more concerned about the man knowing we're here than whether Seth and I dined together," I said, miffed.

"I am concerned, but there's nothing I can do about it. Ram man wouldn't break in here and attack us. He does his foul deeds when no one else is around. Seth, on the other hand, is a different story."

"It's not what you think. I was there by myself; Seth came in and sat down uninvited. But that's not the point. The point is..." Before I could finish my sentence, my stomach rumbled loudly. I took a breath and let out a deep sigh. "Are you hungry? Cause I'm starving and left the restaurant before I could take one bite of my fried catfish." I sucked in my cheeks and tried to look as gaunt and famished as possible.

Connor laughed. "Sure," he said.

As we walked through the long hallway and into the B&B's lobby, Mabel was at the front desk, looking at her computer screen.

"I see you found him," she said, her eyes peeking over reading glasses.

"Yes, thank you. Everything's good." My calm demeanor was certainly a change from the frantic one a few minutes ago.

"Glad to hear it. See you two later," said Mabel, returning to her computer screen.

~

"You're back," said Annie as Connor and I walked in. "Your friend already ate and left, but I had the cook keep your plate warm." She showed us to a table.

"Thank you, Annie. You're the best," I said, taking a seat. "By the way, I met a friend of yours today."

"I've got lots of friends, honey. Who was it?" Annie's green eyes twinkled.

"Mary Anne. I met her at the Florida Cracker."

"Isn't she a sweetie? We're BFFs, you know. Let me get Mia to bring your sweet tea and dinner and take Connor's order." Annie left and returned to the hostess station.

Mia came by a few minutes later and brought us our tea and my meal. Connor ordered pulled pork, sweet potato, and green beans. I figured his mouth must be feeling better; his face looked better every day.

Being famished, I couldn't wait for his order to arrive, so I apologized for beginning without him and dug into my delicately breaded catfish and golden hushpuppies.

"How were the murals?" Connor asked.

"Fabulous," I said between mouthfuls. "You've got to see them."

"And who is Mary Anne?"

I took a sip of tea, trying to discern how much I wanted to tell him.

"She's a salesperson at this little gift shop called the Florida Cracker, where I bought something to remember our trip."

Connor glared at me as I gnawed on my lightly seasoned corn-on-the-cob. I'm sure his mouth was watering.

Just as he was about to ask me another question, thankfully, his food arrived. I wasn't ready to give him the low down on my conversation with Mary Anne just yet. I'd save that for when we returned to the Inn, and we could discuss it in private.

More than satisfied with our meals and service, Connor left a nice tip, and we walked to the door. While Connor settled up with the cashier, I said goodbye to Annie.

"We'll be leaving tomorrow, but I wanted to thank you for being so friendly and helpful." I gave her a hug.

Annie scanned the restaurant, turned her back to the customers, and pulled something from her pocket. She leaned toward me. "Mary Anne came by while you were eating and asked me to give this to you." She handed me a sealed envelope.

"What is it?" I asked, turning it over as though doing so would reveal its contents.

"When Mary Anne gave it to me, she told me she was leaving town, that she didn't want the same thing to happen to her as it did to J.J. She said she'd be in touch when she got settled elsewhere. I tried to stop her and get her to explain, but she seemed jumpy and so determined. Almost like she was frightened of something or someone and had to get away as quickly as possible. I don't understand why she'd leave a place she loved and people who loved her without an explanation, especially when J.J. needed her the most. We were best friends." Annie pulled a tissue from her apron and dabbed at her eyes.

"Did Mary Anne say anything else?" Though I didn't know the exact reason she left, I could only surmise that her knowledge of the receipt and what happened to J.J. had everything to do with it.

"Just that you would know what to do with the contents of the envelope. Gotta go," Annie said. She turned around, put on a smile, and greeted the next customer.

"Ready?" asked Connor.

"Sure," I said, stuffing the envelope into my bag.

When we arrived back at the Inn, the sun was just about to set.

"Hey, why don't we go out to the dock, grab a chair, and watch the sun go down?" asked Connor.

"Sounds good to me." After the day I had, I could use some relaxation.

We checked in with Mabel to let her know we were back, then walked down the hallway and out into the garden. Solar lights illuminated the pathway as we strolled toward the marina. At the end of the dock, Connor pulled two Adirondack chairs together. A light breeze floated across the water as the sounds of crickets and frogs began their nightly serenade. The sun tossed a pallet of pastel colors across the sky—pinks, yellows, oranges, and purples—as it set behind a bank of clouds on the western horizon.

"It's so beautiful. Makes you want to stay like this forever," I said, looking at the glorious sunset.

"It is lovely." Connor grasped my hand and pulled me close. My body stretched across the arm of my chair until our faces were but inches apart. His eyes searched mine in the glow of the setting sun. My heart pounded so hard, I could feel it in my throat.

"There's something I've meant to tell you." His hand softly caressed my cheek; his finger gently outlined my lips.

"What?" I asked, looking deeply into his eyes.

"We make a good team, Randi. What do you say we…"

Just then, Mabel hurriedly walked toward us, bringing our intimate moment to a screeching halt.

Darn!

"What's up?" asked Connor.

"Annie called. She asked to speak to Randi. Said it was urgent. She's waiting on the line." Mabel stepped aside. Connor and I rose and took off toward the Inn.

"Did she say what it was about?" I asked over my shoulder.

"No, just that she needed to speak with you," said Mabel as she jogged behind us.

When we reached the desk, I grabbed the phone.

"Annie, this is Randi. Mabel said you needed to speak to me?"

Annie blew her nose.

"Oh, Randi, it's horrible." Her voice trembled as she spoke. "The Sheriff's office just found Mary Anne's car near Sebring. Somebody ran it off the road and into a lake. Mary Anne's in the hospital. She almost drowned! I think maybe the envelope I gave you had something to do with it. Now I'm scared. What if whoever did this knows she gave it to me?"

"Where are you?" I asked.

"Home," Annie said, blowing her nose again.

"Can you get to the Sheriff's Office substation in Lake Placid?" I wanted her somewhere safe.

"Yes, I know where it is."

"We'll meet you there." I hung up and turned to Connor. "We need to get to the substation. Annie's going to meet us there. And we need to call Clark. He needs to meet us there, too."

"What's going on?" asked Connor.

"I'll tell you on the way."

We rushed out of the Inn. Once in the car, I tossed Connor my bag.

"Look inside. You'll find an envelope. Annie gave it to me as we left the restaurant and said Mary Anne wanted me to have it. When I met Mary Anne this afternoon, she told me she was J.J.'s girlfriend, and he told her about the car repair. He must have told her about the receipt as well. She tried to say more, but her coworker called her back to work, so she never had the chance. Tonight, Annie told me Mary Anne left town very abruptly and seemed to be quite frightened. Now she tells me Mary Anne was run off the road and into a lake in Sebring. She thinks the envelope has something to do with it."

"And just when were you going to tell me about this?" Connor spoke in an accusatory tone as though I was keeping something from him.

"Connor, all this happened just tonight. I have no idea what was in the envelope and still don't. I never opened it. The collateral damage is up to two, and I don't want it to go any higher. Please, call Clark and ask him to meet us at the substation." I could hear Connor accessing his phone.

A few minutes later, I pulled to a stop in front of the substation. Connor and I dashed inside; Annie was already there. I gave her a hug.

"We're so sorry about what happened to Mary Anne. How is she?"

"She's in the Sebring hospital. She almost drowned!"

We all sat down in the small lobby.

"How did you hear about the accident?" I asked.

"The Deputy that found her is my son's girlfriend. She knew Mary Anne and I were close and called me at the restaurant. I was so upset I had to go home." Annie caught her tears in a tissue.

"Of course," I said, trying to console her. "Is Detective Clark here yet?"

The front door opened, and Clark walked in. "Annie, I want to speak with you, but sit tight and let me talk to Ms. Brooks and Mr. Romero first."

Annie nodded.

"I think you two know the way." Clark threw Connor and me a sideways glance.

We walked through a familiar door and into the interrogation room. Connor and I sat on one side of the table while Clark stood.

"The assaults are piling up, Ms. Brooks," said Clark, pacing the room. "Now we have two Lake Placid citizens occupying hospital beds. I hope there won't be any more." He stopped and looked straight at me.

"So do I," I said, grabbing my bag and withdrawing the envelope.

"What's that?" Clark asked.

"I think it's the reason we're here." I gave Clark a rundown on meeting Mary Anne earlier this afternoon and what had transpired since, culminating with Annie giving me the envelope. "That small white packet may hold the key to all of this."

Connor and I stared at the envelope. I wondered what was so important that it got Mary Anne run off the road. I reached for the packet. Clark stopped me.

"We need to preserve everything for evidence. I'll be back in a minute."

Clark left the room and returned several minutes later, wearing gloves and holding two baggies. He withdrew a penknife from his pocket, opened the blade, and sliced the edge of the envelope. Lifting a piece of paper from it, he unfolded it and dropped it into one of the plastic baggies, zipping the top. After placing the envelope into a separate baggie, he placed both baggies on the table in front of us. We leaned in for a closer look. The unfolded piece of paper was a photocopy of a receipt.

The upper lines reserved for the name, address, and phone number of the customer remained blank. Below this was a lined portion where the type of service performed would be indicated. It read: Front end repair—grille and bumper—$1725.19. In black ink stamped to the side was PAID IN FULL.

"I don't understand how knowing what the man paid for his repair is going to help us. Besides, it doesn't say the name of the owner or what make the vehicle was." I picked up the baggie and looked at the figure, then turned it over. "What's this?"

The three of us looked intently at the back of the receipt. Printed on it was a line of letters and numbers—a VIN!

"Smart move, J.J. And smart move, Mary Anne," I said, as I smiled at Connor and Clark. "Now we have a way to track down the owner and the vehicle. Since he knows the law has the VIN and can find him, hopefully, he'll leave Annie alone."

"Unfortunately, that's not the way these criminals work," said Clark. "If he's gone this far to protect his identity, he'll keep going until no one's left standing. I'll put out an APB on this guy and have a deputy keep watch on Annie. It's best you two go back to Boca." Clark picked up the baggie and moved toward the door.

"Can we at least know his name?" Connor asked.

"Sure," replied Clark. "Just take me a minute." He left the room.

He returned a few minutes later.

"I've sent Annie home. A deputy will keep watch over her for a few days. You two might as well go, too." Clark stood at the doorway, waiting for us to leave.

Connor and I looked at each other.

"What about the name?" Connor asked.

Clark tucked his thumbs into his trousers. "That information will stay in the Sheriff's Office, and we won't need you at Rob's questioning tomorrow, either."

I jumped up. "You used us!" If I could have sent flying arrows at him instead of a piercing glare, I would have. "It was my parents who this man killed. Connor spent weeks trying to track him down, and we spent hours with you gathering evidence. Now you tell us you won't give us his name, even though it came from the evidence we provided?"

Connor rose and placed his hand on my arm. "Come on, Randi. We need to go."

I jerked my arm away. "Wait a minute! Are you going to let him get away with this?" I couldn't believe Connor would give up without a fight.

"There's nothing either of us can do. Come on." Connor walked to the door.

Confused and in a huff, I followed. Clark's gaze tracked us until we exited the building.

"You got a piece of paper and pen?" asked Connor as we got into the car.

"What? I need an explanation of what just happened, and you ask for paper and pen?" I shot him an angry look.

"Paper and pen," he repeated, holding out his hand as though I should dutifully comply.

"Humph," I said in disgust. I opened my bag and tossed him a small notebook and pen. He flipped open the cover and wrote something on a blank page, then turned it to face me—the VIN from the receipt.

A wide grin covered my lips as we headed back to the Inn. Clark hadn't had the last say after all. While I drove, Connor accessed the Carfax website on his phone and plugged in the VIN.

"It belongs to a grey Ram 3500," said Connor. "It's the right kind of truck. But we still don't know who it belongs to."

"Can't the owner be traced through the VIN?"

"Yes, but it has to be cross-referenced through insurance companies and license tags. Only law enforcement agencies have access to that kind of information. I'll need to call my buddy and see what he can do." Connor tapped his friend's name in his contact file and left him a text message. "Not much more we can do tonight. I'm sure he'll get back to me when he's available."

As I pulled into the parking lot at the Inn, overwhelming fatigue gripped me. Although energized by the possibility of learning who owned the truck, it wasn't enough to keep my weary eyelids from drooping. All I could do was put one foot in front of the other, climb the steps to the second floor, say good night to Connor, and crawl into bed. I was sure he had done the same two doors down.

In the morning, I packed my bag and got ready to leave. Downstairs in the dining room, I joined Connor, his face still discolored, but the puffiness diminished. He was already munching on crisp bacon, scrambled eggs, and rye toast.

"Have a good night's sleep?" he asked.

"The best. Didn't wake up once. Did you hear back from your friend?"

"Not yet. I left another message."

I went to the buffet and filled my bowl with granola and milk and my plate with fruit and mini cinnamon buns. Connor and I ate without much conversation. A long time had elapsed since I'd had a relaxing meal without drama. The break allowed me to reflect on our time in Lake Placid. While hectic and sometimes scary, it also gave me a chance to get to know Connor better and see how compatible we were. I enjoyed his company, and we worked well together, but I wasn't sure what would happen once we got back to Boca. Then, of course, there was my return to D.C., which, in my estimation, would be very soon, now that my parents' murders, the fire, and theft were in the hands of the police.

After breakfast, we retrieved our bags, bid Mabel farewell, and headed toward home. On the way out of town, we stopped by the retail warehouse of Florida Boys Caladiums. Years had passed since Mother planted any of the leafy ornamentals at Boca Grande, and biotechnologists developed new varieties all the time. We watched a short film depicting the industry's history, how they harvested the bulbs, and proper care of the plants. In my parents' honor, we selected two dozen caladium bulbs to plant around the house. I couldn't think of a better tribute to their memory.

As we headed back down SR70 toward Boca Raton, I considered Connor's and my relationship. At Boca Grande, he was my tenant and gardener. In Lake Placid, Connor and I were peers. The analogy that came to mind was an astronaut traveling to the moon and returning to earth—two completely different worlds. How would I go back to an ordinary routine in Boca after experiencing something extraordinary in Lake Placid?

I pulled into the driveway at Boca Grande around noon. I wasn't sure what to say to Connor as I got out of the car. Fortunately, his phone rang, saving me from an awkward exchange. Connor's buddy was on the line.

"Hey, Lenny, how's it going? You get my message?...Uh-huh...I understand...Well, have a good time. I'm sure we'll talk again." Connor hung up and looked at me.

"He said he'd love to help, but he's going on vacation. I guess we're DOA on the VIN," said Connor. "I think I'll go unpack and do some laundry."

"And I have to check in at the store." We gathered our things, neither of us making plans to see each other later.

Just as I climbed the stairs to my bedroom, my cell rang. It was my boss Steven.

"Hi Randi," he said. "I wanted to touch base and see how things are coming for your return the week after next. We're all anxious for you to get back. You are planning to come back. You haven't changed your mind, have you?"

"Of course not," I said.

"Great. We'll see you then. I'll check in with you at the end of next week, just to catch you up on things you'll need to prepare for when you return."

When I hung up, I tossed my phone onto my bed and looked around my bedroom. It was spacious, colorful, and cozy—home. How could I return to my small cold apartment that I hardly spent time in except to sleep, let alone to D.C. with its mass of people, honking horns, and pressure cooker days? Yet, I truly loved my job there despite its drawbacks. I missed the fast pace, the outstanding reputation I'd built for myself, and my peers' admiration, all the things that made me who I am.

After putting my clothes away and others in the wash, I checked in with Randall to see that Archie's office's unveiling was still on for 10:00 a.m. tomorrow. When he confirmed the event, I told him I'd be there with bells on. Then I called Adele. Things were fine at the store and busier than ever. My next call was to Rachel.

"Hey, girlfriend," I said when she answered.

"Hey, yourself. How was your trip?"

"Conflicting."

"Uh-oh. You had both a great time and a terrible one?"

"That's about the size of it. Being with Connor was wonderful, not finding Ram man, not so much. And then there was Seth."

"Seth was there?" I could hear the surprise in her voice.

"Yeah, and he wasn't happy I'd taken off with Connor and didn't tell him we had a lead on Ram man."

"Well, Seth's going to be jealous no matter what you do if it involves someone else. But forget about him. Tell me about Connor. Any romantic encounters?" Eagerness laced her voice.

"Almost," I said flatly.

"Almost? Sounds like you were interrupted."

"It was a perfect setting, a perfect guy, a perfect moment, and then BAM! I had to run to take an emergency call. It all worked out, though, except for the ending I wished for."

"And that was?"

"A kiss, of course," I said with a laugh.

"So, you like him?"

"A lot. I could care for him, but I'm leaving for D.C. in less than two weeks. What can come of it?" I said, sadness in my voice.

After hanging up, I grabbed a yogurt from the fridge and washed it down with iced tea. Then I walked over to Leslie's to pick up Bigfoot. I'd miss him the most and hadn't quite figured out what to do with him after I left. Time was short, and there were a lot of decisions to make in the next week—ones I'd put off far too long.

"Hi, Tootsie," said Leslie, greeting me at her back door. We went to the kitchen, where we sat at her dinette. "How was your trip?"

"Interesting," I said. Bigfoot jumped onto my lap and nuzzled my chin. I kissed his head and petted his soft fur.

"Okay, spill the beans." Leslie sat across from me, her eyes wide with wonder. As I relayed the entire account of the last two days, not leaving out a single detail, she appeared engrossed.

"Sounds like your trip was productive and romantic, minus the assaults."

"It could have been if there hadn't been so much going on. And now, it seems the spell is broken."

"Give it time," Leslie said, offering me an Oreo cookie along with a glass of milk. Snacks always mitigated stress.

"There's no more time to give. I'll be leaving in ten days to return to D.C."

"So, you're going back to your job?"

"I'm a news producer, Leslie, not a business owner. It's what I do; it's who I am." My tone had an edge of exasperation to it. Bigfoot jumped down.

"Sounds like you're the one you're trying to convince."

I inhaled deeply and let my breath out slowly, hoping my frustration would depart with the air. "What I'm trying to do is figure it all out."

"You will, Tootsie, you will." Leslie gave me a comforting look as she patted my hand.

Bigfoot padded after me as I returned to the house through the secret gate. Being close to his mealtime, I filled his bowl with a half scoop of kibbles and freshened his water bowl, two things that now seemed routine.

Though I didn't have plans for the night, I didn't contact Connor. I wanted to give both of us time to reflect on our trip to Lake Placid and our time together. In a way, it had been magical, but now we were back in reality. We both needed space to evaluate our relationship and figure out where to go from here.

I hadn't checked the mail in days, and as I gathered the pile from the mailbox, a large manila envelope protruded from under the usual pile of flyers and junk mail. I knew what was inside. I'd been expecting it for weeks, ever since the meeting with my attorney and Todd. I dropped the rest of the mail onto the kitchen island and opened the envelope as I made my way to the den. There, I carefully reviewed its contents—the sale and partnership agreement for the upholstery shop.

Satisfied everything was in order, I tucked the contents back into the envelope, placed it in the top drawer of the desk, and went upstairs to take a long hot bath. It's where I always seemed to do my best thinking and hoped I would emerge from the afternoon's soaking refreshed and with a clear path.

Chapter 16

"Isn't this exciting? And I can't wait for Archie to see his new office. He's going to love it." Adele stood next to me as the staff of around twenty and Archie's wife Karen waited anxiously for Randall to open the building.

"Please, everyone, come this way into the new Service Center." Randall ceremoniously opened the doors and directed us into the room, Archie in the lead.

A collective "Oooo" rose from the group as we took in the bright office with its large attractive photos of upholstered furniture hanging on the walls.

"And this is our new upholstery shop," said Randall.

We all filed through the door that led to the refurbished shop. It was awash in light from new ceiling fixtures to the walls painted in an attractive shade of light blue-grey. The stations and equipment, laid out in a logical pattern, allowed the workers to quickly transfer each piece of furniture they were working on from one station to another. As the staff meandered through the workspace, Archie beamed with pride at his son's accomplishment. Everyone seemed most impressed, but the best was yet to come—Archie's office.

After about fifteen minutes of touring the upholstery shop, Randall gathered us toward the back of the warehouse.

"To top off our tour, I'd like to ask my father to come up." Randall waited while Archie made his way to the front of the crowd. "To honor my father, his commitment to A Stitch in Time, and to give him the best environment one could work in, I present Archie's new office!" We let out thunderous applause as Randall opened the door and let Archie be the first one to step inside.

A few minutes later, he came out. Facing the crowd, Archie wiped the tears from his eyes.

"This is the most elegant office I've ever seen. Thank you, everyone, for making my years at the shop so enjoyable. And thank you, Randall, for turning the shop into something that could rival an art gallery." Archie gave Randall a big hug, then clapped his hands. "Now, let's get to work!"

Everyone laughed, hugged Archie and his son, and showered Randall with accolades for his beautiful work. Over the weekend, the rest of the equipment would move over from the leased warehouse. The shop would be back in business come Monday. With Rachel's magic touch, we'd have an open house for our customers on Wednesday.

While the staff went back to work, Archie, Randall, Karen, and I stayed behind admiring the new office. Archie sat in his new chair behind his desk, getting acquainted with his attractive surroundings, while Randall and Karen sat in chairs facing him.

"The surprises aren't over," I said. From behind a file cabinet, I pulled out a large rectangular package covered in brown wrapping paper. I handed it to Archie.

"What's this?" he asked, feeling the package. "A picture?"

"Not just any picture. Open it." I stood back, waiting for his reaction. He carefully peeled away the paper. As he did, his eyes grew large, and tears spilled down his cheeks.

"What is it, Dad?" asked Randall.

Archie slowly turned the picture around. It was an enlarged photo of Archie and his father in the shop with several upholstered pieces beside them. Their arms wrapped around each other's shoulders, and they sported giant smiles. Archie was about thirty-five at the time.

"Grandpa would be so proud of what you've accomplished," Archie said to Randall. "And with your permission…" He went over to one of the pictures Randall had hung on the office wall, took it down, and replaced it with the photo. "There. Now that's what I call a comfortable office." We all laughed.

"One more thing," I said. "Please sit down."

Archie complied.

"As you know, I'll be returning to my job in Washington soon, and I've done a lot of thinking about what to do with the business. Do I sell it, keep it and let others run it, or give up my job and come back here to run it. After a lot of thinking and trying out several scenarios with my attorney and financial advisor, I've decided the best thing to do is split the business into two entities—the fabric store and the upholstery shop. The problem is, I don't know a thing about upholstery, and even if I did, I couldn't run the shop as you two have done. So, I've decided to sell a substantial interest in it."

Archie shot out of his chair. "You can't, Miss Randi! Not after all of Randall's hard work." Archie's eyes narrowed; tears welled in them.

"Actually, I can," I said calmly. "After all, I am the owner."

Randall and Karen looked at each other dumbfounded.

Archie slumped into his chair, his brow furrowed, and his expression was one of disbelief. "I don't understand. Why would you do that?"

"Because I can't manage both parts of the business long distance, so I've decided to sell part interest in the upholstery shop to someone who has admired it for a long time."

"Not Mr. Barlos!" Archie shouted, jumping up again.

I laughed. "No, Archie, not Leo Barlos. I'm talking about you." I withdrew the manila envelope from my bag. "I'd like you, Randall, and Karen, to review this agreement over the weekend. I've tried to make your partnership in the upholstery shop as financially comfortable for you as possible with payments over time. I'm sure you'll want to pray about it. If you agree, I can have the business agreement signed before I leave."

This time Archie plopped into his chair like a spent rag doll, speechless. He accepted the envelope without a word.

"I've got to run. I'll see you tomorrow." I left the father, mother, and son staring wide-eyed at each other.

As I left the upholstery shop and walked back into the fabric store, Detective Kester called.

"Can you meet me at the station? I have an update on your case, or should I say cases." Kester's voice sounded hopeful, as though there was finally something to report.

"Any news would be great. I'm just up the street at the fabric store and can be there in about ten minutes." I looked at my watch—11:00 a.m.

"See you then."

After checking in with the police receptionist at the station, I waited for Kester in the lobby. He didn't keep me waiting.

"Hi, Randi, nice to see you." Kester extended his hand.

"You, too, I think." I extended mine as well.

Kester looked at his watch. "Close to lunchtime. How about a bite at Tom Sawyers? My treat."

"I didn't know detectives had expense accounts for lunches with victims, or is this your way of trying to soften me up for some disappointing news you're about to deliver?" We walked down the station entrance stairs toward the parking lot.

"Nothing like that. You've been through a lot lately between Boca Raton and Lake Placid. Besides, we have a lot to talk about, and I'm hungry." Kester hiked up his pants as we walked toward his car.

I laughed. "So that's the real reason—you're hungry. But I haven't been to Tom Sawyers in years, so I'm game."

The restaurant had been a staple in Boca Raton since 1985. More like a diner, it only served breakfast and lunch but had a dynamite pastry shop. We ordered lunch.

"So, where do we stand on the fire and theft at A Stitch in Time?" I asked.

"We've had some triumphs and some defeats. This is where we are. We've gathered enough information on the accounting theft to arrest Ron. Adele wasn't involved, but we're holding back on arresting Ron until you've had time to make arrangements at the store since there will probably be some fallout."

"What kind of police department considers the side effects of something like this?" I was amazed they'd give me time to make arrangements at all.

"We're not uncaring," said Kester. "As soon as you're all set on your end, we're ready to move. But, we need to make the arrest no later than Monday afternoon."

I almost choked on my cheeseburger. "Monday! That doesn't give me much time, and I've got the move to the warehouse tomorrow."

"Sorry, but that's all the time we have. Now, for the next item. Through your surveillance cameras, we were able to identify the blue truck and the man who assaulted Connor. We've arrested him. When we confronted him with the boot prints at the guest house and the warehouse fire, he confessed to throwing the Molotov cocktail into the upholstery shop. He was also the one who killed Kenneth Donovan by rendering him unconscious before he put him in the car and turned on the ignition."

"That's such good news. How come you don't look happy?" I asked.

"Because unfortunately, he doesn't know who hired him for the fire, to kill the professor, or assault Connor. He worked with an intermediary who spoke to him only by burner phone and paid him in cash at various drop-off points."

"Bummer," I said, taking a sip of tea.

"We figure Leo Barlos is the mastermind behind all three crimes, but we don't have ample evidence to arrest him.

We'd like nothing better than to put him in cuffs, but we just can't prove his involvement. So far, we've only got circumstantial evidence tying Ron and the professor to Barlos. That won't make a case."

"What about Ron? Once you arrest him, wouldn't he give up Barlos?"

"We're hoping that's the case, but once he's out on bail, he may wind up with the same fate as Donovan. There's no telling what Barlos would do to keep someone from testifying against him. We took one killer out of circulation, but I'm sure Barlos could find another one if the price were right."

"There's no doubt I'm furious with Ron for being involved with the theft, but he is family. Can't you protect him?"

"You mean, like witness protection?"

"Sure."

Kester laughed. "We're not the FBI, and this is not a federal case dealing with national security or a large conspiracy."

"So, where does that leave us?"

"Unfortunately, back where we've been for decades—supposition but no concrete proof, at least to arrest Barlos."

Somehow, I'd lost my appetite. We all knew Barlos was at the helm of these crimes, but how could we tie him to them?

Just then, my phone pinged. I apologized for interrupting our lunch and looked at the phone. An urgent text message from Seth said he needed to see me right away.

“So sorry,” I said, “but it looks like it’s my day for getting together with the police. Detective Morgan wants to meet me. Says it’s urgent.”

“Hopefully, he has better news than I delivered. Just don’t forget to keep in touch, so we’ll know the exact timing for Ron’s arrest on Monday.”

Kester paid the bill, and we returned to the station. On my drive home, my mind went into overdrive, trying to figure out what to do. Do I tell Adele about Ron? If I do, she’ll be alerted to his arrest, and he may flee. But then, I’m sure Kester considered that before telling me.

On the other hand, do I make arrangements for someone else to run the business because Adele will be so mad at me she’ll quit? I might be able to stay for another week, but then I’d have to return to D.C. or lose my job. I had a lot to think about.

Seth was already parked outside the gate at Boca Grande when I arrived home. I spoke my code word, and the gate swung open; he followed me in. We settled in the sunroom. Bigfoot sat close by, his head pivoting between Seth and me as we spoke, as though he was not only listening but understanding every word.

“So, did you find the guy that killed my parents?” My tone was one of resentment, one he earned by eliminating Connor and me from his communication chain.

“Both the Lake Placid PD and the Palm Beach Sheriff’s Office are working together on the case. Clark followed the VIN and put out an APB on the truck. So far, we haven’t found it or its owner.”

“Humph. So even with all our efforts in Lake Placid, you guys couldn’t make an arrest.”

"It's not like we were right on his heels. He had more than twenty-four hours to make his getaway. We'll find him, but it will take time."

"When you talked to Clark, did he say anything about J.J. and Mary Anne? How they're doing?"

"Thankfully, J.J. is out of his coma and recovering. Clark said he should be fine and back at work in a few weeks. Mary Anne was released yesterday."

"I'm so relieved. What happened to them was terrible. I'll send them each a card."

Seth fidgeted in his seat and cleared his throat. "Randi, I didn't come here to talk about your parents' case or Lake Placid."

"Oh?" My eyebrows knitted together, and I shot him a questioning look.

He eyed me sheepishly as though he was reluctant to have this conversation. He held out a thin pack of stapled papers.

"What's this?" I asked, taking the papers.

"Your parents' autopsies."

I leafed through them. The documents included the medical examiner's report on the cause of death—drowning—along with a toxicology report, diagrams of the bodies with notes from the M.E., and other pertinent information regarding their physiological condition when they died. What I held were reports that reduced my parents' lives to a few pages of transcript. Tears trickled down my cheeks. I looked at Seth; he offered me a tissue from the box on the coffee table.

"Was there something I was supposed to do with this information?" I wiped my tears.

"I wanted you to take a look at page three on both your mother's and father's report. There you'll find the results of their DNA tests."

I flipped to the page in each report and put them side-by-side on the coffee table. The title in bold print read "DNA Results." Beneath it, two columns with seven lines each contained a series of numbers and letters.

"I'm afraid I don't remember much from biology class, so I'm not quite sure what all this means."

"Well, I'm not a DNA expert by any means, but let me explain as best as I can. Here, take a look at this diagram." Seth handed me a single sheet of paper with what looked like a twisting ladder with multicolored rungs and supports. "DNA is made up of two long strands of genetic information called genes. Twenty-three pairs of chromosomes that we inherit from our parents store the genetic information. One pair comes from our mother and the other from our father. Autosomal testing reveals genetic genealogy by checking a person's numbered chromosomes. These are compared to others who have been tested to see if there are any similarities. These matches indicate ethnicity and family relationships. The higher the number of matches, the closer you are to that ethnicity or relation. With me so far?"

"Yep." Though I had no idea where this was going.

"These letters and numbers indicate the result of your parents' DNA tests. The medical examiner tests the DNA of every victim of a violent crime. Likewise, we try to gather DNA from the crime scene or people of interest so we can figure out who to eliminate, who might be connected to the crime, and whether they are or have been part of the criminal justice system."

"Makes sense."

"Now, this is what I wanted to show you."

Seth handed me another DNA report. This time, mine.

"How'd you get my DNA?" I asked.

"It's standard operating procedure to gather all the DNA we can in a case like this so that we can eliminate some people and question others. We got yours from one of your old hairbrushes when we went through the house after the accident. Now, I can't sugarcoat this, Randi. You need to know what we found."

My stomach lurched at his ominous words.

"Pay close attention to your parents' patterns and yours. Do you notice anything?"

I looked intently at my parents' patterns, then mine. I rose from my seat and paced the room, trying to understand but not believing what the tests revealed.

"There's some mistake, Seth. What it says here can't be. It just can't be!" Tears welled in my eyes.

"I thought there was a mistake as well; that's why I had them rerun the tests, this time with another lab tech. The results were the same."

"So this report tells me my chromosomes match my mother, but not my father? My father wasn't my father?" The tears spilled from my eyes and ran down my cheeks.

"Not biologically."

"Well, if the parent I grew up with and called 'father' wasn't my biological father, then who was?"

Seth stood. "We don't have the name of that person, but his DNA is part of your pattern, Randi. We can only trace DNA from DNA banks, criminals, and crime scenes. Suffice it to say he wasn't in the criminal justice system."

“Is that supposed to be some sort of comfort?”

Seth wrapped his arms around me. “Look, Randi, I’m sorry to deliver this news. I know it’s a blow, especially considering all you’ve been through.”

“Why didn’t they tell me? Why keep it a secret all these years?” My body shook as Seth held me.

“Maybe they didn’t know.”

I pulled away, wiping my cheeks. “What are you saying?”

“I’m saying, perhaps they believed you were their daughter, but maybe something happened to your mother before she got married to your father.”

“Oh my gosh!” I exclaimed, bringing my hands to my wet cheeks.

Seth looked at me in surprise. “What? Do you know who it is?”

“I’ve got to go, Seth.” I ushered, more like pushed, him to the door. “Thanks for the information. I’ll talk to you soon.” He was trying to ask me a question when I closed the door.

My parents kept originals of their important papers—birth certificates, marriage license, house titles, and the like—in their safety deposit box at the bank and copies in a file drawer in the office. I pulled out their marriage license and my birth certificate and compared the dates. The documents confirmed my suspicion–my parents conceived me the night of their wedding.

I grabbed my digital recorder and dashed out the back door to head to Leslie’s house. As I did, I practically ran headlong into Connor.

“Hey, why the rush?” he asked.

"Can't talk just now." I hurried past him down the patio toward the secret gate.

"Wait a minute, Randi. I haven't seen you since we got back. Can't you stop a moment? I have important news."

"Later," I called over my shoulder, Bigfoot at my heels.

Leslie was in her yard, fussing over an uncooperative tendril of Allamanda that had taken up residency on a hibiscus bush instead of the arbor.

"Hi, Tootsie. You look like a woman on a mission." Leslie locked her clippers, slipped them into the pocket of her garden apron, and pulled off her gloves.

"I need to talk to you." My hands trembled as I held the papers.

"Of course. Tea?" She grabbed her cane and headed toward the house.

Once inside, I sat at the dinette table while she filled two mugs with water and popped them into the microwave. Then she sat down. I took a deep breath, pulled out my recorder and turned it on, then spread out the documents in front of her.

"What are these?" she asked. Her thin fingers caressed the papers.

"My parents' marriage certificate and my birth certificate. Look at the dates."

Leslie slipped on her reading glasses and peered at the papers. "So? You were a honeymoon baby. Nothing wrong with that."

Leslie rose and brought each mug to the table, along with spoons and tea bags. The sugar bowl was already on the table.

"That's not the whole story, is it?" I looked at her, hoping I wouldn't have to drag it out of her.

"I told you before, Tootsie, things aren't always what they seem." She put her tea bag into her mug and let it steep. I did the same.

"I just found out my father isn't my biological father. Tell me what happened between my mother and Leo Barlos."

Leslie wriggled a bit in her chair. "I wish I could, but I don't know the whole story. Your mother never told me any specifics. I read between the lines of what she told me."

"And?" I prompted.

"Before I tell you what I think happened, rest assured that regardless of who your biological father is, your father and mother loved you as though you were their flesh and blood. They never for a moment thought someone else fathered you."

Leslie expanded upon the story she told me earlier of how my mother used to date both Leo Barlos and my father and how she was very fond of both of them. In the beginning, they would joke with each other about dating the same girl, but later, when the discussion became more serious, that stopped. She reiterated that when my mother chose my father over Leo, it caused a severe rift between the men's once best friend status. Leslie also said that Leo became very angry with my mother and said he came to see her several days before she and my father married.

"After that," said Leslie, "your mother's demeanor changed. Just days before her wedding, she became withdrawn and perhaps even frightened when she should be excited. I believe that during Leo's time with your mother, he forced himself on her. Your mother never told me exactly what happened, and I don't believe she ever imagined she was pregnant. She and your father simply figured you were a product of their marriage consummation on their honeymoon."

I sat back, contemplating what Leslie said. "So, Leo may have gotten my mother pregnant?"

"It's possible."

"Do you think he knew he might have fathered me?" I couldn't imagine him as my father and was beyond thankful the man I called 'dad' brought me up.

Leslie looked at me, her eyes reflecting love and concern. "I don't think any of them knew. And, really, Tootsie, we don't know for sure if Leo is your biological father. You only know what the reports say and what I've told you. That isn't proof. It would take a paternity test to know for sure."

"If that's what it takes, then we'll have to figure out some way to prove or disprove what we surmise." I switched off the recorder and got up to leave. I had what I needed on the voice recorder in case I ever needed it.

Leslie put a gentle hand on my arm. "Just remember what I said, Tootsie."

"I know—things aren't always what they seem."

Leslie gave me a reassuring smile as I left her house and walked home, Bigfoot beside me.

As I passed through the secret gate and headed toward the house, I found Connor stretched out in a chaise lounge by the pool, waiting for me.

"There you are. Is everything alright?"

"Sorry. I didn't mean to be rude, but I needed to see Leslie." I slumped onto a chair next to him.

"Anything I can do to help?"

"What do you know about paternity tests?"

Connor jerked to an upright position and swiveled around to face me. “Where’s this coming from?”

I told him the story. “I need to find out if Barlos impregnated my mother and whether he’s my father.”

“Geeze, Randi.” Connor drew his hands through his hair. “With everything else that’s going on, you have to deal with this, too?” Connor moved next to me on the chaise, put his arm around my shoulder, and pulled me close.

I began to weep. “It seems a life-changing event hits me every time I turn around. Now, this.” I brushed the tears from my cheeks.

“If you want to know, I can help, but you’ve got to understand the legal ramifications. If you want the test to hold up in court for any reason, you’ll need to have the test done in a certified lab so they can verify and document the person giving the sample. Meaning, Barlos would have to show up there, register, and be swabbed by a lab tech. I doubt that he’d do that voluntarily. You can always get a court order, but if you just want to know for personal reasons, an in-home test would do. But, you’d still need to collect the DNA. That’s usually done by a swab run along the inside of the mouth.”

“Can’t we get it another way? Like on the lip of a coke can or glass?”

“It only takes a few skin cells to perform the test. Those can come from hair, saliva, blood, semen, skin, sweat, mucus, or even earwax. Depending on the sample we get, I could talk to my buddy and get him to run the test. Twenty-four hours is all it takes for the lab work, but labs are usually backed up. That’s why the results typically take weeks.”

“Weeks! I don’t have that long!”

"Randi, I'd be asking this guy to put off the lab work he's already scheduled to work just on yours."

"I'll pay him, and handsomely if that's what it takes."

"I'll call him and see if he can do a rush job."

"Then you'll help me? I've got to know, Connor." My eyes pleaded my case.

"Of course. We'll just need to figure out a way to collect the DNA."

"I'll get it somehow."

"What if he is your biological father? Then what?"

"I haven't projected that far ahead," I said. "Right now, I just need to know. I'm sure the statute of limitations has run out on reporting the sexual assault, but maybe I can use the information in another way."

"Like?"

"I'm not sure. I just need to get the information first. Now, what is this important information you wanted to tell me?"

"It can wait," Connor said. "First things first."

He moved to the chaise opposite me, placed his hands on either side of my face, and looked at me tenderly, his gaze filled with desire. Drawing me to him, his gentle yet passionate kiss sent ribbons of heat through my body, releasing the pent-up tension and craving I'd held in check until now.

"I've wanted to do that for such a long time," he said, lifting me to my feet and wrapping his arms around me. He pulled my hair to one side and kissed my cheek, my neck, my clavicle.

I melted into his arms.

Chapter 17

I awoke the next morning feeling reinvigorated, tensions from the weeks before having dissolved. Although I still faced a lot of uncertainties, somehow, they didn't seem so overwhelming. Even the revelation from last night took a back seat to the euphoria I felt after Connor's and my romantic encounter.

After pulling on my grubbies, I drove to the warehouse to help Archie, Randall, and the staff move the upholstery equipment, furniture, and fabrics back to the shop. Archie had already made arrangements for trucks, and with so many people on hand, the move didn't take us long. By midafternoon, Archie and Randall had tested all of the stations and pronounced the shop set up and ready to go. That would give everyone Sunday to rest up before the shop opened for business on Monday. On Wednesday, we'd have our Open House to the public.

To celebrate our completed move, I ordered barbeque with all the fixings from Toms, Boca's iconic barbeque grille started by an early settler. We sat in the warehouse and enjoyed the new surroundings and delicious food. The meal brought perfect closure to a five-week-long determined effort to get back to normal.

After most of the staff left and I was about to leave, Archie stopped me.

"Miss Randi, thank you for your help today and your generous arrangements for us to become partners in the upholstery shop. The family and our attorney are looking over the offer and will have an answer for you by Monday. It's a big step for us to go from employees to co-owners, and we want to make sure we're up to it."

"I have no doubt you're up to it. The process and accounting won't change. It's just that now you'll be more involved in decisions affecting the shop, and you'll receive a percentage of the profits. We'll even add your name to the sign."

"We couldn't do that, Miss Randi. It's been A Stitch in Time Upholstery Shop forever. People know the name," said Archie.

"Well, it's your choice, and I'll support you on whatever decision you make." I gave Archie a reassuring hug.

"When are you leaving?" he asked.

"Next weekend. I'll miss you and all the fun we've had."

Archie let out a high-pitched laugh. "Yes, Miss Randi, we've had fun, that's for sure. Well, I pray the Lord will keep you safe and bless you in your job."

"He's already blessed me beyond measure. Returning to Boca was a welcome change, despite the circumstances that brought me back. I've become reacquainted with old friends, made new ones, and had a rather exciting time. But I'm ready to go back where it isn't so exciting." I rolled my eyes.

"And the investigations? I'm assuming you aren't returning before those are finished."

"Closure is just around the corner, Archie. I'll be glad when it's all over."

We gave each other a parting hug.

~

Connor grabbed my hand as we walked through the parking lot toward Boca Raton Church to attend the early morning service on Sunday morning. I couldn't help but glow as he squeezed my hand, brought it to his lips, and planted an extended kiss on it. Sitting next to him while listening to contemporary Christian music and Pastor Drake preach an uplifting sermon on forgiveness seemed so right.

"Hey, you up for a few hours at the beach and a picnic lunch?" Connor asked as we drove back to Boca Grande.

"Are you trying to woo me, Mr. Romero?"

"Woo-hoo is more like it, especially after last night," he said with a laugh.

"So you liked kissing me?"

"You bet, and someday I'd like more than that."

"Yeah? Well, maybe someday. But I'm not an easy catch."

"No, you're not. What you are is a woman with principles. I respect that."

We spent several hours at the beach, ate a late lunch, and simply relaxed by the pool. I hadn't spent such a peaceful and uneventful day since I landed in Boca. We said good night with the same intensity as we did the night before, coming close but short of intimacy.

I knew Connor was aware I'd be leaving soon. It became a silent topic that hung like an invisible dark cloud over us. Next week would be full of events that would bring closure to many pending situations. In between them, I simply wanted to enjoy Connor's company. I'd face my departure when I had to.

I spent Monday morning at A Stitch in Time, where I spoke to Adele, making arrangements to meet her at 4:00 p.m. at the house. With that settled, I called Detective Kester. We agreed that while I was meeting with Adele, he would arrest Ron. That way, Adele wouldn't have any foreknowledge. If she became angry and quit the company, I would have four days to manage the fabric store while I trained and promoted one of the sales staff to take over. I knew it would be a tough week, but I prepared for any of the alternatives.

"Hi, Aunt Adele. Thank you for coming. Let's sit in the sunroom." My heart pounded as I led her to the couch; we both sat. The coffee table in front of us held the documents I'd need as I went through my explanation.

"It sure is wonderful to have the upholstery shop back in business and be up and running again at full speed. And that photo of Archie and his father is priceless. He's so proud of it. Such an ideal gift for the occasion." Adele leaned back and seemed grateful to relax. Bigfoot jumped up and curled next to her.

"He and Randall did an incredible job working around the fire and overseeing the reconstruction. I wanted him to have something personal for his office. May I get you something to drink? Iced tea, perhaps?" I got up to go to the kitchen.

"Yes, that would be wonderful. You know, as I look around the sunroom, I can almost see your mother sitting there across from me. I can't tell you how many times we sat here after work and chatted about the business and our lives. I cherished the time we spent together and was so thankful she asked me to come down and join her at the store. It helped me more than it helped her."

"How's that?" I asked.

Adele and I had never been close. She lived in Philadelphia, and we lived in Florida. Although she and Ron visited occasionally, she and I never really connected. Then when I went away to college, I hardly saw her. Her visits to Florida never coincided with my school breaks, and in the summer, I always worked. When she moved to Florida, I was in D.C., rising through the ranks to become a producer. We never had a truly personal conversation.

"Well, I'm sure your mother never told you this, but Ron and I haven't exactly had the ideal marriage. He had some personal issues in Philadelphia, and we were hoping the move to Florida would get us away from those. Unfortunately, the availability of South Florida distractions only made things worse. I've coped the best I know how, but it's been your mother and the fabric store that's kept me sane these past years. Without her and my job, I don't know where I'd be. I miss her more than you know. Thank goodness I can pour my heart and soul into the store because although we may do a good job at faking it, there's not much between Ron and me anymore." Adele looked up with watery eyes.

I went over and sat next to her. “Aunt Adele, I never knew any of this. I’m so sorry.” I put my arms around her in an embrace.

“So, where’s the iced tea?” she asked, pushing back the tears.

I went to the kitchen and brought back a tray with two glasses of iced tea along with plates of crumb cake.

“This is so much like what your mother and I used to do after work.” Adele smiled as she took a sip of her tea. “Now, what is it you wanted to tell me?”

After what Adele had just said, I hardly knew where to start. I mentally prepared myself for the worst. As I explained everything, I showed Adele the documents and photos backing up the claims from copies of Archie’s ledger, the forensic accountant’s report, and the pictures I took at the dog track. I also explained Ron's association with Leo Barlos and the Southeast Florida University professor, his death, Connor’s assault, and the real reason the police came to her home. Through it all, Adele sat quietly, asking few questions and merely nodding.

“I’m so sorry to be the one to tell you all this, but I wanted it to come from me, family, instead of the police.”

Adele got up and paced the room, her shoulders hunched. I could see the pain in her pinched face.

“Why didn’t you come to me sooner? Why didn’t you tell me what was going on? I could have helped you.”

“Neither the police nor I had any idea if you knew of Ron’s involvement. They couldn’t risk having their investigation go south by my telling you, and I couldn’t jeopardize the store.”

"You must have considered the possibility that I gave Ron my password."

"No, Adele, I never did. I figured he found it or watched you use it sometime. Who would think their husband would sabotage the business that provides their livelihood, or that he would blackmail family into covering his gambling addiction?"

"I knew something was going on and had my suspicions, but I never thought he'd be so deceptive." All of a sudden, Adele stood tall and threw back her shoulders. "I'm relieved now that it's out in the open. The fact is, I've been contemplating divorce. I was just waiting for the right time. That time is now."

"Adele, there's one more thing." I hesitated, building up my courage. "The police are arresting Ron as we speak."

"After what you just told me, I'm not surprised. But I'm not bailing him out if that's what you think. I'll be kind and do what I can because we used to love each other, but for years he's put me through hell. It's time he grew up and took responsibility for himself. No time like the present."

"You're welcome to stay here if you don't want to be alone tonight," I offered.

"Yes, I think that would be nice. We can go out to eat and get to know each other better, something we should have done a long time ago. I'll just run home and get some things so I can go to work tomorrow." Adele picked up her handbag.

I rose and went to her. "You don't need to do that. Mother's clothes are still in the closet. I haven't had the heart to get rid of them. You're the same size, so I'm sure you can find something to wear."

Adele kissed me on the cheek. "Sounds like a plan."

Connor and I had arrangements to go out, but I called him and explained the situation. He understood, and we decided to get together tomorrow night. While Adele and I got ready, Archie called and accepted my offer to become part owner in the upholstery shop.

Adele and I drove north up Military Trail to Farmer's Table, a recently opened farm-to-table restaurant. It served free-range meats and organic vegetables from its garden. We sat outside on the patio, where lights dangled from a large pergola, giving the outside seating area a cozy glow. Chardonnay warmed us as we talked and waited for our entrees.

"As you know, I've been struggling with what to do with the business, but I think I've come up with a viable solution. I wanted you to be the first to know."

"You're not selling it, are you?" Adele's brow creased as she gazed at me.

"Nothing that dramatic, I assure you. I offered Archie part ownership in the upholstery shop. He accepted. This way, he can manage that aspect of the business while you concentrate on the fabric side. I think it will be a win/win for all of us."

"Congratulations!" said Adele. "It seems a perfect solution. You retain ownership while feeling confident the store and shop are well managed." She lifted her glass in the air for a toast.

"I'm so glad you understand. I'll announce the partnership at the Open House." The clink from our glasses rose in the air.

"Randi, I've meant to tell you how much I appreciate your understanding of my situation with Ron and how grateful

I am for your support of me as store manager. If it weren't for my job right now, I don't know what I'd do." Adele dabbed at her eyes with her napkin.

"I understand your personal life is in a bit of an upheaval, but please know I have the utmost confidence in you. Actually, I have a proposition for you. I realize that you don't want to go back to your condo under the present circumstances, so I'd like to suggest an alternative—move into Boca Grande. You'd be helping me by looking out after the house and Bigfoot, and it will give you a place to think things through. Please consider it." I gazed at Adele, hoping she'd say 'yes.'

"Oh, Randi, that's the perfect solution. Now I can put the condo up for sale and take my time finding another place." Adele lifted her glass toward me. "Salude."

"I also wanted to tell you that as soon as your divorce is final, I'll gladly sign over Mom's stock certificates. That way, you'll have the money free a clear without Ron having access to it."

We finished our dinner and drove home. When I went to sleep that night, I heard Adele crying. I didn't know if it was from sadness or relief. Maybe both.

~

On Tuesday morning, I spent most of my time in the fabric store. Occasionally I'd pop into the upholstery shop to see how arrangements were coming for the open house on Wednesday. While Archie and the staff worked to reupholster furniture, Rachel oversaw the setup by the catering company. The event would take place from 9:00 a.m. to noon, with folks dropping in and out during that time. At 10:30 a.m., I would pronounce the dual celebration—completion of the warehouse's refurbishing and Archie as a partner in the upholstery shop. The occasion would be glorious.

Connor and I headed out to dinner around 7:00 p.m. We held hands as we strolled along Delray Beach's Atlantic Avenue and window shopped among the art galleries, clothing boutiques, and footwear shops. Then we headed for Casa Rosa, an Italian Restaurant on A1A across from the beach. We ate upstairs on the balcony, where we had a commanding view of the ocean while we enjoyed the night breeze and excellent cuisine. I told Connor about yesterday's conversation with Adele and Ron's arrest and invited him to the Open House tomorrow. I also told him I had extended an invitation to Leo Barlos.

"So, that's where you're going to collect his DNA?" Connor dug into his fresh catch of the day, Mahi Mahi, with a side vegetable medley and herbed rice with lemon sauce.

"Yep. On a coffee cup. How long will it take for your buddy to get the results?" I enjoyed my jumbo crab cakes, brown rice, and asparagus spears.

"By Friday, we might hear something."

"Friday? That hardly gives me any time to confront Leo, and I need to take care of this before I..."

Oops!

I had just pricked that dark cloud I didn't want to disturb.

Connor put down his fork; his gaze held mine

"Look, Randi, I know you're returning to D.C. this weekend, so let's not pretend it's not happening."

I put down my fork and wiped my mouth. "It's my job, Connor. If I don't get back, Steven will demote me or worse, let me go. I've invested a lot of years and energy at the station and worked myself up to a prestigious position. I can't just walk away."

"I understand," said Connor, "and for that reason, I need to tell you something." He fidgeted in his chair.

"What?" I asked, suddenly feeling a drizzle of rain from the cloud I'd punctured.

"I've accepted a contract job. I need to be in Texas by the end of next week."

"You're leaving Boca Grande?"

He stiffened. "Did you expect me to stay forever?"

"Yes. I mean no. I mean, I just figured you'd stay on here. We just started enjoying each other's company. Can't it continue?" I asked.

"Let me get this straight. You want me to go on being your tenant, your gardener, your pool man, and your romantic interest when you come home, whenever that is?" Connor glared at me.

I put my hand on his arm. "Connor, that's not what I meant." The lack of drama I was just beginning to enjoy had come to an abrupt end.

"Well, just what did you mean?"

"I could fly down now and then, and you could fly up."

Connor shook his head. "As you know, I don't do extended long distances very well."

We looked deeply into each other's eyes, torn between the desire to give ourselves to the other and protecting our hearts.

"So, that's it?" I asked.

"I guess so."

"What about the last two days? Didn't they mean anything to you?"

"Didn't they mean anything to you?" he asked, challenging me.

"What about your promise to find my parents' murderer? Did you forget about that?"

"I've done all I can, Randi. The police will have to take it from here." His admission was the first time he spoke of defeat.

We finished our dinner without further conversation and returned home amid politeness without substance.

My peaceful night's sleep lasted all of one night. All I did was toss and turn, thinking about the myriad things I still had left to do and, of course, my conversation with Connor. Now that our relationship was over, as short and pitiful as it was, at least I could move on and concentrate on other priorities.

I awoke with my mind on the Open House and my scheme to obtain Leo Barlos' saliva on a coffee cup. How I was going to do that, I wasn't exactly sure, but I was determined. If he sexually assaulted my mother, he needed to confess and atone.

When I reached the shop, I helped the staff and catering company put last-minute touches to the event. When we were through, the warehouse looked fantastic. Workstations were cordoned off with stanchions and red velvet ropes, while red carpets like they have at movie premieres directed guests around the facility. Drink and food tables set with linens and flower bouquets stood just inside the warehouse entrance, where guests could mingle and talk.

At 9:00 a.m., Archie opened the doors. Customers and visitors trickled in, becoming a steady stream by 9:30. When 10:30 a.m. arrived, the warehouse was brimming with folks. I took my place at the podium and gathered everyone for the big announcement. As I panned the crowd, my gaze stopped when it landed on Connor. He simply nodded. I held back tears.

After welcoming everyone and introducing myself, I thanked the guests for coming, then gave them a brief history of A Stitch in Time and my role with the company. I also introduced key members of the staff.

"And of course, heading up the upholstery shop is long-time employee Archie Withers." Raucous applause rose from the crowd as Archie humbly made his way to the podium. "But he couldn't do it without his son Randall. And in fact, Randall's the one who put the upholstery shop back together. Didn't he do a wonderful job?" Another loud round of applause rose from the guests as Randall came up. "But that's not all. Since I came back to Boca and found myself a business owner, I've had to make many decisions. Thankfully, one of them wasn't difficult. I'd like to announce that tomorrow Archie Withers will be a partner in the upholstery shop. It will still be called A Stitch in Time but with a new tag line."

Archie stepped to the podium. "A Stitch in Time Upholstery Shop with Archie & Son," he said, holding up the new logo for all to see.

Spontaneous applause and whoops echoed off the ceiling.

"Thank you, everyone, for coming and celebrating with us. Enjoy your tour of the upholstery shop. And don't forget to congratulate Archie." I stepped away from the podium.

"So, you're giving up command of the ship?" asked the familiar voice of Leo Barlos.

"Just adding another captain," I said. "Had refreshments yet? Please join me." We walked together to the refreshment table.

"Two coffees, please," I said to the server. "How do you take yours?"

"Just cream," said Leo.

I handed him his coffee and smiled.

"I must say, Randall did a bang-up job with this place." Leo scanned the warehouse with his watchful eyes and took a sip of his coffee. I couldn't wait for the chance to get my hands on his cup.

"Yes, he did. Now he and Archie can do their jobs more efficiently."

"I'll bet your new partner will be more reasonable about selling the place than you've been."

"I wouldn't bet on it. I still retain majority control." I maintained my composure, though the suggestion that he would approach Archie about selling the shop after he and Randall had poured their hearts and souls into it sent a surge of rage through me.

"Randi, you're so naïve. What I can offer him is more money than he'd see in his lifetime of working here in the shop. Why work when you can live a comfortable life without having to? Once I have him in my pocket, it'll be just a matter of time before you cave. Really, how long do you think the fabric store would survive without the upholstery shop?" Leo gave me a wry grin.

Had I been a man, I would have wiped that smirk right off his face.

"Done with your coffee? I'll take the cup," I said, reaching for it.

Leo pulled away. “Not yet. I think I’ll take it with me.” He turned and strolled down the red carpet, followed by a string of guests. Defeat enveloped me as I stood there transfixed, glaring at his back.

“Something wrong?” asked Leslie, who had moved next to me.

“I think I just blew my chance with Barlos,” I said.

“To get his DNA?”

“Yes. I need that coffee cup with his saliva.”

“Leave it to me.”

Before I could stop her, Leslie followed Barlos down the red carpet with a determined hobble just as other guests surrounded me and wanted to chat. About ten minutes later, Leslie returned.

“Clumsy me. I accidentally lost my balance and bumped right into Mr. Barlos. It made him spill his coffee and drop his cup. It was only right that I should pick it up and offer to dispose of it. Do you have somewhere I could put it?” Leslie gave me a mischievous grin as she suspended Leo’s coffee cup carefully pinched between her thumb and index finger.

I asked one of the servers to hand me a large baggie.

“And do you have a place where I can clean up?” Leslie asked.

I looked down at her blouse. A large random brown stain covered it.

“I know just the place,” I said. We both laughed as I wrapped my arm around her shoulders and escorted her to the restroom.

~

When I got home, I knocked on the guest house door. Connor opened it wearing a low-cut pair of jeans; his tanned, muscular torso remained bare. A shiver ran through me, seeing him like that. Just two nights ago, passion consumed me as I ran my fingers over his taut muscles and caressed his contoured torso. Tonight, I had to quash those feelings.

"I got it," I said, dangling the plastic baggie with Leo's cup inside.

"Please come in." Connor stepped back so I could enter the cottage.

"I didn't want to disturb you. I just wanted to drop this off." My voice was calm, but my insides trembled to be so close to him.

He took the bag and put it on his table. "I'll get it to the lab tomorrow. We should have the results on Friday. I've asked my buddy as a special favor to do a quick turnaround."

"Thank you. I'll check back with you on Friday." I turned to go.

"By the way, it was a nice event this morning," said Connor, "and the shop looks great. How come you didn't tell me you were thinking about partnering in the upholstery shop with Archie?"

I shrugged. "I guess it slipped my mind with everything else going on. I knew I couldn't handle it, and the fabric shop long distance. It was strictly a business decision. Adele's going to stay on at the store, and now that Ron's out of the picture, she's going to move into Boca Grande when I leave to watch over it and take care of Bigfoot. I'll decide later what to do with the property, but as long as someone's living here and maintaining it, I won't have to worry so much."

"The house does need someone to take care of it. And I suppose you'll need another gardener and pool man."

We gazed at each other as we had so many times before, not knowing what to say, yet both our hearts aching.

"Well, I'll talk to you on Friday," I said.

"Friday," Connor repeated.

Chapter 18

I spent all day Thursday and most of Friday morning at the store overseeing the installation of new accounting software onto the company server and approving password changes. These would get us back to normal, at least with our company accounting. Following the fraudulently transferred money, it first went to Ron's checking account, where he took a percentage off the top. Then he repaid Barlos in cash through a go-between so there wouldn't be any trace of the transaction. The commercial real estate mogul had insulated himself well, and Ron would take the fall. Thankfully, we lost only a few thousand dollars, reimbursed by the insurance company, not the tens of thousands envisioned had this scheme gone on longer.

Besides the business, I arranged for pool and landscaping companies to maintain Boca Grande and organized myself to return to D.C. Coming down had been a rush job, and now it seemed going back was a rush job as well. My time in Boca seemed like a whirlwind, and when I looked back on everything that had happened, I was amazed my sanity remained intact. While my job at the TV station was always busy, at least it had some consistency. Being in Boca had no consistency. There seemed to be a crisis every day. Thankfully, most of that was now over. I looked forward to getting back to something more routine.

Wanting an update of my parents' case before I left, I phoned Seth on my way home.

"Hey," I said as soon as he picked up.

"Hey, yourself. I was just about to call you. I hear from Kester that you're heading back to Washington on Sunday. You agreed to go out to dinner with me before you left. What about tonight?"

"That would be very nice, Seth, but tomorrow would be better. I still have a lot to do."

"Tomorrow it is. I can catch you up on the investigation then, and you can tell me what you found out about your DNA match. I'll pick you up at 6:30 p.m."

Through the afternoon, I cleaned up the house, packed, and got ready for my Sunday morning flight. Bigfoot seemed to know something was amiss. He followed me from room to room as I waited to hear from Connor. At 3:30 p.m., his text came.

HAVE RESULTS. MEET ME AT THE GUEST HOUSE.

I made my way over to the cottage, Bigfoot padding after me. My emotions were raw—a mixture of expectation and trepidation. The result of the test was a matter of chemistry, not of heart or feeling. Nothing would change the love I had for my parents, but the test result could enhance the intensity of the dislike I had for Leo Barlos. My hands trembled as I knocked on the cottage door.

"Come on in," said Connor. "Have a seat. I'll get the items." He walked to the bedroom.

I sat on the couch and stared at the coffee table. The photo of Connor and Sarah in the desert was no longer there. In its place was Connor's selfie in the pool with the lush tropical garden in the background and Bigfoot nuzzling his nose. The image was so Connor. So Boca Grande. So Bigfoot. My eyes teared at the scene, and an unexpected lump formed in my throat. The picture was the perfect image of what I envisioned for the man in my life. Now it was over. I could hardly keep my composure.

"Here's the result of the test." Connor handed me a sealed envelope. "And here's the cup. I didn't know if you wanted it back, but I had my buddy put it in a plastic baggie just in case. I hope the results are what you expect."

"Honestly, I don't know what to expect," I said, keeping my gaze on the envelope so he couldn't see my tears. "I only know I can't thank you enough for what you've done for my father, for Boca Grande, and me." I got up to leave.

Connor walked to the door. "I'll let Adele know when she can inspect the cottage, and I'll leave the keys with her."

"My plane leaves Sunday morning, but I'll come by to say goodbye before I go." I went to kiss Connor on the cheek.

"Don't," he said, turning his face away. "It only makes it harder for both of us."

My heart broke at his rejection. I turned and walked out the door knowing in my hand was the answer to where I came from, but it wouldn't answer the question in my heart—why were Connor and I both leaving Boca Grande?

As soon as I got back to the house, I opened the envelope and scanned the result. To make sure I was analyzing the information correctly, I took out my DNA report and compared the markings. There was no mistaking what I saw—Leo Barlos was my biological father.

I ran to the bathroom and heaved.

~

"Ms. Brooks, Mr. Barlos will see you now. Go on in." Leo's administrative assistant gestured toward his office door.

Before entering the building, I'd sat in the parking lot for fifteen minutes, held back by a jumble of emotions—anger, resentment, confusion, disbelief, hate. Yet, for all those negative feelings, one positive sentiment rose to the surface—thankfulness. Without Leo, I wouldn't be here. I'd have never experienced the unconditional love of my parents, the thrill of graduating from college, the pride in doing a good job, and the bond of friendships. All those magnificent memories and relationships were the reason I could walk into his office.

Leo was comfortably seated behind his desk. He nodded toward a chair and for me to sit. My blouse clung to my moist torso, and I prayed I could keep my voice from shaking. I needed to get through this. I took a deep breath.

"I'm sorry to call you so late, especially on a Friday, but I'm heading back to D.C. on Sunday morning, and I wanted to catch you before I left." My hands trembled. I folded them tightly and placed them on my lap.

"Don't tell me you've had second thoughts and are willing to sell the store?" Leo gave me a confident grin as though what he suggested was true.

"Afraid not," I said, a nervous laugh escaping. "I came to talk to you about something else."

"And that would be?"

"You and me."

Leo pulled back. "I'm afraid I don't understand."

"Do you remember the day I told you that I knew about you and my mother?"

"I do." His arrogant smile had morphed into a straight line of thin lips.

"Well, I think there's something you left out."

"Just what are you getting at?" Leo shifted in his chair.

He had alerted the spider, and she was about to pounce.

"Let me show you something." I pulled a folder from my tote and opened it, withdrawing copies of my parents' marriage license and my birth certificate. I placed the papers on the desk in front of Leo. "Notice anything about the dates."

The real estate mogul's gaze bounced between the two documents. "You were born nine months after the wedding."

"That's right. Now here are a couple of other documents." I pulled out two other papers and handed them to him. "This information shows the results of my parents' DNA tests analyzed as part of their autopsies. Pay special attention to the highlighted areas. Those are their DNA markers."

He scanned the reports with narrowed eyes and a creased brow, then let them drop onto the desk.

"So." He splayed his hands.

I handed him the last document.

"And this is the result of my DNA test. Again, note the highlighted area. Notice any similarities?"

He gazed back and forth between the documents. "You have your mother's markers, but not your fathers."

"Exactly. Why do you suppose that is, Leo?"

"Well…I, uh…I'm not an expert on these things," he huffed. He tossed the papers onto the desk with the others.

"I know you sexually assaulted my mother just days before her wedding to my father. And I can prove it."

Leo hesitated, then let out a cheeky laugh. "Randi, dear, you've let your imagination run away with you."

"Really? What I have here is a coffee cup with your saliva on it from the open house. If I had it analyzed, what do you think the DNA would show?" I dangled the baggie with the cup in front of him.

"You couldn't possibly have that cup. That busybody Leslie Davidson bumped into me, and my coffee cup fell to the floor. She picked it up and put it…"

"Yep, right into my hands."

Sweat beaded on Leo's brow; his tension filled the air. He took out a handkerchief and wiped his forehead, then sat back and looked in deep concentration. He put his elbows on the desk, folded his hands, and glowered at me.

"Are you trying to blackmail me, young lady?"

"Call it what you like. What do you suppose your wife would say, or your friends, or your business associates, or your neighbors if I made the results of these reports public along with your DNA results? Wouldn't they want to know why your DNA matches mine? I'm sure they could put two and two together and come to the same conclusion I did—that you forced yourself on my mother just days before her wedding."

"Are you saying I'm your father?" Barlos' eyes twitched at the corners. He pushed himself from his desk and paced behind it. I couldn't help but think his devious mind was trying to find some crumb of an excuse for his actions.

I had his DNA results and could have pulled the document from the folder and shown him, but it wasn't official. With one phone call to his attorney, he would have disputed the results, had a legal field day with how I obtained his saliva, and laughed right in my face. This way, I could enjoy watching him squirm.

Leo abruptly stopped pacing and faced me.

"I loved your mother to the depths of my soul," he said, his eyes moistening. "When she chose Carl over me, I became enraged. I couldn't let her marry him without showing her what she was missing."

Righteous anger surged through me, hearing what he'd done to my beautiful mother.

"And you believed that forcing yourself on her would make her love you?" My voice escalated, and my knuckles turned pale as my hands clutched the chair arms. Yet, I couldn't let his admission or my anger derail my plans.

"Alright, young lady, we're reasonable business people. I'm sure we can come to some sort of agreement. What do you want?" Leo drew the handkerchief across his eyes.

"Not much. Just two documents. The first will state that you agree never to harass Archie or me again about buying the upholstery shop and fabric store."

"Done," he said without argument, as though he'd gotten off easy. "And the second?"

"Your signed confession that you forced yourself on my mother."

Leo put his palms on his desk and leaned toward me. "Are you crazy?" His nostrils flared, his eyes bulged, and his face turned beet red.

Keep it together, girl.

"I don't intend to make your confession public unless…" I suspended the baggie in front of him.

A whoosh escaped Leo's executive chair as he plopped into it like a defeated prizefighter after a knockout.

"I'll need the documents signed, notarized, and in my hand at Boca Grande by 3:00 p.m. tomorrow," I said. I placed the baggie in my tote and left the documents, so he could mull over my terms after I departed.

While walking to my car, the numbing cold enveloping me was a stark contrast to the heat that pulsed through me while sitting in Leo's office, listening to his disgusting confession. I gulped air and prayed with each step that my trembling legs would sustain me before I collapsed. Sliding into the driver's seat, I gripped the steering wheel, took a deep breath, and exhaled loudly. I repeated the process until the tension dissipated, and I returned to some semblance of control.

Lifting the digital recorder from my tote, I turned it off, proud I'd managed to capture Leo's confession. Though I now had the truth, I wasn't quite sure what to do with it. My parents' deaths had forever altered my life, and it was being changed again by a despicable man. With so much to deal with, all I could do right now was push the revelation back in my mind and draw comfort from the fact that my return to D.C. would restore a familiar and stable routine. I'd still have to face the emotional fallout, but I'd be hundreds of miles away, the distance acting as a potent salve to jump-start the first step in my healing.

~

Adele came to the house on Saturday morning, so I could explain the house's nuances, give her a list of vendors that provided services, and show her where I kept the keys to

Mom's car. I would continue paying the bills, but Adele insisted on reimbursing me for the utilities.

"Of course, if you need anything else, you can just phone me. And Connor will be here until next week. He can help out if necessary."

"Aren't you going to miss this place, the store, Bigfoot, and Connor?"

"Of course. These have been the most wonderful and terrible two months of my life. But right now, I need some routine and consistency. As hectic as my life is in D.C., at least I have those."

"We all have our challenges and must deal with them the best way we know how," said Adele.

"Well, I need to finish packing and get ready for my dinner date with Seth."

"He's still in the picture?"

"It has to do with the case. Seth's going to give me an update."

"Over dinner on a Saturday night?" Adele tilted her head, raised her eyebrows, and eyed me skeptically.

I laughed. "I'm leaving tomorrow, Aunt Adele. Just what can happen on my last night?"

"Well, I've still got lots of things to do at the condo. Have a nice evening. I'll be here at 7:00 a.m. to take you to the airport." She gave me a parting hug and hiss.

In the afternoon, as I was packing, I heard a buzz from the front gate.

"Yes," I said into my phone.

"I've got a package for Randi Brooks from Leo Barlos. You'll need to sign for it," said the man's voice. He held up a large envelope toward the camera.

"Come on in." I pushed the button on my phone to open the gate, then took several bills from my bag and met the courier at the door.

"Sign here," he said, handing me a tablet.

After signing with my finger, I returned the device along with the tip. The courier offered me the packet.

Climbing the stairs, I sliced open the envelope with my finger and withdrew several documents. The first was Leo's letter, stating he would cease pursuing the fabric store and upholstery shop property. The second was his confession. Yet it was the third document that caused me to drop onto my bed with round eyes and a slackened jaw—a Quit Claim Deed.

I sat there blinking, reading the document a second and third time until reality set in. Leo had deeded me the vacant lot next to A Stitch in Time free and clear, a parcel probably valued into the hundreds of thousands of dollars! Did he consider this atonement for his shameful actions and the damage he'd caused? Or was it a bribe to keep my mouth shut?

I took the papers downstairs and placed them in the safe along with the card from my digital recorder. I wasn't sure what I'd do with these items or the property, but I knew I couldn't deal with any of it now.

~

As I got ready for my date with Seth, my boss from the TV station phoned. Steven caught me up on all that he planned for next week's news broadcasts and said he couldn't wait until I was at the helm again. I assured him my return would be like I never left, but I knew that wasn't true. I had experienced events that both carried me to mountain tops and stabbed me to the core. I would never be the same.

Seth picked me up at 6:30 p.m. We drove down A1A to Fort Lauderdale, where he pulled into Seven Oceans, a seafood restaurant on the beach. Just one more I hadn't been to in years. We sat at the bar and sipped a glass of wine until our table was ready. After a fifteen-minute wait, we were seated on the main floor, where we enjoyed a commanding view of the gently rolling ocean as we savored our entrees.

"I'm sorry I couldn't attend the Open House. I had a ton of paperwork to catch up on and two new cases to start. I hope it went well."

"It was wonderful," I said. "And now Archie is a proud partner in the upholstery shop."

"I don't want to pry, but did you get closure on the DNA results?"

"I did," I said, swallowing my emotions.

"And?"

"I'll tell you sometime," I said, my voice quavering.

"Just know, Randi, no two people loved you more than your parents, regardless of what the DNA says."

"I know, but it certainly came as a blow and will take time to accept and fully understand."

"I'm here if you ever want to talk."

"You've been so kind and helpful. Please know how much I appreciate your friendship." I smiled, put my hand on Seth's, and squeezed it.

"Speaking of friendship, now that you're heading back to Washington, I'm guessing Connor is out of the picture."

"Yes, he's moving to Texas next week for contract work." I pushed rice around the plate with my fork.

"Well, I'd like to see if we couldn't get to know each other better after all we've been through. Who knows where the relationship might go?"

"So the high school torch has been reignited?"

"The flame never went out," he said, staring at me, his eyes filled with desire.

"Seth, I'm very flattered, but I don't know when I'll be back, and my life in D.C. is very hectic." I didn't want to give him any false hope.

"I have issues of my own to deal with over the next few months. I just wanted you to know how I felt and if there was an inkling of a chance for us to see where this relationship might go, I want to take it. Even if that means flying up to D.C. to see you."

"No promises, Seth, but I'll keep it in mind."

"That's all I ask, Randi."

Since there was no news regarding my parents' case, Seth and I ended the night early with a friendly kiss goodbye. It was nice but didn't compare to Connor's soft sensuous ones.

Needing to say goodbye to Leslie, I went over to her house about 9:30 p.m. We sat at her dinette and had tea.

"All ready to go, Tootsie?" Leslie asked.

"Just about. Adele will take me to the airport in the morning then return to the house. I'm so thankful she's consented to live there and take care of Bigfoot."

"I'm sure that's a huge burden off your shoulders."

"It is," I said, reaching across the table for Leslie's hands. They seemed so frail in mine, yet they also radiated strength. "I'm sure going to miss you. You've been the best friend ever."

"You're special to me, too. You brought a lot of joy back into my life. I can't wait to go on another escapade next time you're in town." Leslie smiled; her eyes sparkled.

I squeezed her hands and rose to leave. We walked to the secret gate arm in arm. When we got there, Leslie cupped my face in her thin hands and gazed tenderly at me.

"Tootsie, I know you've had a severe blow, but remember this. While Leo may have given you life, your parents shaped your future. It's up to you what you do with it."

"Stay well, my friend," I said.

We gave each other a parting hug and kiss.

My next stop was the guest house. Since I had an early flight, I wanted to see Connor tonight. When he didn't answer his door, I checked the driveway. His truck was gone. The disappointment and empty feeling overwhelmed me. Tears dropped onto my phone as I sent him a goodbye text and returned to the house.

I hadn't seen Rachel since the open house. Her kids were sick the rest of the week, so seeing her one-on-one before I left had been out of the question. I phoned her to say my goodbyes, knowing we'd FaceTime from D.C. like always. I'd wanted to share my findings with her, but it was something I wasn't ready to do. I needed time to understand my own feelings, let alone articulate them to someone else, even my best friend. Maybe someday.

Bigfoot jumped on the bed before I went to sleep and cuddled next to me as he did every night. I ran my hand down the length of him, memorizing every contour of his svelte body and the feel of his soft, silky coat.

Meow.

I'd miss him terribly.

~

I sat on the plane and gazed out the window. Checking my phone before boarding, Connor hadn't called or texted. My leaving had been painful for both of us, and as I flew thirty thousand feet over the continent, I knew I'd never be the same after all that happened in the last two months.

As I unzipped a pocket in my purse to double-check for the keys to my D.C. apartment, I felt something made of paper—an envelope. On the outside was a handwritten note:

Connor asked me to give this to you. I stuck it in your purse so you would see it.

Love, Aunt Adele.

Pulling open the flap, I found a thin piece of cardboard backing a photo. I withdrew the image and turned it over. It was the picture from Connor's coffee table—so Connor, so Boca Grande, so Bigfoot.

I smiled at the image; my eyes brimmed with tears. Had Connor given me this photo to remind me where I truly belonged? Resting my head against the back of the seat, I closed my eyes. Leaving Boca and returning to D.C. resolved one set of issues—restoring independence and continuity to my life. Yet, my departure left three frayed ends—my parents' unsolved murders, my unsettled feelings toward Leo Barlos, and leaving the man I could love.

I knew it would take time to come to grips with everything I'd experienced, but two of the greatest gifts my parents gave me were strength of character and determination.

As the plane touched down in D.C., I vowed to use those gifts to step onto the road of my unpredictable future with resolve and hope.

NOTE TO THE READER

Thank you for reading *Frayed Ends,* the first book in A Randi Brooks Mystery series. I hope you enjoyed it. As reviews are important to every author, please take time to leave a review at Amazon.com.

The second book in this series is entitled: *Uncovered* and continues where *Frayed Ends* left off.

Uncovered

When Randi realizes the job she once loved doesn't fit her anymore, she heads home. This time for good. Little does she know her new life in Boca will be anything but quiet.

While working with an elite Palm Beach customer, a small bronze statue ignites an unexpected mystery. Since the figure is tied to a seventy-year-old double homicide cold case and the theft of all the sculptor's work, Randi sets out to uncover the whereabouts of the stolen pieces. Shrugging off anonymous threats to stop snooping into the past, she plows ahead only to discerver her zeal places her in the unknown person's crosshairs.

To further complicate things, the man who murdered Randi's parents is discovered to be part of the Mexican drug cartel and is now after Connor who is in Texas. As well, Seth, now single, heaps fuel on the fire in his quest to secure Randi's heart.

Can Randi recover the missing statues without putting her life in jeopardy? And can she resolve her love interests while not getting her heart broken along the way?

ABOUT THE AUTHOR

Sally J. Ling, Florida's History Detective, is an author, speaker, and historian. She writes historical nonfiction, specializing in obscure, unusual, or little-known stories of Florida history and mysteries with a Florida connection.

As a special correspondent, Sally wrote for the *Sun-Sentinel* newspaper for four years and was a contributing journalist for several South Florida magazines.

Based upon her knowledge as well as excerpts from her books, Sally has appeared in three feature-length TV documentaries—"Gangsters," the National Geographic Channel; "The Secret Weapon that Won World War II," and "Prohibition and the South Florida Connection," WLRN, Miami. She served as associate producer on the latter production. She has also appeared in and served as a production consultant for several short documentaries on South Florida history produced by WLRN, Miami.

Sally has been a repeat guest on South Florida PBS TV and radio stations, guest presenter at the Lifelong Learning Society at Florida Atlantic University, and guest speaker at numerous historical societies, libraries, organizations, and schools.

Sally lives with her husband, Chuck, and splits her time between South Florida and western North Carolina.

For information on Sally's current projects, or to become a "Preferred Reader" and receive notices on upcoming books. please visit her website at:

sallyjling.com

To engage Sally as a speaker, or to send her an email, contact her at:

info@sallyjling.com

Sally's books include:

Fiction

- *Frayed Ends: A Randi Brooks Mystery (Volume 1)*
- *Women of the Ring*
- *Who Killed Leno and Louise?*
- *The Twelfth Stone: A Shea Baker Mystery (Volume 3)*
- *The Spear of Destiny: A Shea Baker Mystery (Volume 2)*
- *The Cloak: A Shea Baker Mystery (Volume 1)*
- *The Tree and the Carpenter*
- *Spies, Root Beer and Alligators: Phillip's Great Adventures (Children's Novel)*

Nonfiction

- *Deerfield Beach: The Land and Its People*
- *Al Capone's Miami: Paradise or Purgatory?*
- *Out of Mind, Out of Sight: A Revealing History of the Florida State Hospital at Chattahoochee and Mental Health Care in Florida*
- *Sailin' on the Stranahan (commissioned coffee table book)*
- *Run the Rum In: South Florida during Prohibition*
- *Small Town, Big Secrets: Inside the Boca Raton Army Airfield during World War II (First and Second editions)*
- *A History of Boca Raton*
- *Fund Raising With Golf*

Made in the USA
Middletown, DE
19 August 2021

46383014R00156